Mystery Man

Second Edition

Mike Faricy

Library of Congress Control Number: 2023915500
paperback ISBN: 978-1-962080-33-0
e-Book ISBN: 978-1-962080-34-7

MJF Publishing books may be purchased for education, Business, or promotional use. For information on bulk purchases, please contact the author directly at mikefaricyauthor@gmail.com

Published by

MJF Publishing
https://www.mikefaricybooks.com

To Teresa

“Revenge is a dish best served cold.”

Acknowledgments

I would like to thank the following people for their help and support:

Special thanks to my editors, Kitty, Donna and Rhonda for their hard work, cheerful patience and positive feedback.

I would like to thank Ann and Julie for their creative talent and not slitting their wrists or jumping off the high bridge when dealing with my Neanderthal computer capabilities.

Special thanks to Ann for her patience.

Last, I would like to thank family and friends for their encouragement and unqualified support. Special thanks to Maggie, Jed, Schatz, Pat, Av, Emily and Pat for not rolling their eyes, at least when I was there, and most of all, to my wife Teresa whose belief, support and inspiration has from day one, never waned.

Prologue

Artie Walker finished his tonic water with a twist and pushed the empty glass across the bar. He was facing the stage but not really watching, more intent on checking out the few remaining clientele before heading for the men's room. They'd announced last call over the sound system about ten minutes ago. Just two other guys were seated around the bar, three more sat in front of the stage. The crowd had been thin, even for a Tuesday night.

The last dancer was shaking everything she had up on stage in an effort to get a halfway decent tip, but it wasn't going to happen tonight. She had to pay a hundred and twenty bucks just to dance and then give thirty percent of her tips to the manager. There was no way she was going to make any money dancing in a place owned by Tubby Gustafson. The last song finally ended, and she swung around the brass pole two more times. She quickly picked up the tips lying on the edge of the stage, seven dollars, and a piece of paper with a phone number. She tossed the phone number on the floor and headed back to the dressing room.

Artie headed into the restroom, waited until he was alone, and then hurried over to the maintenance closet next to the back stall. He quickly picked the lock and stepped into the closet. He pulled the mask on the top of his head, put the stethoscope around his neck, slipped on his latex gloves, and quickly screwed a sixty-nine cent hook and eye latch into the wooden closet door. He pulled the Snickers candy bar from his pocket, opened the wrapper, and took a bite. So far, so good.

The bartender locked the front entrance. He poured a bourbon and a glass of red wine for the two dancers. They sat at the bar and sipped while he picked up glasses and napkins from the empty tables and set them on the bar. He loaded the dishwasher behind the bar, turned it on, and then turned off the outside neon lights. He poured half a glass of sparkling water and joined the two dancers. They chatted for twenty minutes before he shut everything down, and they all headed out to their cars. Artie Walker waited another half-hour in the closet before he quietly unlocked the door and peeked out.

It was dark, which was a good thing because, if the lights were off, it suggested the place was empty. He placed a hand against the wall and slowly made his way to the door in the dark. He listened at the door for a number of minutes and didn't hear anything. He pulled the clown mask down over his face, opened the men's room door, and headed past the dressing room to the back office.

The office door was marked private, and the lock on the door was a Mul-T-Lock, a state of the art lock that was pick and drill resistant. Fortunately, Artie had a special tool sent all the way from Australia, and he was in the office in thirty seconds and standing in front of the door to the vault.

The vault was what had given him the idea. A walk-in vault in a strip club? That seemed like a lot of overkill. The vault was at least a hundred years old, and maybe the owner, Tubby Gustafson, even got it for free, but the installation had to have cost a small fortune. Artie pulled the combination from his pocket, placed his stethoscope against the steel door, and slowly began to turn the dial. It took no more than ninety seconds before he pulled the door open.

There were two heavy black canvas cargo bags, leather, and heavy, that were sitting next to one another on a shelf. Two cash register drawers from behind the bar were next to them. Artie grabbed the cargo bags. He tossed them out of the vault and into the office. He closed the vault door behind him, spun the dial, and hurried out of the office with the bags slung over his shoulders. He relocked the office door and hurried out past the bar toward the front entrance.

He was almost to the door when he saw the flashing red and blue lights cross the intersection and race across the parking lot headed toward the entrance. That was more than enough warning. He spun around and ran toward the back door.

He flew through the small kitchen. One of the cargo bags bumped into a plastic tray full of glasses, sending everything crashing to the floor. He made it to the rear door, peeked out, and ran across the alley into a backyard just as more flashing lights entered the far end of the alley and sped toward the rear door of the club.

Artie ducked down behind a hedge and heard chatter that he couldn't understand on a radio as two cops jumped out of the car and entered through the rear door. They stepped inside, and a moment later, the lights flashed on. He pulled the clown mask off and waited another two minutes, which under the circumstances, seemed like two hours. He crouched and made his way across the backyard, past a swing set and a sandbox. He hurried up the street toward his car. Fortunately, at this hour, no one drove past.

One

As I opened the door Louie said, "You certainly seem to be in a good mood. I heard you whistling all the way up the stairs. Things must have gone well on last night's date."

"Let's just say, not as bad as it could have been."

"Huh? Not as bad? What does that mean?" Louie asked. He tossed a file on his picnic table desk and leaned back in his chair. Morton settled onto his bed in front of the file cabinet and placed his paws over his head. He'd heard this story before.

"It just means that Sharon didn't say don't ever call me again. She didn't go into the ladies' room and climb out the window. She didn't tell the bartender to call the cops on me."

"This is what makes a good date in your mind?"

"Louie, it was our second date. She's going by the playbook. I met her at that wedding two weeks ago and got her phone number. We met for lunch the following Wednesday. I took her to the restaurant last night and offered to provide dessert at my place. She declined; she's supposed to decline. It's in the women's playbook. She has to prove she's not a slut. Okay, now she's done that. The three-date rule, mission accomplished."

“What?”

“Yeah, she’s proven she has morals or at least can pretend she has them. Our next date is tonight, and I’m pulling out all the stops. I’ve got a dinner reservation at Antonio’s for tonight at eight.”

“Whoa, big spender.”

“This is how it works. After last night when she got the ‘I’m not a slut’ bit out of the way, now we can have a great time. She can spend the night. She’ll no doubt be wearing something super sexy. I’ve got clean sheets on the bed and clean towels in the bathroom. She can be as wild as she wants to be because she’s already demonstrated she’s not easy. It’s the third date, Louie. This is the way things work.”

“Gee, who knew? Well, keep me posted.”

“Yeah sure, reporting in to you will be the first thing I think of. Just remember, I might be a little late coming in tomorrow morning. In fact, I might not be in until noon, you never know.”

Louie had an afternoon full of court dates, and I had a stack of job applications I had to wade through for an insurance client. I was online all afternoon, checking property tax records, looking for arrest histories, and speeding tickets on close to fifty job applications. Mercifully, everyone checked out just fine. We were home a little after five, and I took Morton for a walk. I set a bottle of pink Prosecco in the fridge. Sharon loved the stuff. I showered, shaved, put on a reasonably clean shirt, and a dark sweater to hide the shirt wrinkles. I was seated at Antonio's at 7:45, fifteen minutes early.

Sharon arrived stylishly late at 8:10 and looked like a million bucks. She wore a tight, black cocktail dress with lace sleeves and a scoop neck. Nothing was left to the imagination, and a number of heads turned as she waved and then strutted to our table. Her dark hair was swept back over her shoulders, and she looked like she was going to bounce out of her top at any moment. I loved it.

"Hi, Dev, sorry I'm late. My car's in the shop, so I had to Uber over here," she said, then leaned down and kissed my cheek. "Mmm-mmm," she moaned softly and lingered a second or two before she sat down.

Uber over? Yeah, right, how perfect. She probably had a friend drop her off. Now it would just be natural that I'd offer to give her a ride home. Then once we're in the car, I'll offer a glass of pink Prosecco at my place, and that will start the clock ticking to try out my clean sheets.

"Well, you're certainly worth the wait. You look great," I said.

"Thanks, I was running short on time after dropping off the car, so I just threw on any old thing. Hope you don't mind."

"Mind? You kidding? You look fabulous."

"Oh, thanks, you're so sweet," she said, shrugged, smiled, and gave my hand a squeeze.

Yeah, the third date was it. I could tell. We had dinner. I ordered pasta, and Sharon had lasagna. We ordered a bottle of wine with dinner, took our time, no rush. I kept her glass filled and listened to everything she said. She only answered two text messages during dinner, so that was a plus. I paid the bill, and we headed out to the parking lot. Once again, Sharon turned all sorts of heads as we walked out, holding hands, and she rested her head against my shoulder.

The entrance to Antonio's has a twenty-foot red canvas awning over the top. It was a lovely early fall evening, a warm temperature, but not hot. We walked out the door and stopped to let a car pass before stepping into the parking lot.

My first thought was, who knew there would be two red 2011 Chevy HHR's in the parking lot? Then I glanced at the license plate as it sped past and out onto the street. I recognized the number on the plate. It was mine.

"Hey, asshole," I yelled.

"Excuse me?" Sharon said and pulled her arm away from mine.

"That car that just shot past, that was mine."

"Yours?"

"Yeah. Someone just stole it. What the hell? I can't believe it. They just stole my car from right in front of me." I pulled my phone out and dialed 911.

"911 Emergency services."

"Yeah, I'm standing out front of Antonio's restaurant, and some bastard just drove off in my car."

"Did you know the individual?"

"Know him? You gotta be kidding. Hell no, I didn't know him. What the… Look, my car was just stolen, right in front of me. He's headed east on Fifth Street."

"Do you know the license number?"

I gave her the license number.

"Color and make of the car?"

"Yeah, it's a red Chevy HHR. The year is twenty-eleven."

Sharon had her phone out and was texting someone. I was on the phone with 911 for another four or five minutes. A shiny black Toyota suddenly pulled into the lot. Sharon waved her hand, and the car came to a stop.

"Sorry about your car, Dev. I'm going to grab this Uber and head home."

"The cops said they'd be here in thirty or forty minutes. I was thinking we could maybe grab another glass of wine. Check out the dessert menu if you wanted to—"

"Thanks, but I've got a crazy day tomorrow. I should probably just head home."

"Well, um, do you want me to stop by once I file my report with the police? I could bring the bottle of pink Prosecco." It wasn't what I'd planned, but a night at Sharon's or even just an hour or two was better than the dry spell I'd been going through.

"Oh, that's sweet of you," she said, sounding like she didn't mean a word. She followed up with a fake smile. "Maybe we both need a little break."

A little break? So far, I paid for a night of drinks and dinner on the last two nights. I'd certainly put in the time, not to mention the money.

She opened the back door on the Uber and slipped in, then looked at me and locked the door. No kiss, no hand squeeze, not so much as a wave. I read her lips as she spoke to the Uber driver. '*Just go, please, and hurry.*'

TWO

I watched the Toyota turn the corner and disappear from sight. Great, just great. What could be worse?

A black SUV in a distant corner of the parking lot turned on its headlights and pulled out of the parking space. It pulled up alongside me as I stood beneath the canopy waiting for Sharon to come to her senses and return. The passenger window on the SUV lowered, and unfortunately, a familiar voice said, "Get in, Haskell."

Fat Freddy Zimmerman. Righthand thug to the city's crime lord, Tubby Gustafson.

"Perfect timing, Freddy. Like things aren't bad enough. Hey, it's turned into a pretty lousy night, and right now I don't really need to—"

"I'm asking nicely, Haskell. Get your worthless ass in here while you can still do it under your own power." With that, the backdoor opened, and a very large individual stepped out, smiled, and extended his hand toward the inside of the car.

I'd had just about enough. "Hey, Freddy, sorry, but I'm going to take a pass. It's been a lousy night. Someone just ripped off my car. It was my third date with a woman, the night everything was supposed to happen, and she ended up going home in an Uber. For the record, just in case you're not picking up on it, I don't feel like talking to Tubby tonight. How about we set an appointment for some time tomorrow and I can just—"

"Get his worthless ass in here," Freddy said and raised the window.

The thug started toward me, minus the smile. "Hey, Freddy, were you even listening. I said—" The thug placed a hand the size of a ten-pound ham on my shoulder and started to force me toward the open door.

I slapped his arm away, made a fist with my right hand, and put everything I had into a punch headed straight for his solar plexus. He caught my fist in his massive hand and began to squeeze, all the while smiling. I started to groan as he slowly increased the pressure, and then just when I thought he was going to break all four of my fingers, he wiped the smile from his face and gave me a head butt. I saw stars just before everything went black.

"We're almost there. Wake that idiot up," a distant voice seemed to echo somewhere in my thick skull. I felt some not so gentle slaps across my face.

"All right, all right, knock it off. I'm awake. I was just resting my eyes," I said. I could barely recognize my own voice.

My statement brought a chorus of laughter from all four thugs in the car. I opened my eyes and focused in on the guy who had head-butted me. He didn't smile, and

I noticed a red welt on his forehead after coming in contact with me. Let that be a lesson to him, although it didn't seem to bother him all that much.

"Nice of you to join us again, Haskell," Fat Freddy said without turning around. "You'll be in front of Mr. Gustafson in just a minute, so pull yourself together."

I couldn't breathe through my nose. I glanced down at my sweater. Fortunately, it was black, so the blood from the head butt I'd received more or less disappeared. The thug with the forehead welt held out some sort of a baby butt-wipe in my direction.

"I'm fine."

"You might want to clean the blood off your face and chin," he said.

I dabbed and wiped and asked for another butt-wipe and then another one after that.

Fat Freddy laughed and said, "I knew you were always a shit head, Haskell." He followed up with another laugh as we turned into a crowded parking lot and headed for the building at the far end. The neon sign across the top of the building flashed the name of the place twice, Bare Facts. After that, the sign went dark for a moment before the letters flashed on one at a time until the entire sign was lit up. Then the sign flashed two more times before returning to one letter at a time. I recognized the place and had even visited a few dozen times, at least until I learned Tubby Gustafson owned the place, after which I pretty much stayed away.

The driver pulled the SUV to a stop opposite the front door. Actually, a set of double doors with neon lights designed to look like a pair of female legs in cowboy boots, one on either side of the doors. A childish idea that was probably great for business based on the three guys standing just outside the entrance having their picture taken.

"Let's go," Fat Freddy said as he rolled out of the front passenger seat. The large thug next to me opened the door and stepped out. He gave me a quick nod of his head, indicating I had better get out and fast. I thought it best to comply. Another thug joined us.

Fat Freddy said, "All right, Haskell, I don't want you talking with anyone along the way. You just keep your fat head down, keep that big mouth shut, and follow me. When we get to the office, I know you'll act the perfect gentleman. All right, let's go."

As we stepped in through the neon legs, the SUV pulled away and headed into the crowded parking lot. Inside, the place was jammed. Guys stood two-deep at the bar, all the tables around the stage were filled, and guys were standing against the walls on either side of the stage. The crowd was attired in everything from three-piece suits to shorts and work boots. Three women were currently on stage. One spun around on a brass pole while the other two danced along the front of the stage. Four more women, clad in see-through negligees, were working the crowd offering lap dances.

“Keep moving,” one of the thugs behind me shouted over the music. He pushed me forward just to make his point. Everyone was focused on the three women working the stage, and no one noticed us as we headed down the hall past the dressing room and toward an office door marked private. Fat Freddy knocked on the door, smiled, and held it open for us.

“Behave,” he said, issuing a warning as I stepped past him.

Three

Another muscular thug with a neatly trimmed beard and an open collar white shirt beneath his dark suit stood in a corner. He had his hands politely clasped in front of him, and he nodded at Fat Freddy as he stepped into the office. Fat Freddy nodded back. The thug looked at me, snapped his fingers, pointed to a chair in front of the desk, and I sat down.

Tubby Gustafson was seated behind the desk and didn't bother to look up. He was busy pushing keys on an adding machine. His fingers were moving in a blur, and there must have been at least five feet of partially rolled adding machine tape draped across the desk. Behind Tubby was a large steel door leading into a vault. The door was painted black and looked about a hundred years old with elaborate leafy gold trim around the edge of the door and the combination dial. The door was only partially open and was made up of a number of inch-thick steel plates.

Tubby's fingers flew across the adding machine keys for another minute or two before he hit a button, causing the machine to crank for a bit before it fell silent. He pressed a key, advancing the paper tape a couple of inches, then tore off the tape and glanced at whatever number was at the bottom.

"Damnit to hell," he half-shouted and tossed the tape onto the desk. "I'll kill whoever did— Well, if it isn't Private Investigator, Dev Haskell. How nice to see you. Perfect timing."

"Always nice to see you Tub… err, Mr. Gustafson."

"Tell me, Haskell. How is that business of yours working out?"

"My business? It's keeping me busy. I've got a few major clients now that provide regular work."

"Really?" Tubby raised his eyebrows. "Regular clients. You don't say. Are you making any money?"

"Oh, you know how it is, sir. I manage to keep the wolf away from the door, and then just about the time things seem to be going well, something unexpected happens."

"Unexpected?"

"Yes, sir. As a matter of fact, just tonight I came out of a restaurant with a friend, and my car was stolen right in front of my eyes."

Tubby smiled. "A friend, interesting. A business friend?"

"Umm, not exactly," I said.

"Well, I know how things go, Haskell. You get a hundred dollars in the bank, and suddenly, you need a hundred and ten to repair the furnace or pay the water bill."

"Yes, sir, something like that."

"Haskell, I'm going to give you the opportunity to experience a decent client. Without a doubt, the best client you will ever work for. What do you say?"

"Well, sir, umm, yeah, that sounds nice. What company would this be?"

"Not a company, Haskell. An individual. A wonderful individual. Namely, me," Tubby said and then extended his hands, palms up as if he was welcoming me into a church or something.

"You, sir?"

"Correct, and let me be the first to say congratulations. Lucky you."

"What exactly is it that you would like me to investigate?"

"Just one little thing," Tubby said, sounding like he was dangling the only option for freedom in front of a desperate prisoner.

"One little thing?"

Tubby nodded as he pushed his chair back and stood. "Come over here, Haskell," he said, urging me forward and wiggling his index finger.

I slowly stood and walked around the desk as Tubby pushed the vault door open. I looked inside the vault. The walls, floor, and ceiling were all steel. The vault was maybe ten feet long, six feet wide, and one side had a series of shelves. The shelves were all empty.

"Did you want me to paint this or move the shelves somewhere?"

Tubby shook his head then said over his shoulder, "You were right, Frederick. Why do I even bother? Haskell, the opportunity I'm presenting to you is to locate the items that are missing from this vault. To be specific, two black cargo bags that disappeared barely twenty-four hours ago."

"Someone took them out of this vault?"

Tubby smiled and said, "Correct. You're beginning to catch on."

"Who has access to the vault? Do you lock it?"

"It's always locked. It was opened last night at seven minutes after two in the morning, and the cash drawers from the registers behind the bar were placed in the vault. Like they are every evening after close. At twelve minutes after three, an individual opened the vault and left with both cargo bags. Show him," Tubby said and snapped his fingers.

The thug with the neatly trimmed beard and white shirt ran his fingers across the computer keyboard on the desk. An image appeared of an individual in a clown mask, wearing blue latex gloves and dressed all in black. He had a stethoscope plugged into his ears and was slowly working the combination dial on the door to the vault.

"Any idea who this is?" I asked.

"That's for you to find out," Tubby said.

"Who knows about this vault? Obviously, it's not original to the building. Did you have it put in?"

"Just for starters, certainly anyone who has ever ventured into this office knows about the vault. I had it installed three years ago for the express purpose of preventing just such an incident. Damnit to hell. Whoever did this is going to pay, big time!" Tubby's temper was suddenly ramping up. "I want you to find out who in the hell did this and find out fast."

The individual on the computer screen opened the vault and disappeared inside. A moment later, he stepped out of the vault with two large, black cargo bags slung over his shoulders. He seemed to look up at the security camera. The clown mask suggested he was laughing, and then he raised his middle finger and waved it at the camera before he disappeared. Tubby's face went crimson.

"Have you contacted the police?" I asked.

"The police? Really, Haskell? Please, use your head and don't make me think you're as stupid as everyone keeps telling me."

"I'll try to see what I can find out. I'm going to need a list of your employees. Anyone you can think of who has been in this office. I'll need the name of whatever company installed the vault and the names of anyone with access to the vault. Oh, and there's one other little problem, sir."

"And what in God's name is that?"

"My car was stolen this evening at—"

"At Antonio's. I'm aware of that, and for your information, we've already recovered it, and it's waiting for you out in the parking lot. I only hope you will return the favor and be as efficient when dealing with my particular problem."

"Recovered it? But how did you even know? I—"

Tubby held up his hand and said, "Silencio. If you would please simply focus on the task at hand."

Four

I left Bare Facts armed with about twenty pages worth of names and addresses of employees, former employees, dancers, the company that installed the vault, a number of accountants and attorneys who worked for Tubby, vendors, and various individuals who, for one reason or another, had seen the inside of Tubby's office. Not to mention the image of the guy wearing the clown mask and giving Tubby the finger, talk about living dangerously.

One thing became crystal clear, this was mission impossible. And then there was the question of who stole my car. Obviously, Tubby arranged the whole episode. Thanks to him, my third date with Sharon had been ruined.

When I walked out of Bare Facts, my red car was parked directly in front of the place. Two thugs smiled, and one of them opened the driver's door for me. Once I was inside, the thug who had opened the door took a pocket square from his suit coat and rubbed it across the door handle, pretending to make it clean. It wasn't lost on me that what he was really doing was removing any fingerprints.

Still, it didn't make sense. Tubby could have grabbed me anywhere at any time. Ever the eternal optimist, I drove past Sharon's condo, thinking if there was still a light on, it might make sense to call her and offer to come up and give her a back rub or something. Alas, the lights were off, and the place was dark. It was now approaching midnight after all.

I drove home, parked my car in the garage, then went inside and let Morton out into the backyard. I got the coffee ready for the morning, let Morton back in, and we went to bed. Nothing against Morton, but he wasn't who I'd hoped would wake up next to me in the morning. I tortured myself thinking about Tubby as my new client for the next twenty minutes until I drifted off to sleep.

I was up two hours before Morton made his way downstairs. I let him out the back door and returned to the laundry list of names and addresses Tubby had printed off for me. Twenty pages worth, and I knew there had to be more. I went through the list, checking the names of potentials. Certainly, Tubby's band of desperados, starting with Fat Freddy Zimmerman, were all potential culprits. Of course, there was also the company Tubby got the vault from and the crew that installed it. I was overwhelmed, to say the least.

Morton and I were in the office a half-hour before Louie arrived. I was on my computer looking up folks on Tubby's list, and it wasn't going well.

"Dev?" Louie said. He stood in the doorway with his hand still on the doorknob. "Oh my God, what happened to your nose?"

"Nothing good." I went on to tell him about my car being stolen, Sharon taking an Uber home, the thug's head butt, and Fat Freddy Zimmerman taking me to see Tubby at Bare Facts.

"So, you're going to take on the investigation?"

"Louie, this is Tubby Gustafson we're talking about. You don't tell him no."

"What did the police say?"

"The police? He's not going to report this to the police, and I sure as hell won't. God only knows where this stuff came from, but two canvas duffle bags filled with cash or drugs or diamonds or something. It's gotta be worth a million, plus."

"And what are you going to do if you find it? Who knows how many people you'll be up against?"

"If I'm so lucky to find out who is involved, I'm giving their names to Tubby and running for cover. Let him deal with it. I just want out of this whole thing as soon as possible."

"Yeah, I get that. But do you think Tubby will go for it?"

"I think he'd like nothing better."

"Any chance of linking up with Sharon again?"

"Mmm, might be a good idea to give her a couple of days to calm down, and besides, I don't want her anywhere near Tubby Gustafson and his group of bottom feeders. I can't think of a faster way to end my chances with her. If she ran off because my car was stolen, can you imagine what she'd do if she knew Tubby Gustafson was now my biggest client? In fact, my only client. I just want to get some answers on this deal and get the hell away from it as fast as I can."

Five

I spent the better part of the day online checking backgrounds. If I'd looked at one individual, I looked at a couple hundred. One thing came through loud and clear. This was not the group you'd want your kids hanging with. My thought had been to eliminate those individuals that did not have criminal records. There was only one thing wrong with that plan. It didn't work.

Everyone had a record of some sort. The women invariably had been arrested for solicitation, shoplifting, and oftentimes assaults. The men had universally spent time in the workhouse, if not a minimum of three to five years in state or federal prisons, for a variety of crimes. There was a whole range of financial scams, a few disbarred attorneys, possession and intent to sell charges, insurance fraud. The list went on and on. But that didn't begin to cover murder and non-negligent manslaughter, rape, robbery, aggravated assault, and gang violence, not to mention all the property crimes like burglary, larceny, motor vehicle theft, and arson. The handful of people who had been charged but not convicted began to look like boy scouts.

I kept coming back to the idea that someone had to actually open the vault door. If the robbery took place in the early morning hours, someone had to have access to Bare Facts. Did that mean they worked there? Or were they maybe a delivery person? But then, who made deliveries at that hour of the morning? Was this a onetime deal, or was it a regular occurrence that these cargo bags would be stored in the vault?

I put Morton in the car, and we drove home. I let him out the backdoor and filled his water dish. After twenty minutes, I lured him back inside with the promise of a treat. He caught the dog biscuit before it hit the ground, then hurried over to the far corner of the kitchen and inhaled the thing in three quick bites so he wouldn't have to share with me. I headed out the door to my car and drove to Bare Facts.

It was the tail-end of rush hour, and the normal twelve-minute drive took ten minutes longer. The parking lot was full, but I was able to grab one of the last spots, actually a parking place right next to the dumpster. I sat in my car and watched five different cars pull into the lot and guys hurry into Bare Facts. It was a sunny evening, so no one was dodging rain or lousy weather. It was more like no one wanted to be spotted going into the place. And, who could blame them?

After the fifth car, a guy in a starched shirt and tie talking on his cellphone, parked and went inside. I climbed out of my car and did a quick look around the lot, checking for Tubby's Cadillac Escalade before I went inside. Thankfully, I didn't see it. Once inside, a good two-thirds of the clientele were wearing ties. Half of that group still had their suit coats on.

There were two women with a group of a half-dozen men, and I figured they were there on an office dare. The women were seated next to each other with their backs to the stage. Right now, they looked like they might be having serious second thoughts.

The tables were full, so I grabbed one of the empty stools at the bar.

"What do you want," one of the three bartenders asked. He didn't smile, and the way he asked the question suggested he was in a hurry and didn't have time to waste.

I glanced at the half-dozen beer taps and said, "Give me an IPA." He immediately departed without so much as a nod or even saying, "Okay."

He was back a couple of minutes later and set two beer mugs down in front of me. "Fifteen dollars," he said.

"I only ordered one."

"Two drink minimum while there's someone on stage."

"Seven and a half bucks for a beer?"

"It's good beer," he said without cracking the slightest hint of a smile. I tossed a twenty on the bar. "You want change?"

"Yeah, I'd like my change," I said. If it was possible, he looked even less happy.

I finished the first beer over the course of fifteen minutes, then picked up my second mug and walked past the end of the bar and down the hall to Tubby's office door which was marked private. I knocked on the door, but no one answered. I tried the doorknob, but it was locked, so I walked back to the bar.

I looked around for a logical place to hide if I was planning to break into the vault. Maybe the stage or the dressing room would work, but how would you get in either place without someone spotting you and telling you to get out? Especially if you were a guy. Maybe that pointed to an inside job or accomplices. I finished my beer and headed into the men's room. There were four other guys in there. One combing his hair, one in a stall, one just leaving, and one standing at a urinal. I walked down to the far end, and stood at the urinal, looking around. It wasn't until I finished that I noticed the door to the maintenance closet on the back wall.

I pulled on the doorknob and the door opened. The closet was full of exactly what one would expect; trash bags, brooms, a mop, a shelf with spray Clorox bottles, urinal cakes, and maybe two dozen rolls of toilet paper. Oddly, there was a hook and eye latch screwed into the door frame. It looked like a recent addition. Why would you lock the closet door from the inside? There was no place to sit down in the closet. I noticed a wrapper from a Snickers bar on the floor. I unrolled a length of toilet paper and used it to pick up the wrapper. Melted chocolate was on the inside of the wrapper. I pulled a trash bag off the roll and placed the wrapper inside. I folded up the trash bag, walked out to my car, placed the trash bag in my glove compartment, and went back into Bare Facts.

Six

The bartender gave me a look like he was daring me to order something as he said, "Last call." It was a different bartender from the earlier guy and even less charming. I had been sipping my beer for the last two hours, and it was now more or less flat.

"No, thanks, it's time to head home," I said. The place was emptying out. There were six guys at the bar, three of whom were together. Only four occupied tables, two of those by just one person. Four guys sat at the stage, one appeared to be asleep or maybe passed out. I set my half-finished mug on the bar and climbed off the stool. I waited until the two bartenders were busy before I strolled into the men's room. It was empty, and I hurried into the maintenance closet, hooked the door, and waited.

I heard someone walk into the men's room a half-hour later. After a minute or two, I heard the faucet on the sink running, and then they started whistling. As they left, they must have turned off the lights because the shaft of light shining at the bottom of the door suddenly disappeared. I pulled my cell phone out and checked the time. It was two-twenty. I waited for another thirty minutes before I unhooked the latch and opened the door. The room was pitch dark. I couldn't hear any music coming from outside the restroom.

I slowly made my way in the general direction of where I thought the door might be. I took tiny steps as I walked with one arm out in front of me, and my head tilted back expecting to hit the top of a door frame.

I eventually came to a wall and then followed the wall to the right until I came to a corner. The door was one foot over, and I opened it slowly, no more than an inch. A dim light lit the hallway. I couldn't hear any noise coming from the bar area. I stuck my head out and looked around. Just three dim lights were on, the one in the hallway was just above the private office door.

I hurried down to the door and took out my lock picking set. I'm not the greatest, but I'm pretty good, and I was getting nowhere with the lock on the door. After a couple of minutes, I made my way to the front entrance and looked out. The parking lot was virtually empty, and based on the complete lack of flashing lights outside, I guessed the neon lights on either side of the entrance must have been turned off.

I pushed open the door and hurried to my car. I climbed in, started the car, and headed out of the lot. I was maybe three blocks away when I saw the flashing lights racing toward me. There was no siren, but I pulled to the curb as the squad car shot past me headed in the opposite direction. I figured the squad car was probably responding to silent alarms in Bare Facts along with motion detectors. So whoever broke into the vault was better than I was at picking door locks, and that didn't even begin to account for the time it would take to open the vault.

I drove home, pulled into the garage, and went inside. Morton wasn't at the door, and he wasn't on the couch in the front room, although based on the napkins and trash scattered around, he'd been there. It took me the better part of a half-hour to clean up the mess he left and get the coffee made for the morning.

I climbed the stairs and debated taking a shower. I decided I would wait until morning for the shower and went into the bedroom. Morton was stretched out on the bed. A steak bone rested next to his head. I couldn't really blame him. I set the bone on my dresser, got undressed, and climbed into bed. Thirty seconds later, I was sound asleep.

Seven

Morton woke me the following morning at half-past eight. I let him out the back door, turned on the coffee, then went upstairs and grabbed a shower. Once I was dressed, I went downstairs, filled Morton's food and water dish, and let him inside. I poured myself a coffee and turned on my laptop. I went through the list of Tubby's employees and associates and made a second list of individuals who'd been convicted on burglary charges. Most of the individuals were thugs who kicked in a door or stole a set of keys. I eliminated them. There were five guys who appeared to have maybe picked a lock. I typed up a shortlist, turned off the laptop, and made breakfast.

Once we ate, Morton and I headed down to the office. Louie was nowhere to be found, but in the back of my mind, I seemed to remember he had a court appearance this morning. He was the go-to attorney in town if you were fighting a DUI, and he was busy doing just that all the time. I tossed the trash bag with the Snicker's wrapper from Bare Facts onto my desk. Yesterday's coffee was still in the pot. I dumped it and made a fresh pot. I filled my mug and sat down at my desk. I happened to give a casual glance out the window just as a black Cadillac Escalade pulled alongside the curb and stopped.

I kept my fingers crossed, even though that never seemed to work. Sure enough, a moment later, Fat Freddy Zimmerman slid out from behind the wheel and opened the rear door. I could see Tubby Gustafson sitting in the back seat, red-faced and apparently screaming into his cellphone. When he was finished, he disconnected, shook his head, and barked something before oozing out of the back seat. He handed Fat Freddy an empty white bag that looked like it was from a bakery and made his way across the street. Fat Freddy tossed the bag in the front seat and hurried across the street to catch up with Tubby.

A moment later, I heard the staircase leading up to the second floor begin to creak and groan. The noise grew louder, and then just as suddenly, it stopped. Morton glanced toward the door, whined, then curled up and placed his front paws over his head. A moment later, a flushed-faced Fat Freddy opened the office door. Tubby was right behind him, gasping for air and shaking his head.

"Honest to God, Haskell. I'm trying to think of a better way than that staircase to eliminate potential clients, and I can't come up with one. No wonder your business is a losing proposition. No one can make it to your office without risking a heart attack."

I didn't feel the need to suggest that the vast majority of my clients weren't two to three hundred pounds overweight. “Maybe I could rent from you, Mr. Gustafson.”

“Who are you trying to kid?” Tubby said as he collapsed into one of the two client chairs in front of my desk. “Good Lord, I’ve told you before, absolutely not. I’d lose an entire floor of tenants no matter where you moved in. Rent from me? No. You seem devoid of any business sense, Haskell. Yet another problem with you.”

“To what do I owe the pleasure of this visit?”

“Oh, believe me, it’s anything but pleasurable,” Tubby said, then gasped and, with a wave of his hand, signaled Fat Freddy to continue the conversation.

“We had another break-in last night at Bare Facts,” Fat Freddy said. “Fortunately, it doesn’t look like anything was stolen this time. We brought you on board to put a stop to this sort of thing. But here we are, a little more than forty-eight hours later, and you haven’t done shit. I’m warning you, Haskell, either you get a handle on who is doing this, or you’ll pay, and I’m talking big time.”

I ignored Fat Freddy and focused on Tubby. “I know all about the break-in last night, sir. As a matter of fact, I was there.”

“You were there? What the hell are you talking about? That place gets locked down tighter than a drum. Our crew hadn’t left more than twenty minutes when the alarms were going off. And you were there, for the love of—”

"I think I figured out how he did it, the man with the clown mask who stole the two cargo bags."

"What do you mean figured it out? We already know. He picked the lock on the office door and then the combination to the vault. Hello. We had that information. Good Lord, in case you've forgotten, we even have a security tape."

"But I think I've found out how he got in the building to begin with."

Tubby leaned forward. For once, he appeared genuinely interested. "Really?"

"I think so. I was there last night looking around and came across something. By the way,Sir, seven and-a-half dollars for a beer, that's pretty expensive."

"That's why we keep the price high. The whole purpose is to keep out trash like you. What did you find out?"

I went on to tell him about the maintenance closet with the hook and eye latch. How I had time to fool with the office door but couldn't get in and how I was three blocks away when the police car passed me going in the opposite direction.

Tubby sat back and seemed to think. "So you were in the maintenance closet, and you found a candy bar wrapper. I don't suppose you hung onto it."

"As a matter of fact, I did." I pushed the trash bag across the desk to him. "I'm guessing whoever it was ate the candy bar while he waited in that closet. He screwed in the hook and eye latch, that probably took all of thirty seconds, and then he felt comfortable enough to bide his time until everyone left."

"And no one saw you go in there?"

"They might have, but who keeps track of people coming and going from restrooms? It's the end of the night. They're too busy getting things put away and shut down."

Tubby pulled the trash bag with the Snicker's wrapper toward him, opened it up, and peeked inside. He looked up at me, nodded, and said, "It pains me to say this Haskell, but well done. You seem to have finally accomplished something. Your services are no longer needed, and I'm releasing you from your contract."

"Thank you, Mr. Gustafson. Um, exactly where should I send my bill?"

"Bill? For what? You were entertained for the evening, and now I'm supposed to give you money on top of that? Really? Come along, Frederick. We've other things to accomplish today."

"But, I don't know who left that wrapper in the closet, Mr. Gustafson. I don't even know if it was the individual in question. I mean, I think it was, but I—"

"Enough. Quit while you're ahead, Haskell. For the love of God. I should send you a bill for the lessons in life I always seem to have to give you. Let me ask you this, Haskell. Just how in the hell have you made it this far knowing what little you know? How is it even possible for you to survive? Now enough. We're out of here. Come along, Frederick."

Fat Freddy jumped up and pulled the chair back as Tubby stood, then he followed Tubby, flashing me the finger behind his back as they hurried out the door. I watched from my window as Freddy held the door open while Tubby climbed into the back seat of the Cadillac Escalade, holding the trash bag with the Snickers wrapper. Freddy gave me the finger as he climbed in behind the wheel. He waited for a pickup truck to pass before he sped up the hill and onto the interstate.

Eight

As Louie walked into the office he said, "Well, don't you look like the cat that swallowed the canary. Someone call you for a date tonight?"

It was after 2:00, and I was just finishing the last of the onion rings I had with my cheeseburger in celebration of getting Tubby Gustafson out of my hair. "Mission accomplished. No more Tubby Gustafson."

"He's been arrested?"

"No, Louie, but he's taken me off the case. Apparently, I said something that made him think he knew who broke into the vault in his office at Bare Facts. I didn't bother to question him. I'm just glad he thinks he can handle things from here, and he left with the only clue I had, a Snickers candy bar wrapper."

"What?"

"Look, he said he was releasing me from my contract, not that I ever signed anything, but who am I to argue? There are at least a hundred ways I can think of that would make that job a no-win situation for me. I'm just thrilled to be done with it. You got time for a little celebration at The Spot?"

"I will in about an hour," Louie said. "I just have to tidy up some loose ends and email a bill to my client."

"Things went well for you?"

"Yeah, they gave him a year in the workhouse instead of jail. He can go to work during the day and attend weekly AA meetings. If he sticks with that, his record will be expunged in thirty-six months. Under the circumstances, rear-ending a police car, yeah, he got off easy. He's paying for repairs to the squad car, and over the next seven years, he'll fork out maybe ten grand extra for risk auto insurance, but all in all, he's damn lucky."

"Well done, Louie."

"I'd love to take all the credit, but fortunately, the cop he rear-ended was a grade school pal, and he testified on my client's behalf. Nice thing to do, and he didn't have to do it."

"Well, then we both have a little something to celebrate," I said.

"Just give me an hour, and I'll be ready." Louie pulled his laptop out of its case, flipped it open and started tapping keys.

It was more like two hours, but who's counting? We were both in a good mood. Louie finally switched off his computer, and we headed over to The Spot. We beat the evening rush. There were just four people at the bar and two couples seated in one of the booths. We grabbed our usual stools at the end of the bar. Morton curled up at my feet and looked up in anticipation. Mike was bartending. Louie ordered a whiskey. I just ordered an IPA and a bag of pork rinds for Morton.

"I got this, man," I said and handed Mike a twenty-dollar bill as he set the drinks in front of us and pushed them across the bar.

"You two celebrating? What is it, Dev? The paternity test turned out to be someone else?" Mike said and laughed as he tossed the bag of pork rinds on the bar.

"Very funny, not. No, I was just able to finish up a lot faster than I expected with a client. And without mentioning any names, I'm glad to be done with it. Here's to you," I said and raised my glass just as my cellphone rang. I took a sip and answered without looking at the screen. "Haskell Investigations."

"Oh, hi, Dev. I hope I'm not interrupting anything."

"Sharon? No, no interruption at all. Just winding up a business meeting. You made it home okay in the Uber the other night?"

"Yeah, that's one of the reasons I'm calling. I wondered if the police ever got your car back?"

"I got it back. Umm, it turned out a friend took it. He owed me a favor, and he just got it washed and waxed for me. Thought he was doing a good deed."

"A friend? I thought you said you didn't recognize him when he drove past."

Damnit. "The whole thing sort of caught me off-guard. He's always been kind of a different sort, but he had the best of intentions. Things just didn't exactly work out the way he intended."

"Oh my, that is really weird. Well, the reason I'm calling is I wondered if you might have time to join me for dinner. I'm sorry it's so last minute. I thought I'd be tied up tonight, but that didn't work out as planned, and I'm about to head home. If you wanted to come over in, oh, maybe an hour or so and join me for dinner I think we'd both enjoy it. I feel bad about the other night."

It wasn't lost on me that she didn't specifically mention feeling bad about her leaving in an Uber, but I didn't care. Besides, tied up? If that's what she wanted. "Yeah, I should be able to finish up here by then. I'd love to join you. What can I bring?"

Louie shot me a look over the rim of his glass.

"Just bring yourself. If you wanted to pick up a bottle of wine, that would be okay. I'm doing a chicken dish."

"Chicken. Okay, see you in about 90 minutes. I'm looking forward to it. Thanks for the call, Sharon."

I turned off my phone as Louie shook his head.

"What?"

"She wants something," Louie said and took a sip.

"Yeah, hello. I'll say. She wants your boy here, and I'm more than willing to fulfill that particular desire."

"I'm sensing some form of bad luck about to happen," Louie said.

"Are you kidding? First, Tubby Gustafson tells me my services are no longer needed, and now beautiful, drop-dead gorgeous Sharon calls and offers to cook me dinner if I'll come over and provide my special services. What I should do is go buy a lottery ticket right now while my luck is still running this hot." I tore open the bag of pork rinds and gave three to Morton and one to myself.

"What you should do is run in the opposite direction. When was the last time a woman called you, and there wasn't some major hook involved?"

"That isn't the way—"

"Connie. Misty. Molly. That Kate woman whose husband came home early from his business trip."

"Her name was Kitty, and yeah, okay, you're right on that one. But I didn't know she was married."

"Oh, really?"

I drained my beer, left a couple of bucks on the bar as a tip for Mike, and said, "Well, we better go. I should probably get cleaned up and get Morton home and settled in. See you in the morning?"

"Yeah. I've got a court appearance at ten-thirty, but I'm just asking for a continuation, so I should be back before noon."

"See you tomorrow. Come on, Morton. Let's go."

"Good luck," Louie called. As we headed out the door, he raised his glass to Mike for a refill and attacked the bag of pork rinds.

Nine

When we got home, I let Morton out into the backyard and then hurried upstairs to shower and shave. I pulled on my cleanest pair of jeans and slipped into a reasonably clean Saint Paul Saints jersey. I called Morton in, tossed him a biscuit, and headed out the door. I stopped at Solo Vino, picked up two bottles of white wine, a bottle of pink Prosecco, and headed over to Sharon's condo.

She buzzed me in the door, and I hurried up the stairs. Sharon's condo is on the third floor of an older building, and there isn't an elevator. I'd never been in the place before, so it would be interesting to get the lay-out. When I reached the top of the stairs on the third floor, Sharon was standing in the open doorway at the end of the hall. She was wearing a short, dark, lapel shirt dress with long sleeves. The thing was unbuttoned down almost to her navel. A small gold cross dangled right at the top of her cleavage, not a complaint on my part.

"Hi, Dev, right on time," she said, never looking up from her phone as her thumbs flew up and down.

I stopped in front of her and waited for fifteen sec-onds before she finished texting and looked up at me. "Mmm, sorry about that. Just a question someone had."

She leaned forward, gave me a kiss, and said, "Oh, wine. You didn't have to do that, but it's so nice. Thank you."

"Little something extra in there for you," I said and handed her the bag.

She glanced inside, and her eyes literally sparkled. "Oh. My. God. Pink Prosecco and I don't have an early morning meeting tomorrow. Thank you. You are such a dear. It's shaping up to be an interesting night," she said and gave me another kiss before she turned and headed into her unit.

We entered a living room with a Persian rug and three windows that looked out onto the street. The windows had a rounded top that was a stained glass panel. Each panel was a similar floral design and most likely original to the building. The far wall had a gas fireplace that was off at the moment. I followed Sharon through the living room and across a hallway into the kitchen. There was a wonderful garlic smell as we entered.

I stepped behind one side of the granite kitchen counter, and Sharon walked around to the business side with double ovens, a range, a brushed chrome refrigerator, and a large white porcelain sink. She opened the refrigerator, laid the three bottles I'd brought onto a shelf, and pulled out a chilled bottle of white wine.

A pair of stemmed crystal glasses, probably Waterford, rested on small linen napkins, and she proceeded to fill both glasses. She pushed a glass across the counter toward me and raised her glass.

"Here's to a lovely evening. And thank you for coming on such short notice. I hope I didn't interrupt any plans you had."

Drinking at The Spot with Louie or standing here with drop-dead gorgeous Sharon, gee, let me think. "No, I was just finishing a meeting with a client, giving him the final results of my investigation."

"Oh, no," she said and set her glass down. "A client? I thought you said it was a friend? I'm sorry I would never have interrupted if—"

"No, please, we were all finished, and I much prefer to be here with you. You look wonderful, by the way."

"Oh, that's so nice of you to say." We raised our glasses and clinked them together, giving off a little crystal sounding chime. As she sipped, Sharon gave my St. Paul Saints jersey the once over. At least I had shaved.

"What do you have on the stove? It smells delicious."

"Oh, thanks. It's a garlic chicken recipe of my mom's. I hope you're hungry. The recipe serves six, and I've never taken the time to cut it down, but it always tastes so good I don't care."

"Well then, here's to you and your mom and a delicious dinner. I'm looking forward to it."

"What do you say we head into the living room? This needs to cook for another twenty minutes, and I want to hear about you getting your car back. It sounds absolutely crazy," she said, then stepped around the counter, took my hand, and led us into the living room.

She flicked a switch along the side of the fireplace, and the flame jumped on. Two winged-back chairs were positioned on either side of the fireplace, and she settled into one. I headed toward the other.

"So, your car?" she said and took a sip.

"Oh, yeah. In the end, not a big deal. My pal, I've known him since we were kids. He's actually a nice guy," I lied, making it up as I went along. I piled it on thick and said, "He um, suffers from a bit of Asperger's, so he doesn't have the best handle on time frames and maybe what's appropriate. So he just wanted to do me a favor, have the car washed and waxed, never realizing that once we finished dinner, you and I would be leaving. He didn't mean any harm, and it was great to get the wash and wax. It was just lousy timing. Hey, I have to say you have a very lovely place. How long have you been here?"

"Here? Oh, not really all that long. I was in St. Louis before moving up here, and, before that, New York."

"New York City?"

"Yeah, investment banking. That's what I do. We like to joke and say we'll manage your money until it's all gone."

Ten

I poured more wine as Sharon dished up the garlic chicken. She placed two delicious smelling, steaming plates on the dining room table, added a basket of ciabatta rolls, dimmed the lights, lit a candelabra holding three red candles, and placed her cellphone on the table just to her right. If it was possible, the garlic chicken tasted even better than it smelled.

"I have to tell you, Sharon, this is so good. It's absolutely delicious."

"Aw, thanks. Like I said, it's my mom's recipe. She served it on special occasions, and she'd make a giant batch. My aunts and uncles and my grandparents would all be over. They'd all tell stories about my mom growing up, and we'd want to hear all the details. You can just imagine."

"A wonderful memory. You're blessed to have it. Here," I said, raising my glass. "A toast to your family, your folks, aunts and uncles, and your grandparents." I made sure Sharon's glass was never empty throughout dinner as we chatted, and she responded to two text messages. She placed the dishes in the dishwasher as I brought them in from the dining room table. I topped up her wine glass with the last of the first bottle of wine and then opened the bottle of pink Prosecco. When the cork popped off, it flew into the kitchen sink.

"Oh, well, you know what that means," she said.

"What? That I have good aim?"

"Hardly. It means we'll have to finish the bottle. Let me get my special Prosecco glasses. Oh, this will be great. I haven't had Prosecco for a couple of weeks." She opened a cupboard and took out two long tall glasses. They sort of looked like wine glasses only taller and thinner. "Fill 'em up," she said and grinned. I poured the bubbly liquid into the glasses, giving Sharon maybe a third more than me. "Oh, you don't like it?" she asked.

"No, it's not that. It's okay, but it's obvious you love it, so I'll just sip a little, and you can have the rest."

"You're just trying to get me drunk."

"No, actually, I'm just saving room for dessert. Besides, I probably need the sweetening."

"Well, you're going to love it," she said and opened the refrigerator door. She took out two white dessert plates with a chocolate looking dessert. "Tiramisu," she said as she set the plates on the kitchen counter and took a healthy sip of the Prosecco. "Oh, honest to God, Dev. This is to die for." She followed up with another sip then picked up the dessert plate and her glass of Prosecco. "Come on. Let's sit by the fire."

I followed her into the living room. The fire was going, and by now, it was dark outside. The street light in front of her building shone through the stained glass windows illuminating the three images on the distant living room wall. The soft music playing in the background made everything just that much more perfect.

"This is really lovely, Sharon," I said.

"I'm just glad you could come over. If you weren't here, I'd either be watching a movie I wasn't interested in, or I'd be working. This is much better."

We finished the tiramisu in about two minutes. I was immediately on my feet. I hauled our dessert plates into the kitchen and returned with the bottle of Prosecco. I topped up Sharon's glass and added about a teaspoon's worth to mine. We chatted on about everything and nothing over the next hour. Sharon answered another text message and basically finished the bottle of Prosecco. By this time, we were both sitting on the Persian rug with our backs against the winged back chairs.

Sharon had assumed a very unladylike pose and seemed oblivious. I certainly wasn't going to say anything. She was at the point of intoxication, where she had trouble focusing on me just three feet away. Her head was weaving, and she held the stemmed wine glass at an angle that almost poured the contents onto the Persian rug.

"Okay," she said, suddenly sitting up straight. She placed the glass between her thighs and ran both hands through her hair. "I think it's time for bed. You about ready?"

"Oh, yeah. Very ready."

"Well, good. Come on. Do me a favor and help me up." With that, she attempted to get up. I quickly snatched her wine glass from between her legs and set it on the end table just as she dropped back to the floor. "Give me a hand here, honey," she said and raised both her arms as her head drooped down.

I took hold of her hands and slowly raised her up onto her feet. She staggered down the hallway with my right arm around her waist and my left hand hanging onto her arm. The bedroom was illuminated by three scented candles lined up across her double dresser and reflecting off the mirror above the dresser.

The four poster double bed had off-white silk drapes hanging at each post and then what looked like a red silk scarf hanging from either side of the headboard. Sharon turned toward me and in a slurred voice, said, "I think it's time you show me what you're made of."

She staggered a step or two in an effort to regain her balance but instead fell backward onto the bed. She started to laugh as she sat up and struggled with the buttons down the front of her dress. By now, I was standing in my boxers and black socks.

"Can I help you with those buttons, Sharon?"

"Maybe that'd be a good idea. A very good idea," she said. She looked at me as I began to undo her buttons, but even though I was just a foot away, I don't think she could actually see me. I unbuttoned her dress and spread it open, revealing a black bra and thong. "Perfect," she said and pulled back the covers on what looked like silk sheets. She was suddenly up on all fours and crawling toward the head of the bed.

I hurried around to the far side of the bed, kicked my boxers off, quickly tossed my socks onto the floor, and hopped into the bed. I curled up next to her, and she greeted me with a loud snore.

"Sharon? Sharon, you awake? Sharon?"

Another loud snore.

Eleven

Based on the digital clock on Sharon's dresser, it was a little after four in the morning. At first, I thought I heard the radio, but then it was clearly Sharon's voice. "Oh, God. My head is killing me."

It took me a moment to realize the voice was coming from down the hall, probably the bathroom. I waited for her to slip back into bed, but I drifted off to sleep before she returned.

I woke again as she climbed on top of me. She still wore her undergarments and the unbuttoned dress. She was more or less asleep and still intoxicated. Nice try, but it wasn't working for me. I rolled her off, and she settled in with her back to me and resumed her snoring. I thought I heard something in another room but then remembered that she was only separated from her neighbors by a shared wall.

I woke again at around six, this time for good. Even asleep, she looked stunning. I purposely bumped up against her. I pretended to flop my hand on her face, but nothing seemed to wake her, and eventually, I quietly slid out of bed, dressed, and headed into the kitchen. The wine glasses were nowhere to be seen, the kitchen pans were washed and drying in the sink, and the coffee was perking. Incredible. She basically passes out as we're getting undressed and then is up in the middle of the night cleaning up the kitchen. What a piece of work. I sipped coffee for a half-hour, hoping she might wake up and suggest we have an early morning tumble in the hay, but it never happened. I took a pen and tore a piece of paper from a pad attached to the refrigerator and left her a note. I wrote that I loved the meal, and hopefully, we could consummate the evening activities sooner rather than later. I placed my note in front of the coffee pot, where she would be sure to see it and then drove home.

Morton was still asleep, which was a lot better than having him whining at the back door to be let out. I put the coffee on, cleaned up the mess Morton made the night before, and went online. He was downstairs about forty-five minutes later. I gave him the usual morning head scratch and let him outside. I filled his food and water dish and let him back in. We ate breakfast together and then headed down to the office.

Louie was nowhere to be seen, but there was a reasonably recent pot of coffee on the burner, and I poured a cup. I sat down behind my desk and placed a call to Sharon. As I got dumped into her voicemail, I turned around in my desk chair and looked out the window. Someone had parked a classy looking, dark blue, Acura NSX behind my car. Not bad, my almost ten-year-old bomb that I paid four grand for and the NSX that goes for something north of a hundred and fifty grand. I could hear the stairs creaking outside the office door, but I was pretty sure Tubby Gustafson couldn't fit into that sporty looking car on the street. There was something familiar about the vehicle, and I was racking my brain trying to think of who I might know that would drive such a thing.

I stared at the car while I left my message. "Yeah, hi, Sharon. This is Dev. Just checking in to see how the head is. Thanks for a lovely evening. Lesson to me, next time you can have pink Prosecco or white wine, but not both. Call me when you're able. Bye, bye."

As I disconnected, the office door opened, and all my positive thoughts went down the drain.

Private eye, Scarlett Raunchnoble, Scarlett for short, aka Raunchy Scarlett. She was a major pain in the ass and, on more than one occasion, had vowed to never interact with me. She was also very good looking, auburn hair, incredible figure, highly successful, and the last time I checked, had something like a dozen investigators on staff and four offices throughout the metro area.

"Hi Scarlett, the hairdresser is across the hall. Sorry, but I'm kinda busy."

"Yeah, sure you are," she said, stepping into my office and closing the door behind her. She lingered for a moment, giving me ample time to appraise her perfect rear in the tight black leather slacks. No doubt designer labels on the both slacks and the white blouse.

"Yeah, you're so busy you're sipping coffee at your clean desk and begging on the phone to the latest woman who had to drink herself into a stupor just to put up with you. Looks like you've got just a ton of work going on. I'm kidding, of course."

"What do you want, Scarlett?"

"I just wanted to check and see how my sexy competitor was doing. Is there a crime in that?"

"First of all, I'm not your competitor."

"Yeah, true. You're also not sexy, but I thought I'd just throw that in to make you feel better. You know, sort of a version of helping the downtrodden."

"I'm presuming you came here for a reason, I mean, along with the desire to try and ruin my day, which you've already succeeded in doing."

"Oh, I don't know. It sounded like you were scraping the bottom of the barrel once again before you even knew I was here. No surprise, I guess some things just never change. I see you've updated your office decor," she said, indicating my client chair with the duct tape and Louie's picnic table desk with two empty beer cans.

"It gets me by. Besides, I'm more interested in actually solving cases as opposed to fancy office furniture."

"Yeah, sure you are. God, Haskell, even your dog thinks you're nuts. Look at the poor thing."

Morton was lying on his bed with both front paws over his ears. "Morton," I said in a loud voice, and he slowly looked up at me. "Morton, attack. Attack, Morton."

He just hunkered down, settled into the bed, and assumed his former position.

"Who can blame the poor thing?" Scarlett said. She pulled out a client chair and brushed off the seat before she sat down. As she settled into the chair, it creaked, and she got a look on her face. "Is this thing even safe?"

"It'll hold Tubby Gustafson, and he's almost twice your weight."

"Try four times, idiot. And Tubby Gustafson? Are you kidding?"

I ignored her last comment. "So other than casting a dark cloud on whatever positive thought I may have had, what are you doing here?"

"I come bearing gifts, and this is the way I'm treated? No wonder the state wants to revoke your license."

"For your information, they've tried that twice and been unsuccessful in both instances."

Twelve

Scarlett seemed to set her jaw and then said, "All right, so here's the deal, Haskell. I'm working a case and—"

"Who's your client?"

"That's private information at this point. Suffice to say, it's a local prominent family. Oh, and by the way, they're in a legitimate business. Unlike the folks you deal with."

"So, what do you need me for?"

"I need someone on my arm at an event."

"Scarlett, are you telling me that with all the people on your staff, you've got four offices, for God's sake. Are you telling me, all your employees have refused to be publicly associated with you? Wow! Who knew they were that smart? I'll have to take back some of the things I've said about them."

"Ha, ha, ha. Oh, my God, you are so funny, Dev, a real riot. As it happens, we're working more than one case at a time. I know, that's something very difficult for an individual such as yourself to comprehend, but that's just one of the many reasons we're regularly listed as one of the top three firms in the state. Are you, um, even listed? Let me answer for you. No, you are not. In fact, the only time you are even mentioned is the required public notice regarding your latest battle with the state to revoke your license. What's it been barely twenty-four months since the last attempt?"

"It's been almost two and a half years, for your information." My comment only brought a smile to her face.

"So, what do you say? All you have to do is dress up in clean clothes for a wedding, and I'll pay you the city's going rate."

"Which is?"

"I have to check, but I think it's right around twelve-fifty an hour, plus we'll be at a wedding, so it'll be all you can eat."

"Gee, let me think about that for a while. Okay, done. You kidding, no f'ing way. The last time we were together, you left with some guy, and I ended up having to hitchhike home. That was after I waited for you for over an hour to come out of the ladies room, since you never bothered to mention to me you were leaving with someone you just met."

"Mmm, yeah. Well, those were different times. I've changed a lot since then and you, well, sorry. Okay, thirteen bucks an hour, but that's my final offer."

"Good. Your final offer. Does that mean you're going to leave?"

"What is it with you? Did you steal money from someone's cash register so you can just sit here all day and not worry about paying bills this month? Or, are you so far in debt that you're never going to get out, so what's the difference?"

"Neither, and to be honest, Scarlett, it's one of the few perks of being self-employed. Every once in awhile, I get to say no. So, no. I'm not working with you."

"You sure you want to take a pass on this opportunity?"

"Very sure. Here, being ever the gentleman, let me help you on your way out." I stepped out from behind my desk and opened the office door. "As always, it's been a unique experience, Scarlett. Enjoy your life in high society."

"I intend to, Dev. You mind yourself. Now, when whatever gig you're scamming here goes bust, feel free to give me a call." She tossed a couple of business cards on my desk. "I've always got an office or two that needs cleaning."

As she walked out of the office, I ignored the voice inside my head, suggesting I push her down the stairs. I closed the door behind her and clicked the lock. I settled into my office chair and watched out the window as she crossed the street. Tight black leather slacks, an attractive white blouse, and black heels all set off by what looked like a matching black holster holding a nine-millimeter pistol on her belt. I watched her climb into her sporty little overpriced car and drive off. Once she was out of sight, I took her business cards and tossed them in the wastebasket.

Louie wandered in a little before noon. Just to prove Scarlett wrong, I'd spent the past hour and a half being busy cleaning the office. Two white plastic trash bags were filled with shredded papers from old files and a bunch of pictures pals had emailed of wives on a girls weekend at someone's lake place. The ladies were clearly over-served and under-dressed. Since I valued my pals' lives, shredding the emails I'd printed off seemed to be the sensible thing to do. The trash bags were sitting in the wicker basket that had served as Morton's bed for about a week before he chewed it up.

"What got into you?" Louie said. "Did you finally blink first and decide you couldn't stand the mess?"

"I had a visit from Raunchy Scarlett this morning. Among other things, she told me I wasn't busy and then tried to hire me for minimum wage. So, I got busy and cleaned at least part of the place. Don't worry, I didn't touch anything of yours except the empty beer cans on your table."

"Hey, I was saving those cans for a project."

"What?"

"Relax, I'm kidding, Dev. What happened to your sense of humor?"

"I think it left with Scarlett."

"God, that woman can get under your skin. Didn't you have something going on with her a while back?"

"More like a half-night stand that could be measured in minutes rather than hours. She ditched me the same night and went home with some corporate type. I ended up having to walk home about six miles at two in the morning. She's rubbed me the wrong way ever since."

"Can't say as I blame you. Did she really offer you a job?"

"Yeah, I mean sort of. She wanted me to be her partner at a wedding, strictly business, although she didn't say exactly that. She just said I'd be her partner at this thing and get this, she'd pay me thirteen bucks an hour and all I could eat."

"Well, I don't know. I'm not knocking it, but just saying, you got anything else coming in? It seems like things have been pretty quiet except for the references on job applications you had a while ago. What'd that bring in, a couple hundred bucks?"

"That reminds me, I gotta send them a bill, and relax, I'm fine. Hey, you got time to grab lunch? I'm buying."

"You sure you want to do that?"

"What, go to lunch with you or buy?"

"Very funny. Yeah, as long as you're buying, Dev. What do you say to Roosters?"

"Perfect. Let's go."

Roosters was just two blocks away, and we walked up. Louie was breathing heavy by the time we arrived. We stepped inside, walked up to the counter, and placed our orders. Louie ordered the beef rib dinner. I got the barbecue sandwich. Louie's dinner was twice the cost of my sandwich, which is exactly what I get for trying to be a nice guy.

We settled into a booth and waited for our meals to arrive. I'll give Rooster this much, the place smelled wonderful. We inhaled the food when it arrived. Louie didn't even offer to share one of his ribs with me. That actually wasn't a problem because my barbecue sandwich was huge. I was thinking of maybe getting a box to take half of it home, but I somehow soldiered on and ate the whole thing.

I gave the kid my debit card when we finished eating. He was back three minutes later. "Um, I'm sorry, sir, but your card keeps coming up denied. Do you have another one we could try?"

I knew what the problem was, too much month at the end of the money. Well, plus the two bottles of wine and the bottle of Prosecco I purchased the other night, and we know how well that worked out. I was thinking maybe we could split the bill, but I only had three bucks cash.

Fortunately, Louie picked up on my situation and said, "Why don't I pay for lunch? I owe you anyway, so I'll be getting off easy," he said and handed the kid a couple twenty dollar bills.

I don't know who looked more relieved, me or that kid.

Thirteen

Thank God for Louie. "Aw gee, Louie. Sorry you had to pay but much appreciated. I guess my deposit this morning didn't register yet."

"Hey, Dev, relax. We've all been there. I'm just thinking you might want to give Raunchy Scarlett a call, see if you can still take that job she offered."

"Are you kidding me? I'd rather clean toilets at the ballpark than work for Scarlett. Besides, thirteen bucks an hour? You gotta be kidding me."

"Hey, man. She'll pay you in cash. Might be interesting to see what angle she's using for the gig. Maybe it's something you could do."

"Why in the hell would I want to copy what Raunchy Scarlett is doing?"

"Mmm, yeah, good point. I get it. She's got offices all over the metro area, is making a ton of dough, drives an expensive little sports car, and a wardrobe that extends beyond t-shirts and team jerseys. Yeah, you're right. Why waste your time? Things are going so great for you right now. Come on, Dev, a bucks a buck. Take the gig, see if you can parlay it into something bigger. Even if you can't, you'll still get something close to a hundred bucks in cash."

"Yeah, I suppose I could check it out. Let me think on it."

I thought about it for the rest of the four-minute walk back to the office. When we climbed the stairs and stepped into the office, I pulled my wastebasket over, fished out one of Scarlett's business cards, and phoned her.

"Hi, Dev. I was hoping you'd call," was how she answered.

I wondered how she knew it was me since I'd never called her from my cellphone. "Hi Scarlett, hey, I'm thinking about your offer. I might just take you up on it. Can you tell me what's involved?"

"Well, actually, it's gotten a little more complicated since this morning. Seems there's a groom's dinner the night before the wedding. I'd need you to go to that with me. Of course, the actual wedding is the following day along with a reception and then a gift opening the day after the wedding."

"Sounds like a lot of time all of a sudden."

"Yeah, but I'd make it worth your while, Dev."

"Something more than minimum wage?"

"I think we could come to an agreement. Look, what do say we bury the hatchet? I'll pay you your standard fee for three days. If, at the end of this, you don't want to do anything else, okay. I'll still pay you. But if this works out, I have something from time to time that my staff can't handle, but it might be the perfect fit for you. Security somewhere for a night, chaperone someone in town for an evening, deliver subpoenas. You know the gigs. I'd love to turn those over to you, and if you're too busy, okay. I understand."

"I'll try this wedding with you. When is it?"

"Tomorrow night is our first appearance. I'll need you here, in my office, no later than three tomorrow afternoon. We'll take my car, but you'll drive. We act like we're the perfect couple. I can fill you in tomorrow afternoon on the various personalities. You onboard?"

"Yeah, okay, your office tomorrow at three?"

"Correct. Dress code is a suit and tie. These are conservative people. See you tomorrow."

"Same address as the one on your card?"

"Yeah, Fifth Street in downtown Minneapolis. You need directions?"

"I know where you are. I'll see you tomorrow," I said and disconnected.

"There now was that so hard?" Louie said.

"I feel like I'm going to throw up."

"Well, if I heard correctly, you've got three days instead of just one."

"Yeah, and she said she'll pay me my standard fee. So right away, I'll be making okay money."

"Not to mention you're not going to be working for Tubby Gustafson, for free, I might add."

"Yeah, I guess there is that."

"Not a bad result for a four-minute phone call."

"I know. I'm just waiting for the other shoe to drop."

"Dev, if it does, you can always pick up and go home."

Fourteen

The following morning, about all I accomplished was looking at the clock to see what time it was. I scanned the apartment across the street with my binoculars but didn't see anything worthwhile. Everyone had either already left for work, or they were dressed. Morton and I headed home around noon. I let him out in the backyard, then polished my shoes. After that, I shaved and took a long shower. I pulled out a dark suit I hadn't worn for over a year and a starched white shirt. I slipped on a red, white, and blue tie and had to admit I looked halfway decent. I tucked the sticky holster with my nine-millimeter into my belt, buttoned my coat, and was ready to go.

I let Morton in then drove into downtown Minneapolis. There was a parking ramp just around the corner from Scarlett's office, and I parked in there rather than risk a parking ticket or worse, a tow. Scarlett's office, S.R. Investigations, was on the third floor of the Chase building. I rode the elevator up and then walked down the hall to Suite 314. I had to give her this much, she had some awfully nice office digs.

I walked into a reception area with a young woman seated behind a counter. She was busily typing on a laptop but stopped as I entered.

"Hi, my name is Dev Haskell, and I'm here to see Scarlett. She's expecting me."

She smiled as she gave me the once over, maybe it was the suit. "If you want to take a seat, I'll let her know you're here." She picked up the phone and said, "Scarlett, I have a Mr. Hassle here to see you. Yes, okay," she said and hung up the phone. "She'll just be a minute. Can I get you a tea or coffee?"

It was a far cry from Louie offering a can of beer. Just to get as much as possible from Scarlett, I said, "That would be nice. Yeah, coffee, black, please."

"I'll be right back." She stepped into a side room and, a moment later, returned with my coffee. The coffee was in a china cup resting on a saucer. Both the cup and saucer had gold rims, and resting alongside the cup was a little cookie, no doubt imported. Unfortunately, the coffee was very good, and the cookie had an almond flavor and tasted delicious.

I had just finished the cookie when the receptionist answered her phone and said, "Okay." She hung up and looked at me. "Mr. Hassle, if you'll follow me, please. Scarlett can see you now."

I followed her down the hallway past three offices with people busily typing away on computers. Scarlett's office was at the end of the hallway. Her name was on a nameplate attached to the wall next to the closed door.

The receptionist knocked on the door and then opened it in a sort of grand entry style. I followed her in.

Scarlett was seated behind a massive, elegantly carved, antique desk. A leather inlay with gold trim covered the top of the desk. As I entered, she looked up from the file she was reading and said, "Thank you, Catherine," effectively dismissing the receptionist. Catherine smiled and closed the door on her way out. Scarlett stood, picked up the file she had been reading, and said, "Let's sit over here, Dev. It's much more comfortable." She indicated a leather couch and two wingback chairs positioned around a coffee table.

I headed for one of the wingback chairs, and once I settled in, Scarlett took up a spot on the couch and tossed the file on the coffee table. She wore a form-fitting black lace crepe cocktail dress that went just below her knees. The dress had a scooped out top, long lace sleeves, and a lace panel in the midsection. She wore sparkly stiletto heels with black trim. I tried not to stare.

"These are a series of notes, nothing more than general information on attendees and a few of the guests. Read through them. We can talk on the way to the dinner. I have to say, Dev, you clean up well."

"Thank you. Not too bad yourself, although isn't it bad form to look better than the bride?"

"Yeah, right. No surprise, you're still full of it. In a nutshell, this is going to be the clashing of the worlds. On the one hand, you have my client, Hubert Holly."

"The attorney?"

"Yes, his daughter Crystal is set to marry a man named Brendan Bishmann. Apparently wealthy but with no visible means of support. No siblings, family, or really any history that we can ascertain."

"Where did he come from?"

"That's one of the many questions we have," she said and flashed a quick smile. "Supposedly born in Minneapolis in 1983. Oddly, no further information until he washed up on Crystal Holly's shore six months ago. Father was a city employee, passed away in 2014. Mother died the following year, cancer in both cases. No siblings. No fortune to inherit."

"So how did he make his money?"

"Supposedly, investments and financial opportunity. Here's the problem. Crystal Holly is not only infatuated, she's also a couple of months pregnant. Her parents, God-fearing individuals that they are, initially insisted on the marriage only to be having second thoughts now." She glanced at her watch, "Just twenty-five hours before the actual ceremony."

"And you're supposed to get dirt on this guy?"

"I've got everyone working on it, which is why I needed someone to fill in as my escort. That someone is you. There's another reason I chose you."

"My good looks and you hope for some very personal time with me later on?"

"Don't get your hopes up. No. In fact, make that a definite no. However, your interaction with, shall we say, the seamier side of society makes it possible that you might recognize Brendan Bishmann or, barring that, anyone who may be associated with him."

"Have you seen him before?"

She shook her head. "No. There have been three, no wait, four showers where he was invited only to bow out at the last moment due to out of town meetings he had to attend."

"Meetings? While there's no visible means of support?"

"Exactly. Just one of the many warning flags out there. Hubert Holly is beside himself."

"What about his wife?"

"Addison? She can't be bothered. She's immersed herself in planning the entire event. But then again, she hasn't had to face reality in the past thirty-plus years, so why would she want to begin now?"

I shook my head and said, "This sounds like something out of a soap opera. Forget for a moment the girl is supposedly pregnant. Everything I know about Hubert Holly suggests he's a top-notch attorney. What the hell is he doing in this situation? They don't even know where this guy comes from? The whole thing sounds crazy. I remember dating a girl back in high school, and her old man wanted my fingerprints to run through some database."

"And did you give them to him?"

"Don't make it sound so nice. It was more a case of he just took them. He poured me a root-beer in the kitchen. I started to catch on when he slipped a yellow rubber glove from beneath the kitchen sink on his hand and then placed the glass in a plastic bag. I guess he had some federal connections."

"Did you pass the test?"

"I never found out. She dumped me about two nights later."

"Sounds like she was raised right."

"Yeah, well, I got off easy. I think she's on her third or fourth husband."

"Read through this file. I'll be at my desk working. Feel free to interrupt with any questions you might have." She slid the manila file folder across the coffee table and stood.

"One quick question, Scarlett. Who is the best man?"

She scoffed. "Justin Holly, brother of the bride."

"Brother of the— You gotta be kidding me?"

"If only. Mr. Bishmann is clever if nothing else. Go through that file, and you'll see."

Fifteen

It was an impressive file, including what appeared to be the complete guest list. A total of three hundred and fifty names in alphabetical order and numbered. Most of the names had an ‘OK’ penned behind them. There were maybe two dozen names with a checkmark next to the name. A one-page description of the individuals with a checkmark, including a black and white photo taken on the street, followed the list of guests.

Attached to Brendan Bishmann's one-page description was a copy of his birth certificate. He was born in Minneapolis in 1983, making him thirty-seven years old and twelve years older than Crystal Holly. The age difference wasn’t necessarily unique, but it wasn’t all that common for a twenty-five-year-old woman. There were a number of areas where no information had been found, schools, prior addresses, military service, and employment. Three photos of Bishmann were attached to the one page of information.

He looked like an average-sized guy. His dark hair was nearly shaved on the sides of his head, and about an inch long and curly on top. There were actually three photos of him. Two of the photos were of him standing in front of the Top Hat bar downtown, talking to a young blonde woman. One was a close-up, and although a bit blurry, I could detect a dimple in Bishmann's chin, just like Kirk Douglas. I flipped a number of pages to the photo of Crystal Holly, and she was the woman in the photos of Bishmann in front of the Top Hat bar.

The third photo had Bishmann exiting an older brick building, three stories tall with screened in front porches on all three stories. A carved block of stone above the entrance listed the building as St. Regis 77. I knew the building, or at least where it was. The building address was 77, but St. Regis referred to the building name. It was actually located on Oxford Street, maybe three miles from where I lived.

I knew a couple who had lived there a few years back. From what I remember, it was a nice enough building. Given the neighborhood and from what I recalled of the kitchen, it was probably built in the late 1920s or early 30s. Nice place but definitely not a trendy, rich person's location.

Just for starters, there was no parking lot, so you parked on the street, which meant you had to move your car to the side street when the snowplows came through in the winter, and you scraped frost off the windows every morning in cold weather.

Employment information on Bishmann appeared to be nonexistent. I paged through the other photos and names, but no one really rang a bell. On a whim, I phoned Louie.

"Yeah, Dev. What? Did Raunchy Scarlett already fire you?"

"No, not yet, but I'm sure she's about to. Hey, I've got a question for you. Does this name ring a bell with you? Brendan Bishmann." I spelled out the last name for Louie.

"Yeah, something, maybe. Hang on. I'm online. Let me do a search of my files. Should be just a minute to… Oh, yeah, here we go. He filed a character witness statement for a client, Darrin Yardly, arrested for a DUI around last Thanksgiving. I was able to plead it down on the grounds the breathalyzer was faulty. Got a suspended sentence, not that it did any good. Yardly died from an overdose two weeks later."

"How long ago was this?"

"Court date was back in April. That makes it what? A little more than five months ago."

"What was this Yardly like?"

"In a word, trouble. The family was wealthy. Yardly had a trust fund and never really worked. He dabbled in a number of areas and always failed. He'd been arrested for minor drug offenses a half-dozen times. Served twelve months up in Lino Lakes for possession maybe ten years ago. He had an assault charge pled down. Given the lifestyle, his death was only a matter of time. If I recall, Bishmann volunteered the character reference. I didn't meet him for more than a minute or two down at the courthouse, purely happenstance. As a matter of fact, he pulled me aside. I'd just stepped off the elevator heading for a hearing not related to Yardly."

"Do you remember what the drug was that Yardly overdosed?"

"No, not off the top of my head. You need to know right now?"

"No. Don't worry about it. I'll check it tomorrow. You gonna be in?"

"Tomorrow? On Saturday? Not if I can help it."

"Okay, talk to you later."

"If you see Bishmann, tell him hello from me."

"I'll be sure to do that, Louie," I said and disconnected.

"Anything interesting?" Scarlett asked as I placed the phone back in my pocket.

"Not really. Bishmann served as a character reference for a friend who was arrested on a DUI charge. That guy I was talking to was the accused's attorney. He was able to plead the charge down and got the guy a suspended sentence. He seemed to have a positive memory of Bishmann, told me to say hi to him when I see him."

"Interesting. We might like to talk to him."

"My pal? He's an attorney. His name is Louie Laufen. Does a lot of DUI work. Right now, he's one of the top go-to guys if you get caught driving under the influence."

"But Bishmann wasn't charged, correct?"

"That's right. He just made a character statement. In these photos, I recognized the building Bishmann is coming out of. I'm guessing that's his residence."

"Supposedly, it's in St. Paul, just a block or so off Lexington and Summit, although he spends the majority of his time at Crystal's. Mom and Dad bought her a three-bedroom condo in Mendota, overlooking the river, a few months back. I think just to get her out of their house," Scarlett said.

"I had friends who lived in that building where his place is for a couple of years. I was in there a few times."

"We had someone watching the place for the better part of a week. Nothing unusual went on. We never got inside. Was it nice?"

"Of a sort. I have to say, if you're claiming to be independently wealthy, it's not the place I would think of living. Great screened in front porch, but no dish-washer, out of date bathroom, kitchen sink from about 1925. Now, this was maybe six or eight years back or more. Maybe the place has been updated since then, so take it with a grain of salt."

I paged through the file again until I came to Crystal Holly's information. She would have been an attractive looking girl if she dropped a good fifty pounds. "Crystal Holly graduated from the U in 2016?"

"Yes, she graduated with a bachelor's degree in Elizabethan Literature. As you might guess, not really a hot commodity on the job market."

"So, what does she do?"

"Currently, she's working in a daycare facility run by a friend of her mother's. She's earning minimum wage while she figures out which direction she's going to go. That career change may be put on hold with the arrival of a baby in seven months."

"You sure she's pregnant?"

Scarlett nodded. "Yes, at least that's what I've been told. Hence the wedding, compliments of the mother, Addison. I haven't received a confirmation from Crystal and don't expect one."

"Where does one find a job in Elizabethan Literature?"

"You mean with a bachelor's degree? I think right where she is, in a daycare facility run by a friend of your mother's."

"And you said she doesn't live with her parents?"

"Correct. She's in a lovely three-bedroom condo in Mendota overlooking the Mississippi River. Compliments of her parents who can't seem to grasp the fact that their daughter is twenty-five going on fourteen. One of the curses of being wealthy, I'm afraid."

"What about the brother?"

"Justin? It remains to be seen. He's in college, working on an IT degree. He graduates next year and wants to go on and earn a master's. When he's not studying, he's playing games."

"Playing games?"

"The university has a gaming team, online games. I know it sounds crazy, but think about it for a moment.

These kids are working at it just as hard as someone who plays football or basketball and talk about a competitive field. They played for national championships out in Las Vegas for the past two years. Think what that would look like on an internet technology resume. No, Justin is going to go places. He'll cut his own path."

"And Brendan chose him as his best man?"

"You'll have to excuse my suspicions, but I believe Brendan did that simply to please or maybe appease the mother of the bride. From what I can pick up, Justin couldn't care less. He's an okay kid, and he'll be charming over the weekend, but I think deep down, he knows it's ridiculous."

Scarlett picked up a little sparkly purse that matched her heels and checked her watch. "I think it's time we get going. The dinner is out in Sunfish Lake at the Holly home. It might be a good idea to leave that file here. I wouldn't want the wrong people getting hold of it."

Sixteen

The ride out to Sunfish Lake took twenty minutes. I was driving Scarlett's classy looking Acura NSX. Once I pulled onto the interstate, I accelerated and began weaving in and out of traffic just to drive her nuts. At ten miles over the limit, she didn't even blink. I cranked the speed up another five miles per hour and still didn't get a reaction, so I backed off. Scarlett waited about a half-minute before she said, "You trying to yank my chain, Haskell?"

"What are you talking about?"

"You know. You were almost twenty miles per hour over the limit. Go ahead and speed away, but I'm not going to pay for your ticket. I'll just tell the cop I was begging you to slow down. Then once he gives you the ticket, I'll kick you out of the car, and you can walk home."

How nice. I remained at the speed limit, followed the interstate and took the Highway 62 exit, then followed Charlton Road into Sunfish Lake. The Holly residence sat on a five-acre lot on Windy Hill Road and looked more like a castle than a home. A massive two-story stone structure with white trim, peaked slate roofs, an attached three stall garage, a manicured lawn, and a circular drive. The circular drive and Windy Hill Road were lined with parked cars, all of which appeared to be out of my price range.

"Pull up to the front of the house," Scarlett instructed. "They'll no doubt have valet parking."

I turned into the circular drive and made a mental note of the manicured lawn and hedges. As we drew closer to the front door, a young man in a navy blue uniform stepped off the front porch. His trousers had a red military stripe down the side of his legs, and he hurried to Scarlett's door to open it for her. I made a mental note of the odometer reading and stepped out. He closed the door behind Scarlett then hurried around the car to me. I gave him the keys, and he handed me a brass disk with the number fifty-eight carved into it.

"Thank you, sir," he said and smiled. "You can go right in the front door. The guests are gathering out in back around the patio and pool." With that, he slid in behind the wheel and slowly drove away.

I watched him pull around the circular drive for a couple of seconds then stepped over to Scarlett. She linked her arm in mine, and we headed for the front door.

"Nice digs," I said, looking around.

"He told me they picked it up for a song, maybe five years ago. Four-point three."

"Four hundred and three thousand?"

She shot me a look suggesting she wasn't sure if she should laugh or cry. "No Dev, four million three hundred thousand."

My grin gave me away, and she slapped my arm. "Honest to God. Sometimes I think—"

The front door was suddenly opened by a guy in a white shirt with a black bow tie, tuxedo trousers, and a black vest. "Good evening and welcome," he said with a heavy accent.

"Thank you," Scarlett said.

We entered a large hallway with marble floor tiles and elegant looking antique tables on either side of the door. A large crystal vase full of flowers was centered on the tables. Off to the right were two older gentlemen in dark suits, holding drink glasses, and apparently involved in a serious discussion. "Federal judges," Scarlett said under her breath.

We continued down the hallway toward a set of double doors with two young boys at either door. They were dressed just like the guy who opened the front door for us. As we approached, they nodded at one another, stepped outside, and held the doors open. Then together, they gave a gracious swing of their arm as if presenting the back garden, patio, and pool to us. They couldn't seem to wipe the smile off their faces.

"Thanks, guys."

To say we were on a patio didn't really do the place justice. It was large, very large, with raised rose gardens of quarried stone that matched the house. The rose gardens bordered the massive patio. I guessed there were maybe a hundred people standing around, mostly drinking wine. A couple of guys held beers or liquor glasses, but for the most part, it was wine. A four-piece combo was playing nice background music.

"I'll take a white wine and get whatever you want. Just remember you're driving. I'm going to check with my teams. Let's meet over by the band in fifteen minutes," Scarlett said and disappeared into the crowd.

I headed toward the bar. Along the way, I saw a couple of vaguely familiar faces, although I couldn't put a name to them. I smiled, gave a nod and a little wave of the hand, and got a barely visible nod in return. I probably saw them on TV or maybe in the courtroom. No doubt they were wondering how a guy like me was able to crash a party for the upper one percent. The bartender gave me a half-dozen choices of white wine. I decided on two Sauvignon Blanc, keeping up the pretense that I belonged in the group. I wandered through the crowd looking for Brendan Bishmann or, not finding him, Crystal Holly. I didn't see either one, although I did spot Crystal's parents, Hubert and Addison, and I think her brother, Justin, the best man.

As I wandered through the crowd, I occasionally caught a female head giving me more than a glance. None of the men seemed to take note, which was just fine, in fact, it was perfect. Eventually, I wandered over toward the four-piece combo.

Scarlett joined me a couple of minutes later. She flashed a smile as I handed her the glass of wine. "What do you think?" she asked and took a sip.

"It seems like a pretty decent wine, although I don't really know wines all that well and—"

"I didn't mean the wine, you moron. I meant—"

"I know what you meant, crabby. I think, with all these people here, it strikes me as strange that the wedding couple isn't around. I don't know, maybe they're in the house. I saw the parents. They seem to be working the party. Chatting briefly with folks and then moving on to the next group. Did you learn anything?"

"Apparently, the happy couple is an hour and a half late, and the lovely mother of the bride is ready to kill."

"So, in other words, typical family."

"Maybe," Scarlett said just as a few people began clapping near the entrance to the patio, and a moment later, there was cheering and clapping throughout. Apparently, the guests of honor had finally arrived.

"Problem solved. Come on. I want to get a closer look," Scarlett said.

Seventeen

We made our way through the crowd in the direction of the happy couple. Crystal's parents stood on either side of them. Hubert looked rather stern and nodded at various guests. Addison smiled at her daughter with eyes flashing daggers, suggesting she indeed was ready to kill because of their late appearance.

For his part, Brendan Bishmann looked like a nice enough guy. In fact, he looked somewhat familiar, but maybe it was just because of the photo I'd studied in Scarlett's office. He was about six feet tall. Certainly not fat, but I wouldn't have called him muscular. He was dressed in a dark sport coat, a starched, open collar white shirt with pressed, slim-fitting jeans. There was a white carnation in the lapel of his sport coat, and he sported a very nice tan. It looked like two pals were hovering behind Bishmann, I would not have labeled either one as someone particularly dangerous.

Crystal Holly had shoulder-length blonde hair, what looked like diamond post earrings, and a diamond post on the left side of her nose. When I'd looked at her picture, I thought she could stand to lose fifty pounds. After seeing her in person, I upped that to a good hundred. Her white dress looked very expensive and stretched to the max. The dress went down to her knees, revealing the massive white calves on her legs. There was no indication of a waist to speak of, and three rolls of fat led up to large breasts, a cavernous cleavage, and bare, sunburned shoulders. She was supposed to be maybe two months pregnant, but it was impossible to determine that just by looking. She held a plastic bottle of sparkling water in one hand and a half-eaten hors d'oeuvre in the other. She seemed to be chewing the other half.

In short order, people were lining up to shake hands and congratulate the couple. "Care to meet the loving couple?" Scarlett asked.

"It's up to you."

"Maybe stay back here and just take it all in. I'll get in line," she said and headed for the line.

I'd finished my glass of wine and decided another glass was not the best idea. I had a glass waiting for Scarlett when she returned fifteen minutes later. "Were you dutifully impressed with the groom?" I asked.

"Not really, he seemed nice enough, but there's something there. I share Hubert's concern."

"Is that client relationship talking?"

"No, it's genuine. Keep an eye on him. I'd like to get your input at the end of the evening."

"Input? Are you referring to watching Bishmann? Or were you talking on a more personal nature?"

"Don't even kid yourself, Haskell. Come on. It looks like dinner is ready."

Dinner was buffet style, and Addison was busily hurrying people into line after having to hold up dinner for the better part of an hour. A chicken curry, some other chicken dish, shrimp, two types of rice, two different salads, steamed broccoli, roast potatoes, and pasta were presented along the buffet line in heated trays. I skipped the salad, pasta, potatoes, and vegetable and went for the chicken and shrimp main dishes.

"Oh my God. You sure you don't need a second plate?" Scarlett said.

"No. I'm planning to go back for seconds."

"I can't even tell if you're kidding. Let's find a table and sit down. My feet are killing me."

All the tables were arranged with white linen tablecloths and linen napkins wrapped around the silverware. The tables were round and sat eight people. The main table was long and arranged so that the chosen few eating there faced the guests. The soon to be married couple was centered in the middle, with Crystal's mother and father on either side, and then Justin on one end and another woman, I presumed a friend of Crystal's and the maid of honor, at the opposite end of the table. Interestingly, there was apparently no one from the groom's family.

The music combo played for forty-five minutes while everyone ate, and about twenty staff quickly cleared plates as meals were finished. I never had a chance to go up and grab seconds, although it would have been fun just to get Scarlett worked up. Once the plates were cleared, the staff bustled around, delivering flutes of champagne to everyone.

Hubert stood, clinked a spoon against his champagne flute to get everyone's attention, and proceeded to give an extremely short toast. "To Crystal, Brendan, and an honest relationship."

There was a long moment of silence as everyone waited for more, but it wasn't to be said. People quickly looked around then took a sip. A few people clapped half-heartedly. Bishmann sat at the head table and put the champagne flute to his lips, but I'm pretty sure he never took a sip. Crystal seemed focused on the tablecloth and never looked up. With a nod from Hubert, the combo struck up, and gradually, the murmur of conversation returned.

A few minutes later, one of Bishmann's pals walked over to him and whispered something in his ear. Bishmann nodded, tossed his napkin on the table as he stood, and he and his two pals headed into the house. He walked with a slight limp in his right leg, and I wondered if he maybe injured himself just before the wedding. He never said anything to Crystal or her parents. Out of the corner of my eye, I saw two guys hurry around the corner of the house toward the front, and I suspected they were part of Scarlett's staff.

"That was a bit different," a guy across the table from us said to no one in particular and then took a sip from his whiskey glass.

"John, be quiet," a woman I presumed to be his wife said.

Scarlett raised her glass, leaned over and half-whispered, "What did you think of the toast?"

"I think he either got some very recent information, or he's just a lousy public speaker."

Crystal suddenly rose from the main table and said something to her parents that did not appear pleasant. Just about everyone watched, expecting her to head into the house following Bishmann. Instead, she hurried over to the bar, got two glasses of white wine. She gulped down one of the glasses and slammed the empty on the bar. She carried the other glass back to the head table. Once again, an uncomfortable silence spread through the crowd, and all eyes focused on Crystal's mother, Addison, as she reached over and attempted to grab the wine glass. Crystal took hold of the glass, and they wrestled with it, sloshing wine onto the tablecloth and Crystal.

A couple of people at various tables began to stand and head for the door. Hubert stood, said something to his wife and daughter, and headed for the house.

"This isn't looking good," I said.

Scarlett was on her feet, motioning two of her staff to follow Hubert. As they hurried to catch up, she headed for the main table.

"Women. Can you believe it?" the guy across the table said and took another sip from his whiskey glass.

"I've heard just about enough from the likes of you tonight, John Tierney," the woman next to him said and took his whiskey glass.

"Edith, I—"

As she held her hand up, she said, "No, now not another word." She picked up his glass, downed the rest of his whiskey without so much as a blink, and set the empty glass on the table. The couple next to me both laughed and gave a little applause.

"It's been interesting. Nice to meet you all," I said to the other guests at our table as I stood. I headed toward Scarlett and Crystal who were walking away from the crowd toward a picnic table on the far side of the pool. Crystal's mother, Addison, was nowhere to be seen.

Scarlett had her arm around a sobbing Crystal. As I drew closer, Crystal grabbed a dinner roll off a plate as she walked past. Scarlett heard me coming and said, "Dev, get a couple of napkins and give us a minute."

I nodded and headed back toward the tables. The crowd had thinned substantially. There were a half-dozen guys at the bar, apparently all getting whiskeys. Most of the guests were now gathered around the double doors waiting to get into the house and head to their cars. Just about everyone looked like they were fleeing the scene. I grabbed a handful of linen napkins from the closest table and turned to head back to Scarlett just as Crystal let out a scream. It looked like her eyes had rolled back in her head, and she suddenly disappeared beneath the picnic table.

"Dev," Scarlett shouted as she went down on her knees next to Crystal with her arm around her shoulders.

I ran over as the few people remaining at the tables seemed to stand in unison and hurry toward the house.

Crystal had her teeth clenched in an effort to suppress her screams. "Oh, God. Oh, God. Is it the baby? I shouldn't have had that wine. Oh, God, no. Oh, my God."

"What is it, Scarlett?" I said.

"I don't know. She slid across the picnic table bench and then right off onto the ground."

"Help me roll her over," I said, placing my hand beneath Crystal's lower back and thighs. As we rolled her over, a blood-stained tear in her dress appeared along with a growing patch of blood.

"Is she miscarrying?" Scarlett asked.

"A miscarriage? Oh, I knew it. I knew it," cried Crystal.

I took a closer look and cautiously felt her right butt cheek. I could see the bare skin through the torn dress and a wound that was oozing blood, along with a large sliver of wood about the size of a ten gauge nail.

"Relax, it's not a miscarriage. Just calm down. But you've got a hell of a sliver in your ass, Crystal."

"Well, pull it out, Dev," Scarlett said.

"It's in there far enough it will probably break off, and it's fairly deep. If we try to pull it out and it breaks off, she's liable to require surgery, which probably means stitches," I said.

“In my ass? No way,” Crystal shrieked.

I reached into my pocket and gave Scarlett the brass disk with the number fifty-eight. “Go have them bring the car up to the front door. Tell them it’s an emergency.”

“Maybe I should get my team.”

“Scarlett,” I said and pointed to the wound area. The bloody area was now the size of a small plate and growing. “Now go. I’ll carry her to the front of the house. Come on, go.”

Eighteen

As Scarlett headed toward the front door, Crystal said, "Oh, God! What else can go wrong today? This has just been awful. Please don't bring me in the house. The last thing I need right now is my mother. She's too upset. Both of them are," I tried to lift her but only got her about a foot off the ground and couldn't adjust my legs to stand.

"Crystal, you think you can stand?"

"Stand? Yeah, I think so with some help, but I don't think I can walk, at least not very far. God, my dress is ruined. This has just been the absolute worst day of my life."

"I'm going to set you down, and then I'll help you stand. Okay?"

"Yeah, okay, I'm ready, I think," she said, wrapping an arm around my neck.

I lowered her onto the ground and half-rolled her over onto her left side. She gasped but didn't say anything. "Okay," I said, crouching over her. "Let's get you standing up." I took hold of her hands and slowly began to pull her up.

"Ow, ow, ow, ow," she said through clenched teeth, but we got her to her feet. She was barefoot now.

"Okay, deep breath, I'm going to scoop you up. Ready?"

She nodded and took a deep breath.

I groaned as I lifted her up in my arms and headed for the house.

"Oh please, please don't bring me in the house. I can't deal with my parents right now."

You gotta be kidding me. "Okay, hang on," I said and took a left, walking along the patio to the corner of the garage and then out toward the front of the house. We stepped onto the circular drive just as Scarlett's Acura pulled in front of the house.

Scarlett was standing in front of the crowd of guests fleeing the scene. She saw us coming and shouted at the oblivious people. "Move aside. Give them room. Come on. Damn it, move. Get out of the way. Hey ladies, shut the hell up and get your ass out of the way," she shouted at two women and indicated with her arm to get out of the way. They took their time, and I was tempted to shoulder them as I went past, but Crystal seemed to be putting on another ten pounds with every step I took.

Scarlett swung the passenger door open as we approached. People began commenting as we passed. "Oh, my God! What the hell happened? Is she going to live? Oh no. Who did that? I didn't hear any shots," were just some of the comments I heard as we hurried toward the car. I sort of rolled Crystal onto her left hip in the passenger seat then closed the door.

Scarlett handed me the car keys and said, "Take her to the ER at United. It'll be the closest hospital. I'll have one of my staff get me down there."

I was in the car a second later and screeching around the circular drive. I stopped at the entrance onto Windy Hill Road, reached over and pulled the seatbelt across Crystal, careful not to touch the wound, and buckled her up. I glanced at the odometer, twenty more miles on it since I handed the keys to the guy parking cars two hours ago.

"I can't believe this happened. How embarrassing," Crystal said.

"Well, it could be worse. This is fixable, and you'll be fine for tomorrow. Look at it this way, things can only get better."

"Oh, you've no idea. Tomorrow isn't going to happen."

"Sure it will. We'll get you to the ER. They'll remove that sliver, patch you up, and you'll be good to go."

"No, you're not getting it. This is just the icing on the cake. Brendan told me he's not going to go through with the wedding. Told me he wanted out of the whole thing. Can you believe it? Honest to God, I want to murder that prick."

"Not going through with it?"

She nodded and started to tear up. "Yeah. He said he didn't love me. Said he couldn't go through with it because I told him the baby isn't his. God! How embarrassing. Now we'll have to return all those gifts. Oh, my mother is going to have a heart attack. Right after she kills me."

"She doesn't know?"

"Are you kidding? She would have made a major scene at the dinner. I didn't want that. I want everyone and everything to just quietly go away. This is just awful, absolutely dreadful."

"Did you tell your dad?"

"I didn't have to. He already knew. I don't know how, but he did. I'm afraid he'll get that creepy client of his involved, and that guy would just make a bad situation even worse," she said, then seemingly out of nowhere, she brought out the dinner roll she'd grabbed from the plate and took a bite.

We were on Highway 62 at this point weaving in and out of traffic, picking up speed. I took a pen and a small notebook out of the cupholder on the console and handed it to Crystal. "Write down your phone number for me, just in case I need to get in touch with you."

"Why do you need that?"

"Just in case. Besides, the hospital might need it, and this way, they won't have to bother you." She seemed to think about that and started writing.

Eight miles later, we turned onto the interstate. Traffic was light at this hour, and I sped up even though the speed limit dropped down to forty-five on the far side of the bridge crossing the Mississippi River. The brake lights on the car ahead of us flashed on as they began to slow. I passed them in the right-hand lane and wove back into the left.

"Your dad has a creepy client?"I said, just making conversation.

"Yeah, more than one. But this guy has a really big red nose. I mean, it's like the size of a baked potato and all pocked marked and everything. Oh, he's so gross. I can't think of his name. He was over at the house just the other day when Mother and I were choosing the chocolates for the plates at the reception tomorrow. They were going to have our names, mine and Brendan's, on them, two at each place. God, seventy-five dozen."

"Plates?"

"No, the chocolates. Of course, now that's not going to happen. I hope we can return them."

"Might be hard to do with your name already on them."

"I was hoping they could maybe just wash the names off and reuse them."

"I don't think so," I said.

"Hmm-mmm, all those chocolates," she said and seemed to think.

"You know what? Write down Brendan's phone number, too. Just in case they can't remove your names. We can deliver all the Brendan chocolates to his place."

"No, I'll hang onto them," she said, smiled, and wrote down Brendan's number. She took another bite of the dinner roll. Something Crystal had just said was bouncing around in my thick skull, but at the moment, I was focused on the flashing red lights in my rearview mirror. The flashing lights were slowly catching up to us. I pressed my foot down on the accelerator and swung into the right lane again, passing three cars, then into the left as we shot up the slight incline and the Grand Avenue exit. We took the exit, and I hit the brakes as we raced through the curves leading to the stoplight. It was dusk, and I didn't see any lights approaching off to the left, so I made a right-hand turn. The police car was just coming out of the curves.

We raced down to the next corner and made a left just as the light turned yellow. United hospital was on the left, and I skidded into the ER entrance and screeched to a stop.

"Okay, we're here. You undo that seat belt, and I'm going to carry you in."

"I think I can probably walk. I—"

The flashing red lights were about to turn into the ER entrance. "No, let me carry you, just to be safe," I said and hurried around to the passenger door as the flashing lights pulled in behind us.

Crystal wrapped a heavy arm around my neck. I groaned and lifted her out of the car just as the Highway Patrolman stepped out from behind the wheel. "Hold it right there," he said and then hurried past me once he saw Crystal in my arms. "Gunshot?"

"Stabbing, we need a gurney," I said and groaned. My back felt like it was going to break. He held the automatic door open, then raced past, took hold of a gurney sitting along the wall, and rolled it back to us. "Act like you're really hurt," I whispered to Crystal.

"I don't have to act. This does really hurt."

I carefully placed her on the gurney and rolled her onto her stomach. The bloodstain was now the size of a dinner plate and had dripped down her leg. It really did look pretty bad. Crystal stuffed the last of the dinner roll into her mouth and chewed.

"Stabbing," I shouted at the reception desk, where two guys in hospital scrubs were chatting with the receptionist. One of them took a look at me, Crystal's bloody dress, and the Highway Patrolman pushing the gurney and took off. The other guy headed toward us.

"Stabbing?" he said, examining Crystal's large rear.

I just nodded.

"Okay, let's get her to unit three," he said to the Highway Patrolman. He turned to me and said, "You just wait here, sir."

"Thanks," I said to the Patrolman as he pushed the gurney past me.

He nodded, and they wheeled the gurney into a curtained area as another guy and a woman, both in scrubs, hurried behind the curtain.

Nineteen

Scarlett arrived about twenty minutes later with two of her staff. By this time, the Highway Patrolman had left after telling me to keep an eye on the speed limit. Fortunately, he didn't give me a ticket. I thanked him profusely and counted my lucky stars.

I gave Scarlett and company a wave to get their attention. "Where's Crystal?" Scarlett asked. She carried her sparkling purse in one hand and her sparkling shoes in the other.

"They've been working on her ass behind one of those curtains. No one seems to be running around, so I would say everything is fine. She's maybe going to get a stitch or two. Had an interesting conversation on the way in."

"Oh?"

"She told me the wedding's not happening tomorrow. Brendan more or less broke up with her."

"Broke up with her? What? On the night before the wed— Did he just get cold feet? He can't do that. The wedding is tomorrow."

The two staff guys shot a glance at one another.

"Well, not only can he, but he did. Apparently, she thought tonight would be a good time to let him know he really isn't the father. I don't think her mother knows, but apparently, her father does."

"Well, what the hell is she— Never mind, is she okay?"

"Yeah, I suppose. I mean, at the end of the day, it's just a large sliver. She's got a pretty big rear, and my sense is there won't be anyone around anytime soon looking at a scar. She can—"

"Will you ever get your head in the game? No, don't answer that. I know you won't because," she stepped in close to me and lowered her voice. "Because it's so far up your ass you don't even know it. What is she going to do about tomorrow?"

"Right now, her biggest concern seemed to be if they could return the chocolates with their names on them."

"Chocolates?"

"Yeah, seventy-five dozen if I remember correctly."

"Oh, for God's sake. That's the least of her problems. They've got, I don't know, maybe a hundred grand invested in this event."

"Well, it looks like the husband to be, Brendan Bishmann, pulled the plug. Did you talk to the parents at all?"

"No. I couldn't find Addison. She's probably in her bedroom with a cold compress on her forehead watching an episode of Downton Abbey. Hubert has locked himself in his office. When I knocked on the door, he just growled and said he was on the phone, and he didn't want to be disturbed."

"Can I make a suggestion?"

"No, we are not going to some sleazy bar so you can—"

"That's not what I was going to suggest. They took Crystal into unit three in there." I nodded toward the double doors and the curtained areas beyond. "I think, under the circumstances, it might be a good idea if she was kept here overnight for observation just to give both her and her parents some time. If the wedding has been canceled in the eleventh hour, they could probably all use a break from one another. Even just a night apart would maybe give enough of a pause to let cooler heads prevail."

Scarlett seemed to think about that and finally nodded. "Oh, for God's sake. Here, hold this," she said and thrust her sparkly purse at me. I took it, and she took hold of my arm with her free hand. She slipped first one and then the other sparkly shoe onto her feet and grimaced. "Oh, God, these damn shoes are killing my feet." She grabbed her purse from me and took a deep breath.

"I checked your purse. There was no money in it."

Her two staff guys chuckled, and she shot them a look, then turned on me, hit me in the stomach with the purse, and headed toward the double doors and Crystal.

Twenty

We were seated in Scarlett's office. "You mind?" I asked.

"Oh, good lord, no. Help yourself," Scarlett said and pushed the bourbon bottle across the coffee table to me. Scarlett was stretched out on the couch, barefoot. Her feet appeared red and swollen. Her sparkly high heels were over next to the office door, where she'd kicked them off the moment she stepped into the room. I'd taken up residence in one of the wingback chairs. The top button on my shirt was undone, and my coat and tie were draped over the other wingback chair. It wasn't the first drink for either one of us.

"It never ceases to amaze me," Scarlett said and took a sip. "These people, all the money in the world, and they have these children that would drive you absolutely crazy. I mean, Hubert is extremely wealthy, but he's earned it. His folks had a farm that never made any money. He worked his way through college and law school and started out with literally nothing. How come none of his work ethic and brains were passed on to his daughter? I just don't understand it. And he's not alone. I see it in a number of my clients." She shook her head and took another sip. "Did Crystal ever tell you who the father is?"

"No, and I didn't ask. Just based on the way she said it, I'm thinking she may not know."

Scarlett closed her eyes and shook her head.

"You know much about Hubert's list of clients?"

"His clients, you mean the people at the dinner from hell tonight?"

"Actually, not them so much as clients who weren't there. More specifically, maybe clients that he wouldn't want there. Clients he would just as soon not have people know he represented."

"Sounds like you might have someone specific in mind."

"Actually, I do. Crystal mentioned someone with a large, pockmarked red nose who was at the house not too long ago. She didn't know the man's name, but it sounded to me like she might have been describing Tubby Gustafson. Does Hubert represent him?"

"Everyone is entitled to fair and unbiased representation, Dev."

"I'll take that as a yes."

"I'm not sure exactly how or even if Hubert represents Mr. Gustafson, but I do suspect that he has represented him in the past. Fortunately, I've never had to be involved in those matters."

"It might turn out to be profitable for you."

She shook her head. "No, not in the long run. Sort of a guilt by association thing. I've too many well-paying clients who would run, not walk, but run the opposite direction if I was ever associated with Gustafson or any of his operations. Nothing against your business."

I shook my head. "Unfortunately, he's oftentimes involved in an aspect of something I'm investigating. It's just better if I attempt to keep him on the positive side. In some ways, the more I know about him, the easier it is to keep him at a distance."

"Does he pay well?"

I shook my head. "No, payment from Tubby Gustafson consists of you being able to wake up in one piece the following morning. He has his fingers in a number of pies, legitimate and otherwise. It's just that, when Crystal mentioned him, I found it, umm, interesting."

"Well, you know it takes all kinds. Speaking of which. What would you think about working on a private undertaking for me?"

"A private undertaking? Scarlett, who would I tell that you took me to bed?"

She literally stopped and stared. "You know, sometimes I can't tell if you're pulling my leg or if you really are that stupid. What I just said was not in any way, shape, or form an attempt to get you into my bed. No, I can feel this coming. As a matter of fact, I'm a little surprised I haven't already gotten a call. Whether he's out of the picture or not, I literally know nothing about Brendan Bishmann. Something, in fact just about everything, doesn't add up where he is concerned. Hubert had asked nicely for information before this. In short order, he's going to demand it."

Twenty-one

Morton and I were in the office early, very early for a Saturday morning. I went online and tried to find information on Brendan Bishmann. Other than a couple of recent photos that Crystal Holly had no doubt posted and three other guys with the same name, I couldn't find a thing. It seemed obvious there was only one person who could help me. At this hour, he was probably still asleep, so I put Morton in the back seat and drove over to Preston's Leadbetter's house.

Actually, the 1920s white frame house belonged to Preston's mother. Preston lived in the basement, and his mother kept the basement door locked. The old coal chute door was open, and I was just about to climb down the steps when the basement door opened and a woman in tight-fitting shorts and a t-shirt cut off to reveal the lower portion of her large breasts started up the steps. Her hair was wet like she'd just stepped out of the shower. She was focused on counting the handful of twenty-dollar bills she held and didn't see me until she was at the top of the steps.

"Oh, God. I didn't expect to see anyone."

“Yeah, maybe stuff that cash in your pocket and count it once you’re in the car. Is Preston awake?”

“Preston? Is that his name? He told me everyone called him Big Man.”

“Yeah, that would fit.”

“You’re telling me. I’d be squished if he was on top.”

“So, is he awake?”

“Been up all night drinking Red Bulls and playing on his computers when he wasn’t doing me. You looking for some action? I can give you a discount.”

“Oh gee, thanks, but I’m already worn out.”

“Your loss, baby,” she said and headed for the street.

“Yeah, and my shot record isn’t up to date,” I said under my breath.

I went down the steps and entered the musty-smelling hallway that led to Preston’s basement accommodation. The door to his unit was partially open. Preston was seated in his black desk chair facing his three massive computer screens. Some sort of game was on the screen with guys in space suits flying around and shooting at one another.

As I pushed the door open, it squeaked, and without looking in my direction, Preston said, “Forget it, Misty. It was part of the deal. I get to keep your thong.”

“I just want my boxers back.”

Preston half-jumped and spun around in his chair. “Oh, God, dude, you scared the hell out of me.”

"Think how I feel, not getting my thong back."

"Sorry, Dev, I thought you were someone else. Long time no see. What are you doing here?"

Unfortunately, Preston was naked. All three hundred plus pounds of naked Preston Leadbetter oozed out of his desk chair. Rolls of fat from his chins down to his massive, pink, blubbery midsection rolled over the arms of his chair and jiggled as he spoke. I walked over and picked up the damp bath towel slung over the back of the black leather couch. The towel was wet, and I guessed the lovely Misty must have used it to dry off after her shower. I tossed the towel to Preston, who was once again focused on his computer game. I noticed the unopened bag of Snickers candy bars next to the keyboard, just below the red thong hanging from the computer screen.

"Preston, can you turn that thing off so we can talk?"

"Can't right now, Dude. I'm in the middle of this and… What the hell? Where did that come from? Bastard just lasered me, and I'm out. I've been working this off and on all night, and he just won. Damn it."

"Gee, sorry," I said, not meaning a word.

"No sweat, I've got his pattern down. Dude's from Australia. I'll get him next time up, but he's good. So what's up? You just in the neighborhood?"

It was just after 9:00 on a Saturday morning, and I was in Preston's basement abode. The windows were covered with tin foil. The place was littered with pizza boxes, empty Red Bull cans, and smelled like cheap perfume and a sweaty fat guy, and Preston wondered if I was just in the neighborhood.

"Actually, no, Preston. I made a special trip over here just to see if you can help me on a project. I need some information on a guy, any information, actually."

"What's the deal?"

"I'm checking him out, or at least trying to, but I can't find anything. The little I know just doesn't seem to add up. And I—"

"Hang on a second," Preston said and started clicking keys. "Local?"

"Yeah."

"Name?"

"Brendan Bishmann." I spelled out both names for him.

"Age?"

"I think thirty-six or seven."

"You got an address?"

"Yeah, 77 Oxford. It's an apartment building in St. Paul, but I don't know the unit number."

"Yeah, got it. Zip code is 55104." He clicked some more keys and said, "He's in 302. Front unit on the third-floor left-hand side. Resident since the first of June of this year."

"So he's only lived there three and a half months?"

"Yeah, according to this."

"Oh, before I forget, I got his phone number, too."

"Awesome. Way to go, Dude. Now we're getting somewhere."

I gave him the phone number Crystal had written down. "Tell you what, see what else you can find on this guy, and I'll stop back later today. That okay with you?"

"Yeah. Just don't make it too late. I've got another date tonight."

"You have another woman coming over tonight?"

"What? No, another game. I've got a rematch with this guy in Australia."

"I'll be back mid-afternoon. I'll call you first."

"That should work. You want printed copies on everything?"

I thought about that for a moment and nodded. "Yeah, that might be a good idea. Preston, you just keep working on this, and I'll bring you dinner, so you don't have to interrupt your gaming tonight dealing with the pizza delivery guy."

"Super. Much appreciated, Dude. See you later."

"Yeah, and put some clothes on between now and then, please."

Twenty-two

I sat in my car out in front of Preston's mother's house and dialed Scarlett. A gentle, soothing voice answered the phone. "S.R. Investigations. How may I direct your call?"

I figured it was Catherine, the hot looking receptionist. I was surprised she was working on a Saturday morning. "Hi, this is Dev Haskell. I'd like to speak to Scarlett."

"I'm sorry. She's in a meeting just now. If you could give me your number, I'll have her call you just as soon as possible."

"Yeah, that'll work." I gave her my number then said, "Is this Catherine?"

"Yes, it is."

"Yeah, Catherine, nice to hear your voice. This is Dev Haskell. I was in yesterday afternoon. I was Scarlett's partner at Crystal Holly's dinner last night."

"Oh yes, quite the evening from what I understand."

"That might be a bit of an understatement. If you would just let her know I called. No rush. Nice chatting with you, Catherine."

"Always a pleasure, have a nice day, sir," she said and hung up. I wasn't sure if it was always a pleasure for her to chat with me or if she meant me being able to chat with her. Just because I had nothing else to do, I drove past Brendan Bishmann's place. There was a U-Haul rental truck parked in front of the building, and a guy was coming out of the building carrying a cardboard box. He sort of looked familiar, but I couldn't place him. He hurried to the rear of the truck as I drove past. I watched in the rearview mirror as he tossed the box into the truck. A guy in the truck picked up the box and carried it further back. The guy who had come out of the building hurried back inside. I pulled around the far corner and parked out of sight of the building. I clicked the dog leash onto Morton's collar and headed the long way around the block. As we went around the block and headed down the side street to Bishmann's building, Morton decided this would be a good time to do his business. Fortunately, I had a roll of plastic bags attached to his leash.

As we rounded the corner onto Oxford Street, the guy I'd seen before and another man came out of the building carrying what looked like a folded dining room table. I definitely recognized the second guy as the one who had whispered something into Brendan Bishmann's ear just before he stood and left the head table at the dinner last night. It seemed to be a pretty safe bet these were Bishmann's possessions they were loading into the truck.

Morton and I stopped and watched them walk past. Fortunately, the blue plastic bag I was holding with Morton's deposit actually added some credibility to my pretending to be a curious neighbor.

"Moving day?" I said as they hoisted the table up and into the back of the truck. The guy I'd recognized hopped into the truck and took hold of one end of the table as the other fellow in the back of the truck lifted the end, and they moved the table off to the side.

The guy still on the ground flashed a one-second smile and nodded.

"Well, at least you've got a nice day for it. Lots of work," I said.

He gave a slight nod as his partner jumped back down, and they hurried into the building.

"Where you off to?" I called up to the guy in the truck.

"Just helping a friend," he said as he wandered into the rear of the truck and pretended to arrange some boxes.

"I need to help a pal next weekend. You guys get this truck over on University Avenue?"

"Yeah, if he's moving next weekend, you should go call them right now and reserve a truck. It's middle of the month, so we were able to get one right away, but they'll be getting busier starting next weekend."

"No talking to strangers," a voice said, and I turned around just as one of the guys tossed another box into the truck. He smiled and pretended he was joking, but the message was clear to his pal.

"Good luck, fellas. Always a lot of work," I said. I made a note of the license number as Morton and I headed down the street.

"What'd he ask you?" The one guy said, but by then, I was too far away to hear the response. We turned at the corner and headed toward my car. I casually glanced back as we neared the car, and one of the guys was standing at the corner watching us, so we walked past my car and just kept going up the street. When next I looked back, he was gone.

I was still repeating the license number when I put Morton into the back seat, climbed in behind the wheel, and drove off. I pulled over two blocks away and phoned Preston. He answered just before I was going to get dumped into voicemail.

"Yeah, Dev, what is it?" He sounded distracted, and I could hear his fingers on the keyboard. I pictured him with a headphone on and hoped he was dressed.

"Yeah, Preston. Sorry to bother you. Hey, I just drove past Bishmann's address. Three guys are hauling his stuff out. Apparently, he's moving. They're loading everything into a U-Haul truck that they rented over on University Avenue." I gave him the license plate number. "See if you can check it out."

"Okay, dude, I'm on it."

I waited a long moment before I finally asked, "You coming up with anything?"

"Oh, a couple of things I think you'll find interesting. Let me get one aspect nailed down, and I'll have it for you when you come over. I could go for a large pizza with everything on it and double cheese," he said.

Twenty-three

Scarlett phoned me after the noon hour. Other than getting Preston Leadbetter working on background information and stumbling upon Brendan Bishmann's pals in the act of moving him out of the building, I had accomplished absolutely nothing.

"Hi Scarlett, you free to chat?" was how I answered the phone.

"Actually, no, I'm not. I'm about to leave to meet Hubert, but we should be finished up by half-past three. Have you found out anything?"

"Still working on it," I said, hoping Preston would have something later this afternoon. "One bit of information, I decided to stake out Bishmann's place," I lied. "He appears to be moving out. Three guys were loading all his furniture into a truck."

"Moving? Where to?"

"No idea, and it was very clear they weren't going to tell me. But it was the same guys who were with him yesterday at the groom's dinner."

"Oh, God. I'll pass that on to Hubert. Anything else?"

"Tell you what. Let me gather up what I have at the end of the day. You going to be in your office later this afternoon?"

"I can be."

"Let's meet there. If for some reason you can't make it, just let me know. What's happening with the wedding? Were they able to get in touch with everyone and let them know it's been called off?"

"That's where we're going now. We've been working all morning, phoning and emailing people, but there are a number of out of town folks, and we've no idea where they're staying, so we're on our way to the church. Undoubtedly, some people will be showing up there."

"What are you going to tell them?"

"We're pleading an illness and telling them we'll be in touch with a reschedule date."

"And folks are buying that?"

"After last night, by and large, no. Thus far, they've just sounded glad to get off the phone."

"Is Crystal still down at United Hospital?"

"She checked out earlier this morning around half-past seven. She's not answering her father's phone calls."

"And Addison?"

"In the throes of depression. She's booked a one-way flight to Paris on Sunday, fleeing the scene. She's at her therapist as we speak."

"Charming."

"Par for the course. When the chips are down, she's not the person you want to depend on."

"I hope to see you at your office later today," I said.

"I'm counting on it," she replied and hung up.

Preston phoned me a little after three. I'd fallen asleep in my office chair. "Yeah, Preston. How's it going?"

"I think I've gone about as far as I can go today. I'll get back on it tomorrow, but I need to recharge the old batteries, and I'm gaming with the Australian in just over an hour and a half."

"Were you able to print things off for me?"

"Yeah, got a nice sized file for you. Can you get over here in the next forty-five minutes?"

"Yeah, I'll make sure I do. See you soon."

"And, dude, remember, a large pizza with extra cheese."

"Yeah, you got it, not to worry. See you shortly."

Morton and I hustled out to the car. I put Morton in the back seat, slid behind the wheel, and called a pizza place near my house. I followed Preston's instructions and ordered an extra-large pizza with everything and double cheese.

I hurried home, let Morton out into the backyard, grabbed a quick shower, and called Morton inside. I picked up the pizza, along with a banana split, so Preston would have some fruit with his evening dinner. I pulled up in front of his mother's house exactly one hour after we spoke on the phone.

I hustled down the steps to the basement level and knocked on the door. Preston answered a couple of minutes later. He looked exhausted after having to walk all the way to the door. He was red-faced and dressed in a gigantic black silk robe with white lapels. Traces of food stains ran across the white lapels. He wore black velvet slippers that were embroidered with the image of some sort of futuristic character.

"It's about time," he said as his eyes grew wide, and he focused on the giant pizza box. "Oh, there is a God," he said, taking the box from me. As he sniffed the box, his eyes took on an orgasmic look. I followed him back into his lair, trying not to focus on the waddling, jiggling creature taking up most of the hallway in front of me. I carried a brown paper bag holding the box with the banana split.

Preston waddled directly to his office chair and set the pizza box down in front of one of his giant computer screens. Images from some sort of futuristic computer game floated across all three screens. The red thong still hung from the corner of one of the screens. He opened the top of the box and gave another orgasmic smile as he inhaled the scent from the pizza.

I happened to notice the bag of Snickers candy bars next to his keyboard. It had been unopened when I was in here this morning, but now, not only was it open, but there were only three candy bars left in the bag. He grabbed a roll of paper towels, pulled off two sheets, tucked them beneath his chins, and pulled a piece of pizza from the box. Strings of cheese hung from the pizza slice in his hands, and I made note of the fact he didn't offer me any.

"Little something here for your dessert, Preston. I'm just going to put it in your freezer, so it doesn't melt." I carried the bag with the banana split over to the olive green refrigerator and opened the freezer door. Three tubs of ice cream, two bags of candy, a box of fudge, and an empty ice cube tray were scattered inside the freezer. I rearranged them to make room for the banana split box and closed the freezer door.

Preston was just finishing his second piece of pizza. Traces of sauce ran around his lips, and a fine string of melted cheese hung from his chin down to one of the lapels on his silk robe. He appeared oblivious and shoved the remaining half of the piece into his mouth.

"Mmm-mmm, Dude, here check this shit out," he said through a mouthful of pizza and handed me a manila file folder.

As I took the file from him, he left a pizza sauce smear from his fingerprints across the front. "Thanks, Preston." I set the file on the desk and opened it. Preston settled into his office chair and reached for another slice of pizza. I leaned over the file and stared at the top sheet — a copy of a death certificate.

Twenty-four

The death certificate read Brendan Thomas Bishmann, and was dated twelve June 1983. "Who the hell is this, his father?" I said, holding up the death certificate.

Preston chuckled, took another gigantic bite, and shook his head. He chewed for a moment, then shoved the pizza into his cheeks and said, "No, that's actually him."

"What do you mean, it's him? A death certificate from forty-six years ago?"

"Actually, Dev, it was thirty-six years ago but point taken. Brendan Thomas Bishmann died on June twelfth, nineteen eighty-three. One month after his birth, sudden infant death syndrome. The gravesite is over at Calvary Cemetery."

"So, the guy we know as Bishmann, is using a false identity?"

"Bingo. He applied for a California driver's license in February of last year using the Bishmann name, then turned around and, using the California ID, applied for a Minnesota license this past June, listing his address as unit 302 on seventy-seven Oxford Street. I can't prove it, but if I had to guess, I would say he had possibly targeted this Crystal Holly woman right from the start. I know her father is wealthy, and I'm guessing she can wake up on the first of every month and not have any financial worries. To a guy like this Bishmann, she would suddenly become a pretty attractive partner. Give me another day or two, and I can begin to nail it down."

"I went past this address earlier today. Three guys were loading his furniture into a truck."

Preston grabbed another piece of pizza. He was now more than halfway through the large pizza with no sign of slowing down. He took another huge bite and said, "So, he's moving?"

"I'd say it's more like he's fleeing the scene. And this would seem to confirm it. Any idea who he really is?"

Preston shook his head and swallowed. "Not yet. The phone is registered to him, but he's only had the account since last December. It's with Verizon. Give me a little more time, and I'll figure out who he really is. I can tell you this much. Whoever in the hell he is, he's good. Knows what the hell he's doing. Whatever his end game is, I'd say it's a pretty safe bet this isn't his first scam."

"Hang on just a minute," I said and pulled out my phone. I brought up my contact screen and phoned Louie.

He answered after a couple of rings. "What's up?" Bob Seger was singing about old-time rock and roll in the background, and I took a guess at Louie's location.

"Louie, you at The Spot?"

"Yeah. Why would I want to be outside in this weather?" It was gorgeous and sunny, upper seventies and, for a change, no humidity.

"Yeah, I see your point. Hey, the other day, you mentioned Brendan Bishmann gave a character reference for a client of yours. What was that guy's name?"

"My Client? Yardly, Darrin Yardly. Why? What's up?"

"Nothing, just checking some facts."

"Come on down and join me. It's the weekend. You should be drinking, not working."

"I've got to meet someone in a bit, maybe afterward. How late are you going to be down there?"

"Probably till close, unless they kick me out before then."

"I'll maybe swing by. I better run. Thanks for the info."

Louie hung up. Apparently, it was a busy afternoon at The Spot, and he didn't have the time to say 'Goodbye.'

Preston had his head tilted back and was holding a piece of pizza above his mouth. He slowly lowered the piece into his mouth so as not to miss a morsel. Who could blame him? There were only two pieces remaining in the box. I was tempted to grab one but decided that maybe wasn't the best idea, since I needed him to keep working on Brendan Bishmann. Instead, I grabbed a Post-It note from his desk and wrote down Darrin

Yardly's name. I reached over and stuck the Post-It note just below the red thong.

"You mind if I take this file with me?"

Preston shook his head, causing his chins to wiggle from side to side, and one of the paper towels fluttered down onto the table. "No, go ahead. That's why I put it together for you."

I picked up the paper towel from the desk and attempted to wipe off the pizza sauce from the front of the file folder. All I did was smear it across the front of the folder. "Thanks, Preston, much appreciated. That Post-It note I stuck on your screen has a name on it."

"Mmm, Darrin Yardly," he said and reached for another piece of pizza. "Who's he?"

"Supposedly a friend of Bishmann's. He got nailed on a DUI charge late last year. Bishmann filed a character reference before he went to trial."

"Did it help?"

"I think so. He got a suspended sentence, community service, or something, but it didn't really matter. He OD'd about two weeks later. See what you can find out about him."

Preston nodded and stuffed half of the piece of pizza into his mouth.

"Thanks for this file. It'll make for some interesting reading," I said.

Preston nodded and licked his fingers. He pulled the final piece from the box and placed the empty pizza box on top of a half-dozen other empty pizza boxes on the credenza behind him. Chimes suddenly rang across the computer screens, and he clicked on his mouse.

"You ready to go down, mate?" an Australian accent said.

I picked up the file, waved, and headed toward the door. The last thing I needed was to listen to two computer geeks playing some science fiction game. I went down the hall and climbed up the steps into the sunshine and the real world.

Twenty-five

I was leaning against the wall outside of Scarlett's office. The office door was locked, and the lights were off. I'd been reading through Preston's file for maybe twenty minutes when Scarlett stepped off the elevator and headed toward me. She wore a black silk blazer over a low-cut white top and blue jeans that looked like they were spray-painted on. Her chest was in full bounce mode, and as she headed toward me, she blew upwards, fluttering her bangs.

"Oh, God. What an afternoon. Have you been waiting long?"

"No, only a few minutes. Just reviewing the notes I assembled today," I said, holding up Preston's file.

She seemed to focus on the pizza sauce stains smeared across the front of the file for a brief moment but didn't comment. "Come on inside. I could use a drink right about now," she said and pulled a set of keys from her purse. She unlocked the office door and flicked on a light switch. I followed her inside. She closed the door behind me and locked it. "Come on back," she said, heading to her office. She tossed her purse on the couch and hurried over to the bar in the corner of the room.

"Can I get you something?" She opened the small wine refrigerator beneath the granite-topped counter. She pulled out a bottle of white wine, a Sauvignon Blanc.

"No, thanks. Help yourself."

"I intend to. God, talk about unhappy people."

"It doesn't sound like much fun telling folks they made a trip into town for nothing."

"You got that part right. In fact, far from it. On the one hand, you've got the father of the bride standing there, without his wife, I hasten to add. He's telling people that, unfortunately, the wedding will have to be rescheduled due to a medical issue. And of course, the majority of the folks he's talking to have flown in from parts unknown, so they're not exactly pleased with the news. Lots of dark suntans and Botox attributes."

"That last part doesn't sound so bad."

She stared for a second or two before shaking her head and taking a large swallow of wine. "Anyway, what's done is done. What did you learn?"

"A couple of surprises, although, now that I've had a chance to think about it, maybe not so surprising. Come on. Sit down and relax." I headed for one of the wing-back chairs and tossed the file on the coffee table.

"What'd you get all over this file, catsup?" Scarlett asked, spinning the file around to face her as she sat down. She took another swallow of wine, set her glass down, and opened the file. She immediately started coughing as she choked on the wine.

"Jesus Christ, he's dead?"

"Not exactly. Check the dates."

She picked up the death certificate and read through it then looked over at me. "Brendan Bishmann is a false identity? I knew it. I had questions about him from the get-go. I just knew there was something wrong." She picked up the copy of the birth certificate and compared the two. "Sudden infant death syndrome. God, and now he's off to the races." She seemed to think for a moment and quickly pulled out her cell phone.

"Who are you calling?"

"We missed this, completely missed this. Jesus, I can only hope idiot Crystal didn't give him access to her accounts. That's all Hubert needs, the icing on the cake to this entire fiasco. Oh good Lord, if he was able to gain access to accounts, it will be a disaster. I've gotta call Hubert," she said as she pushed a speed dial number. "Oh, God, I can't believe this." She paused, waiting for Hubert to answer, then said, "Hello, Hubert, this is Scarlett. I don't care when you get this, call me immediately, emergency," she said and disconnected. She sat deep in thought, tapping her finger on the arm of the couch.

"What are you thinking?"

"The two of them, Hubert and Addison, they have beachfront property in Hawaii. Haleiwa, Hawaii, to be exact. They were out there from January to mid-May. When they came home, Crystal had Brennan Bishmann in her life. He's the reason they bought her the condo. What are the odds chubby little Crystal let him take up residence in her parents' home, giving the likes of Brendan Bishmann access to her father's office?"

"Wouldn't someone like Hubert Holly be aware of that?"

"Not if nothing had happened. What if he gained access but just sat on information like account numbers and passwords, waiting for the right time? Now Hubert's distracted by this wedding fiasco. Think about it. Someone like Bishmann has months to get everything in order and then has twenty-four to thirty-six hours to pull it off. Oh, this could be absolutely catastrophic." She picked up her phone and pressed the screen. A moment later, she was shaking her head as she left another message. "Hubert, please call me. Brendan Bishmann is an alias. I'm worried he may have gotten access to your accounts."

"He's not answering?"

"Oh, yeah, Dev. He answered, but I wanted to leave a message anyway. Yes, he's not answering."

"Okay, two thoughts. I'll head back over to Bishmann's place. If he's still there, maybe I can delay him. Do you have any idea where Hubert Holly might be? Would he be checking on his wife?"

"Only if he could get her on an earlier flight. He's more than ready to have her travel to Paris. He might be downtown, at his office, maybe at his home office, or even checking on Crystal."

"Can you get your people to check those places?"

She nodded and already had the phone up against her ear.

"I'm heading over to Bishmann's apartment. I'll call you either way." I left Scarlett's office and hurried out to my car.

Twenty-six

I could say I hurried back into St. Paul and Bishmann's apartment, but there was construction on the interstate, which brought six lanes down to two, so I inched my way there. I finally got off the interstate and headed down Lexington Avenue at just the right speed to hit all three stoplights. I finally got into the left turn lane only to find myself stuck behind a tepid driver, who should not have been allowed behind the wheel at any time, let alone when I was in a hurry. She let a half-dozen opportunities to make the turn slip by, and I never honked. But then again, I didn't have to, because various totally frustrated people in the dozen cars lined up behind me were leaning on the horn. One guy about six cars back got out and started heading toward her car. She finally made her turn and sped down the street at a clipping ten miles per hour.

I caught up to her a minute later. She was stopped while she looked both ways at the intersection, searching for a car that might be three blocks away. She finally drove off, and I turned and parked right where the moving truck had been two hours ago.

I hurried into the small entryway. There were a dozen mailboxes on the wall on the left-hand side. No names were listed on the mailboxes, only the unit number. I couldn't tell if any mail was in the box for 302. I picked up the phone and pressed 302. A moment later, it started to ring and continued ringing.

A couple came into the entry. As he unlocked their mailbox and removed a bunch of circulars and an envelope, she pressed a fob on her key and opened the security door. As they began to enter, I said, "Okay, I'll be up in just a minute." I hung up the still ringing phone and followed the couple in. I headed up the staircase, and they walked down the hallway on the first floor, never bothering to look at me.

Unit 302 was the first unit on the left side of the third-floor hallway. I knocked on the oak door that looked old enough to be original to the building. I knocked again and placed my ear against the door — dead silence. I glanced up and down the hallway. I couldn't hear anything coming from the other units. I thought about kicking the door open, and then, on a whim, I simply turned the doorknob, and the door swung open. I stepped inside to an empty living room and closed the door behind me.

My footsteps seemed to echo across the bare wood floor. Other than a grocery store circular and the grey metal Venetian blinds, the room was bare. I walked back through the unit. The kitchen had a stack of four white china plates resting on the counter. I opened the wooden cabinets that looked original to the place, empty. The refrigerator held a half-empty container of milk and a red pepper. I walked past the bathroom, with not so much as a bar of soap. Both bedrooms were empty, as were the closets. I pulled out my phone and called Scarlett.

"Please tell me he's there," was how she answered.

"Okay, I can do that, but it'll be a lie. I'm in the unit. There's nothing in here. I may have told you this before, but for someone who is supposed to be highly successful and wealthy, I don't know. I mean, this is an okay place, but if the daughter was ever here, you'd think she'd start to question his story. Maybe she's in on the scam?"

"I don't think she has the street smarts to come up with that thought," Scarlett said.

"Were you able to locate Hubert, Scarlett?"

"No, and I tried to contact the wife, but she left instructions with the staff, she is not to be disturbed under any circumstances."

"What do you want to do?"

"I want to scream, but that's not going to help. I've got four phone messages into Hubert. I'm going to head over to the daughter's condo. Maybe Hubert's there, or maybe she knows where he is. Otherwise, about all I can do is sit around and twiddle my thumbs."

"Tell you what. I'm going to head over to the rental place where they got that truck. Maybe I can get something there."

"That sounds slim."

"Stay positive, Scarlett. Go ahead and check out the daughter. Call me either way when you're finished, and if you feel like it, I'll gladly buy you dinner."

“Oh, that’s nice of you, but you don’t have to do that, Dev.”

“Scarlett, come on. It’s Saturday night, and we’re in a holding pattern until you hear from Hubert. You’ve still got to eat. If he calls and you have to run off, no big deal. I’ll just buy dinner for some other hot looking woman.”

“Oh, you are such a… Well, never mind. Yeah, I’ll take you up on it. I’ll call you either way,” she said and hung up.

Twenty-seven

I stepped into the U-Haul office about two minutes before they closed. No one else was in the place except the guy behind the counter. He was large, not fat, with a neatly trimmed beard and salt and pepper hair. He looked like he worked out on a daily basis and was not the sort of guy you'd give a hard time.

"We're gonna be closing in about two minutes. If you're bringing a vehicle back, you can just leave it in the lot and drop the keys in the mail slot." He didn't bother to look at me as I came in. In fact, his back was to me, and he was busily stacking boxes on a shelf behind the counter.

"Oh, thanks, but I didn't rent a truck. I was helping some pals load up and had to run to my work for a couple of hours. I just wondered if they brought back the truck or if I should get over there and help them unload the thing."

"Oh, let me just check for you. What was the name?"

"Brendan Bishmann," I said and spelled out the last name.

He was staring at the computer screen and half-frowning. "I'm not seeing that name on here. You sure they got it from this location?"

"Yeah, that's what they told me."

"Let me just check the other locations. We've got six in the city," he said and started running his fingers across the keyboard. He shook his head, typed, shook his head, and typed again. He did that a half-dozen times and then looked up at me. "Sorry, but that name isn't coming up on the system. You want me to check Minneapolis?" he asked, then made a point of checking his watch.

"No, that's okay. I'll head over to the new place and see if they're there. Thanks for your time."

"Not a problem. Sorry I couldn't come up with him." He stepped out from behind the counter and politely escorted me to the door. I heard the lock click as soon as the door closed behind me. A moment later, the 'OPEN' sign was turned off, and a half-minute after that, the lights in the commercial area went off.

It probably made sense from Bishmann's point of view not to use his alias. I thought about knocking on the door and giving the U-Haul guy a description, or better yet, giving him the license plate number, but he'd already disappeared. He was probably watching me on some monitor, and about ten seconds after I left, he'd hustle out the door and drive off. Besides, Bishmann was turning out to be smart enough not to rent the vehicle himself, so he probably had one of his friends get the thing. I thought about staking out the parking lot just in case they returned the truck tonight, but to be honest, that didn't really appeal to me.

My phone suddenly rang. "Hi Scarlett, you find out anything from Crystal?"

"Yeah, she's even a bigger idiot than I thought."

"Oh, that doesn't sound too positive."

"Let me just quote her. 'Under the circumstances, I just can't bring myself to discuss the situation.' Unquote."

"Under the circumstances? Did you tell her this guy has the potential to do some serious financial damage to her father, and by extension, her?"

"Let's just say things became a little heated."

"You want me to come over there?"

"Dev, I didn't even see her. She just spoke to me on the security phone down in the lobby area of her building and wouldn't buzz me in. I tried three different ways of explaining things to her, but she seemed to be a little too busy. I could hear the TV playing in the background. How rude of me to interrupt whatever series she's in the process of watching. God, I just have this image of her curled up on the couch with about a two-pound box of chocolates and a glass of red wine. Speaking of which, is your invitation for dinner still open?"

"It is, and I'd love to have you join me. Just let me call those sexy twins back and tell them they'll have to wait until another night." Dead silence on the other end. "Hello, Scarlett?"

"God, you are an absolute idiot."

"Any place special you'd like to go?"

"You like La Grolla?" she asked.

"I do, but I have to warn you. I live right across the street from there."

"Yes, Dev. Give me some credit. I do happen to know that. But given the way my day has gone, I don't think that's going to be a problem. Besides, if I have enough wine, I won't even care and might just be in the mood for some very personal attention."

"I'll call them right now and reserve a quiet table in the back."

"You do that, somewhere near the wine cellar. See you there in say forty-five minutes?"

"Perfect. I'll see you there," I said and disconnected.

I called La Grolla and was able to reserve a table. I ran outside to my car. I was only ten minutes away but made it home in six. I let Morton out into the backyard, then ran upstairs and changed the sheets on my bed. I picked up the blue jeans, the three pairs of socks, a few t-shirts, the boxers, and tossed them all into a laundry basket in the closet. I hung two fresh, clean towels in the bathroom and picked up the damp towel from the bathroom floor. I hurried downstairs, took the dishes out of the sink and loaded the dishwasher, turned it on, and let Morton back inside.

I gave him a biscuit, checked myself out in the hallway mirror, and decided to go back upstairs and shave. I put on a pretty clean shirt and went across the street to

La Grolla. Christine, the server, had just stepped behind the bar and smiled as I walked in.

"Hi, Dev. Dining alone tonight?"

"No, actually sort of a last-minute thing. Just meeting a friend. I called for a reservation. Do you have a table in a quiet corner? We've both had a pretty dreadful day."

Twenty-eight

It had been a good hour since I'd spoken with her on the phone before Scarlett arrived. As the hostess led her into the rear dining room, she spotted me and waved. She had changed into a tight-fitting black dress with three-quarter length sleeves and a string of pearls around her neck. She looked worth the wait.

"Oh perfect, what a day," she said as I pulled the chair out for her, and she sat down. We were seated in a far corner of the room, and the closest table was empty. At this hour, there was a pretty good chance no one was going to take it.

"You ever hear anything from Hubert?" I asked.

"Don't even go there. Please, let's not spoil what remains of the evening by bringing up his name. In fact, I'll just attend to this while you order the wine. I'd like a red."

At that moment, the waitress came around the corner, noticed Scarlett, and gave me a nod. She was back thirty seconds later with the bottle of red wine I'd chosen when I first arrived. Scarlett had just turned her phone off and shoved it back in her purse. The waitress motioned toward me to sample the wine.

"No, better have her taste it. I'll drink just about anything," I said and nodded toward Scarlett.

The waitress poured what amounted to a large swallow into Scarlett's glass and waited.

She sipped a small sample, smiled, drained her glass, and nodded. "Fill it right to the top," she said.

"Would you like to hear our specials for the evening?"

"I think we need to have a glass or two of wine first, and then I'll give you a wave if that's okay," I said.

She nodded and left. I raised my glass to Scarlett and said, "Here's to you. We at least made it to this point in the evening." We clinked glasses.

Scarlett took a healthy sip then shook her head. "Honestly, I don't know what I have to do to get it across to the high and mighty that they are quite possibly in some really deep shit. No call back. The wife doesn't want to be disturbed. The idiot daughter doesn't want to discuss it. Hubert doesn't answer his phone. I give up. These people think they're the ones calling all the shots, and right now, this Brendan Bishmann character could be stealing them blind. Nothing more I can do," she said and took another healthy sip of wine. "Mmm-mmm, that's good. Really hits the spot."

"Hey, quick thought," I said, pulling out my cellphone. Call Hubert on my phone. Maybe he has your number blocked."

"He wouldn't do that, Dev."

"Humor me."

She shrugged, then dialed Hubert's number and put the phone to her ear. A moment later, she turned it off and handed it back to me. "Same thing, voice mail."

"Well, thanks for trying. Before we go any further, please allow me to say you look really great."

"Dev."

"No, Scarlett, I mean it. Not that you didn't earlier today but, I wish you would have let me know you were going to look like a million bucks. I would have packed some heat."

"A million bucks, oh, you're so sweet," she said as she squeezed my hand. She took another healthy sip and set her glass down. "Speaking of which, I'm sure this Bishmann person has pulled out a lot more than a million dollars by now."

"I thought we weren't going to talk about him."

"We're not. I'm just saying. And by the way, don't you think under the circumstances, Hubert as the father, should have done some due diligence here? You just let anyone date your daughter? Let alone marry her? Especially when she's as brain dead as that little fatty Crystal. A bachelor's degree in Elizabethan Literature. Honest to God." She took another healthy swallow or two and held her glass out to be refilled.

We were eating dinner, and Scarlett was still going on about Hubert. I had ordered one of my favorites, boring Fettuccine Alfredo, and was almost finished with the dish. Scarlett had the Salmon Ripieno, a salmon filet stuffed with fresh crab meat and covered with a lemon-chive sauce. She continued to go on complaining about Hubert and family and wasn't quite halfway through her dinner.

"Bishmann gets Crystal's account details, and he can work backward and drain that trust account. I mean, think about it. If he had the time, which he certainly did while Hubert and Miss Do Not Disturb were in Hawaii, this character could have all sorts of information from Hubert's clients and their accounts."

"You told me one of his clients was Tubby Gustafson, didn't you?"

"I don't know how much of a client Mr. Gustafson was or, for that matter, is. Hubert never mentions him."

"Why should he be any different than anyone else? No one in their right mind mentions they have anything to do with Tubby Gustafson."

"You do," she said and smiled.

"There you go, perfect example," I said. "I mention him only because I'm forced from time to time to assist Tubby in some minor way. Don't assume I have any respect for him. He's a thug who's somehow managed to worm his way into the upper echelons of the high and mighty, and he always seems to have something on them."

"Have something on them?" she asked and took a bite of her dinner.

"Yeah, you know. A version of the old line, behind every fortune, there's a crime. He's maybe pulled some strings to get a DUI expunged, or he's put undue pressure on someone selling a building or a business to accept an offer. Maybe he's got a photo of someone in an indelicate position. Or, if none of that works, he can always send two of his goons around to break both your legs or cut off your fingers."

"Charming. Your client, not mine," she said, flashed a quick smile, and took a forkful of her salmon.

"Would you care for some dessert?" the waitress asked as she cleared Scarlett's plate away. It had taken the better part of two hours, but she'd finished most of her meal.

"I had better say no," Scarlett said, putting her hand up to emphasize the point. "But you go ahead, Dev."

"You sure?"

"Yeah, go ahead and get whatever you like. It's fine with me."

"Okay, I'll have the cannoli. You sure you don't want—"

"No, really. Nothing for me. Thank you."

When the cannoli, two on a plate, arrived, Scarlett stared for a long moment and then said, "Oh, they do look delicious."

"Help yourself."

"I really shouldn't," she said, which always translated to the proverbial 'just one bite.'

I pushed the plate toward her, topped up her wine glass, and waited. It only took her fifteen minutes to finish both cannoli. I didn't say anything. I ordered two glasses of dessert wine, and we sipped and chatted for another twenty minutes. I paid the bill, and we left.

Standing outside, I gave her a peck on the cheek and said, "Thanks for joining me for dinner, Scarlett."

She looked at me and rolled her eyes. "God, when did you get so dense? What, you're not going to invite me in for an after dinner drink?" She inclined her head toward my place just across the street.

"Yeah sure, if you're up for it. I'd like nothing better."

"Finally, we're getting somewhere," she said and linked her arm in mine as we headed across the street. Morton bounded off the couch as I unlocked the door. Once we stepped inside, he immediately thrust his nose beneath Scarlett's dress and wagged his tail.

"Definitely your dog," she said and scratched him behind the ears. His tail seemed to pick up speed in response.

"Scarlett meet Morton. Morton, this is Scarlett, the woman I've been telling you about."

Twenty-nine

We sat in the den and chatted about Brendan Bishmann for the next hour and didn't come up with anything new. I sipped a whiskey, and Scarlett downed three cosmopolitans at the end of which she staggered to her feet and said, "Okay, Haskell, you've got me drunk enough that I don't care. Let's go to bed."

She bumped into the wall three or four times and giggled, "I can't believe I'm going to do this," as I led her upstairs to my bedroom. I closed the bedroom door before Morton could follow us in.

"Unzip me, will you?" she said, turning around. She placed her hands on the bed, promptly fell forward, and giggled some more.

I slowly unzipped her dress, revealing the back of a black bra and then further down the top of a very small red thong. She stood up and pulled the dress off her shoulders, down below her waist, and stepped out of it. She kicked the dress toward the chair opposite the foot of the bed, and then just as she turned around to face me with a big smile, I heard furious pounding on my front door.

Morton started barking as the pounding continued.

Scarlett seemed oblivious to the noise. She staggered back and forth as she ran her tongue across her upper lip, then collapsed onto the bed and began giggling again.

"What the hell? Okay, hold that thought, darling. I'll be right back." The pounding continued as I hurried down the stairs. I turned on the porch light, and there stood two thugs who, unfortunately, looked very familiar, part of Tubby Gustafson's rabble. I opened the door before they decided to break the glass panel. "Hey, look, fellas. I'm busy working a case. Can we get in touch tomorrow morning?"

"Mr. Gustafson wants to see you, now, dumb shit."

"Were you guys listening? I said I was busy working."

"Nothing that can't wait," the larger of the two said. He was blonde, with cold grey eyes and sharp cheekbones. He grabbed me by my shirt collar, pulled me out of the house, and onto the front porch. I pushed him hard, but he didn't really move. Instead, he gave me a sort of disappointed look, shook his head, and then slammed a massive fist up into my chin.

"Mr. Haskell. Mr. Haskell, wake up, we're here," a distant voice seemed to echo in my head. "Mr. Haskell. Hey, douche bag, open your eyes," the voice said. "Okay, better. Now get your act together. Mr. Gustafson is waiting for you in his office, and he's got some questions." The blonde guy snapped his fingers in front of my face a couple of times. "You with it, dumb shit?"

I think I nodded.

"What's your name?"

"Tubby Gustafson?"

"That's who you're here to see, and you better not call him Tubby if you know what's good for you. Now come on. Get your worthless ass out of the car."

He half-pulled me out of the back seat of the Cadillac Escalade and stood me up on the circular drive in front of Tubby's place. A big three-story brick mansion that I sort of recognized because there was another thug standing at the front door. The guy who punched me earlier and just pulled me out of the car snapped his fingers a couple of times in front of my face. "You tracking this, Haskell?"

"Yeah, yeah, I got it."

"Okay, 'bout damn time." He grabbed the sides of my shirt and pulled down, then shook his head. "I'm afraid that's as good as you're going to get. Let's go. You're keeping the big man waiting."

I followed him into Tubby's mansion. As I walked past the thug minding the front door, he chuckled just under his breath and said, "Idiot." We headed down a large hallway, past the grand staircase that led up to the second floor. We passed two doors, stopped at the third, and the blonde giant knocked.

"Hold on a minute," a voice I recognized as Tubby's growled from the other side of the door. After a long moment, Tubby called, "Okay, get in here."

The thug opened the door, and we entered Tubby's office. He usually sat at his desk, but tonight he was at the far end of the room, seated on a leather couch in front of a fire in the fireplace. The three of them were sitting on the couch. Tubby wore what looked like silk pajamas, black silk pajamas. I immediately thought of fat Preston Leadbetter answering the door in that black silk robe with the white lapels. Tubby had a fat hand wrapped around a crystal glass of bourbon. On either side and facing him sat a beautiful young Asian woman in a black negligee. They each held what looked like a glass of champagne.

Tubby took a sip from his glass then indicated with a nod of his head that the women should leave. They kissed him on the cheek simultaneously, stood without a word, and began giggling as they headed for what appeared to be a sort of secret door in the far corner of the wood-paneled room. No one said a word, and all eyes were on them as they disappeared.

"They're gone, Haskell. Thanks to you. So pay attention. Once again, you've created a problem for me."

"Me? What in the world did I do?"

"Were you listening? I just told you, you imbecile, you've once again created a problem for me."

"How? What?"

"Does the name Hubert Holly suggest anything to you?"

"Only that he's a wealthy high powered attorney. He's the client of a friend I was helping. I met him for the first time yesterday at his daughter's wedding, actually not the wedding, but the groom's dinner the evening before. See the wedding was called—"

"Believe me, I'm aware the wedding was called off." He stared at the fire and didn't bother to look up at me. "Seems to me this so-called millionaire the daughter was going to marry wasn't all he's cracked up to be. But there you are, making sure everything goes off without a hitch. Which, no surprise, didn't happen." He took a sip from his drink and, still staring at the fire, said, "So, what exactly do you intend to do about it?"

"I'm not sure what you mean, sir."

Tubby shook his head. "I don't know, Haskell. It always comes down to the age-old question. Why do I even bother? Right now, Frederic is out looking under every rock he can find for this character."

Frederic, meaning Fat Freddy Zimmermann, worthless thug extraordinaire. "By this character, do you mean Brendan Bishmann? The guy who was supposed to marry Crystal Holly? The guy who walked out of the groom's dinner last night and disappeared?"

"Oh, so a one-watt light suddenly flashed on in that thick skull of yours. It's about time. It pains me to say this, but I'm going to need your services. I want you to find Bishmann and bring him to me, dead or alive. You better find him if you know what's good for you. Do you hear me?" Tubby half-shouted.

"Yes sir, umm, just so you know. I've been spending the better part of the last sixteen hours trying to do just that, find him. In fact, I have discovered a few tidbits of information that you may not have."

"Spare me. Do me a favor. Get out of my sight and just find him."

"I think that if—"

Tubby looked up at me and shouted, "Silencio, you moron! You have interrupted my bedtime therapy. Now please, for once, just do as you're told." He nodded at the blonde thug. "Get this fool out of my sight before I take matters into my own hands."

I heard the two women giggling just as the blonde giant shoved me out of the room. Thankfully, they didn't make me walk but drove me home instead.

The blonde guy turned and looked at me from the passenger seat."So this loser Bishmann took off in the middle of the wedding instead of marrying this rich guy's daughter?"

"Yeah, it looks like he maybe lied about a number of things. Everyone is going to be looking for him."

"And I heard Mr. Gustafson say he'd help in any way he could. I suppose he'll get paid."

"I gotta be honest. I wouldn't want him looking for me. You don't cross your boss in this town."

They pulled in front of my place, and the blonde guy said, "Get your worthless ass out of here."

I half-ran up the front sidewalk, across the front porch, and locked the door behind me. I watched to make sure the thugs drove off before I hurried upstairs. I could hear snoring as I reached the top of the stairs. Scarlett was under the covers, snuggled up against Morton, and snoring. For his part, Morton was lying next to her, stretched out on the bed, and looking very content. Scarlett's arm was draped around Morton.

It figured — vintage Tubby Gustafson. My night was ruined. I crawled into bed in the guest room and fell asleep happy I wasn't Brendan Bishmann with Tubby Gustafson and his crew looking for me.

Thirty

At no surprise, I woke early the following morning. At least no one was pounding on the front door. I peeked in my bedroom. Scarlett and Morton were in the exact same position as when I last saw them. Thankfully, she wasn't snoring. I did notice a bottle of aspirin and the glass from the bathroom on the end table on Scarlett's side of the bed, so she must have been up at some point in the middle of the night.

I went downstairs and put the coffee on, turned on my computer, and sent an email to Preston telling him I would be stopping by later in the day for any additional information he had on Brendan Bishmann and Darrin Yardly.

I received an almost immediate reply from Preston saying he was working on it and to stop by sometime after three since he had a game at noon. Knowing him, he probably hadn't been to bed since I was over there yesterday.

I was on my third cup of coffee when I thought I heard Morton jump off the bed upstairs. Sure enough, he wandered into the kitchen about five minutes later. If a dog can look happy, Morton seemed to look overjoyed.

"Well, if it isn't the guy who stole my date last night. How'd you sleep?" I said and gave him the necessary scratch behind the ear. He did his morning stretches and ambled toward the back door. I let him out and filled his food and water dish. We had breakfast together once I let him back inside. I placed my dishes in the dishwasher, washed the frying pan, and got back on the computer, searching for anything on Brendan Bishmann and coming up empty-handed.

It was after ten when I heard noise from upstairs suggesting Scarlett was among the living. She appeared in the kitchen about twenty minutes later. She didn't look the best. Her usually striking auburn hair had a serious case of bed-head and appeared lopsided. Her tight-fitting dress was wrinkled, had a slight tear along the seam, and hung loosely on her shoulders. She didn't look all that happy.

"Well, she has risen," I said.

"Hey, I'm up, and you don't have to yell."

"Whoa, sorry, party animal."

"Just zip me up." She turned around with her back to me. "I should head home," she said as I zipped up her dress. She sort of shrugged her shoulders and shifted the top from side to side.

Morton strolled over, thrust his nose beneath her dress, and began to wag his tail.

"God, he's just like you. By the way, what did you do with my thong, you pervert?"

"Your thong? I didn't touch it. Honest. In fact, when I came home, you were passed out in bed with your arm around Morton."

She gave me a funny look. "Came home? We came home together, didn't we? In fact, don't lie to me. I know we did because you made me a cosmopolitan, and we talked for a little bit."

"Actually, you insisted I make you three cosmopolitans. Which you drank and then we went upstairs. Unfortunately, as I was about to climb into bed, we had some unwanted visitors, and when I came back home, you and Morton were sound asleep. You were snuggled up next to Morton with your arm draped over him, snoring. Snoring loudly, I might add. So I went to sleep in the guest room."

"The guest room? But I remember giving you— Are you sure? This isn't funny, Dev. Don't tell me—"

"Scarlett, I just told you, unwanted visitors showed up. I never got into bed with you. Two thugs beat me up and dragged me over to see Tubby Gustafson last night. When I got home, you were snuggled up next to Morton, with your arm around him."

Morton suddenly put his head down and hurried out of the room.

"Morton? Your dog? Oh God," she said and hurried over to the kitchen sink. She squirted a handful of dishwashing liquid on her hands and ran them under the faucet, scrubbing furiously.

"Scarlett?"

"Shut up and don't you say another word. Tubby Gustafson? What did he want?" She asked, then squirted more soap on her hands and returned to scrubbing furiously.

Thirty-one

While I scrambled three eggs for Scarlett, I gave her a brief description of Tubby's request. Find Brendan Bishmann and deliver him to Tubby, dead or alive. I didn't bother to mention that the way he said it made it sound more like a death threat to me than a polite request.

"Oh, blick! Tubby Gustafson in silk pajamas? I don't even want to think about it, that is so gross."

"You're telling me. And then he had these two hot looking women in negligees on either side of him drinking champagne."

"It would take a lot more than champagne to get me next to that big blob. How did he even find out about Brendan Bishmann?"

"I told you, Hubert's daughter, the jilted bride, described Tubby to me while I drove her to the ER at United Hospital. He was at their house a few days before the wedding. She didn't know his name, at least I don't think she did. But her description of a fat guy with a red, pocked marked nose the size of a baked potato fits Tubby to a T."

"You know, now I'm wondering if that's where Hubert ended up. I don't know. Do you think Hubert was desperate enough to ask the likes of Tubby Gustafson for help?"

"That seems like a bit of a stretch based on what you told me about him being an honest, God fearing, responsible adult. But then again—"

"Yeah, I know, I know. You already told me behind every fortune there's a crime. Hubert doesn't strike me as the type, Dev. He may have done some work for the likes of your friend Mr. Gustafson, but the least bit of criminal behavior would have sent him running in the opposite direction. He's simply too clean to get involved with that sub-class of society."

"Well, all I know is Tubby wants Bishmann in a bad way, and he's got his main creep, Fat Freddy Zimmerman, out scouring the streets for him. Or, as Tubby said, looking under every rock for Bishmann."

"And don't forget Dev. Now he's got you, too."

"Don't limit it to just me. You're looking for him. Which reminds me, you turned your phone off last night. Probably didn't want to interrupt your little adventure with Morton so you—"

"Oh please, promise me you'll never, ever, mention that again. You forced me to drink copious amounts of alcohol to the point I barely knew my own name."

"Oh, no. You're an adult. You could of, in fact, should of, stopped early on. But you didn't, so don't blame me."

"Okay, okay. You don't have to raise your voice."

"I'm not raising my voice. It's just that you're blaming me because you decided to go off the rails. How is that my fault? I wasn't even here, and believe me, the last thing I wanted to do was leave. As a matter of fact, the only reason I went along was because this one jerk hit me and knocked me out as I was fighting off the other four. Then the five of them put me in the car and drove me to Tubby's house."

"Five? A moment ago, you said there were two guys, and one of them had blonde hair."

"There were two that pounded on the door, but it took all five of them to get me in the car and drag me away from you, dog lover."

"Dev, please. Don't ever mention that again. I promise I'll make it up to you. Hey," she said as she put her fork down on the half-finished plate of eggs. "Much as I'd like to stay, I'm going to have to go home and get changed. You learn anything about Bishmann or what your friend Gustafson is up to, let me know." She took a step forward, gave me a kiss on the cheek, and headed for the front door.

Morton suddenly bounded out of the living room and rubbed his head against her leg.

She reached down, petted him, and shook her head. "Okay, Morton. I'm counting on you to keep our little secret. Thanks for breakfast, Dev. Sorry about last night. Call me later." She was suddenly out the door and hurrying across the street to her car.

Morton hurried into the front room, jumped up on the couch, and whined while he looked out the window.

I watched her drive off and then headed upstairs to take a shower. I spent a long time standing beneath the hot water, wondering what, exactly, I was going to do with Tubby Gustafson and his criminal element. I wondered if I was Brendan Bishmann, where would I go? The answer seemed obvious; as far away from here as possible.

I shaved, stood under the shower for another ten minutes, and then dried off. I dressed and was headed downstairs when my phone rang. I didn't want to answer it, let alone look to see who was calling, but I glanced at the screen anyway. Aaron LaZelle.

"Hi, Aaron," I said.

"Sorry to bother you on a Sunday morning, Dev. What are you up to?"

"His question didn't sound exactly friendly."

"What am I up to? I'm about to head down to my office with Morton and do some work. You're working today, Sunday?"

"Yeah, always something to do around here. Did I catch you at home?"

"Yeah, but like I said, I'm about to head down to the office. Always loose ends to tie up," I lied.

"Tell you what. If you've got a couple of minutes, I'd love to have a little chat."

"A little chat? No offense, but that doesn't sound all that positive. Besides, I'm about to head down—"

"Maybe look out the front window. I'll see you in about fifteen minutes."

I glanced out the window just as the second squad car pulled up in front of my place. "Yeah, thanks for the ride, see you shortly," I said and opened the front door just as two cops stepped up onto my front porch.

Thirty-two

As I opened the door the police sergeant said, "Mr. Haskell." He was big, and the protective vest beneath his uniform shirt made him look bigger. The young man behind him was even larger.

"Hi guys, I was just going to run a couple of errands. You mind coming back in an hour or two."

"Afraid not," the sergeant said and shook his head. "Might be best if you just come along nicely. Lieutenant LaZelle and Detective Manning are looking forward to talking with you."

"Am I under arrest?"

"No, at least not yet. But it would be a good idea to join us of your own free will, sir."

"Let me just grab my keys," I said.

"Not a problem," the sergeant said as he moved aside, and the larger officer behind him stepped into the house. "Officer Golden Gloves will help you find your keys."

I smiled and looked at the name embroidered on the officer's shirt, Stassen, T.

"This way, officer. My keys are back in the kitchen," I said and headed toward the back of the house. Morton must have sensed the tension in the air and had enough sense to stay on the couch. The cop followed me into the kitchen, and there my keys were, sitting right on the counter. As I picked them up, I noticed another cop standing on my back porch. I guess he was out there in the event I tried to make a run for it.

"That your partner?" I asked.

Golden Gloves nodded and said, "Yes, sir. His name is Track Star. He's very fast."

I smiled and shook my head. "Any idea how long this might be? Just wondering if I should leave the lights on for my dog."

"Shouldn't be too long, but maybe it would be a good idea to leave them on, you know, just in case."

I flicked the kitchen lights on as we headed back to the front door. I flicked on the front porch light as we headed out to the squad cars parked in the street. As we walked down the porch steps, Track Star came down the driveway and joined us. Thankfully I wasn't handcuffed because a neighbor woman walking past took out her cell phone and photographed us as the sergeant opened the rear door on one of the squad cars and then closed it once I was inside.

She said, "It's about damn time he's been arrested." All three officers laughed. The sergeant crossed the street and climbed into his car as Golden Gloves and Track Star climbed into the front seat, and we drove off.

No one spoke on the way down to the station. They pulled around to the back and parked in a numbered spot, then climbed out and opened the door for me. I slid out of the back seat and followed them inside. We walked down a hallway past the front desk and waited for the elevator to come back down to the ground floor.

"Please, by my guest," Golden Gloves said when the elevator door opened. He graciously extended his hand, indicating I should step onto the elevator. The two of them followed me into the elevator and pushed the button for the third floor. Once on the third floor, we walked past the security door leading into the homicide section where Aaron's office was and turned down a hallway with a half-dozen interview rooms. The two cops opened the door to interview room three and then closed it behind me.

I'd been in the room before. It had cinderblock walls painted a shiny dark grey from the floor to about four feet up the wall. From there, the walls were painted a light grey, almost white. There was a large, two-way mirror on one wall, which I knew housed a room behind it where others could watch. I waved at the mirror and took a seat at the table.

At least the table wasn't metal topped, and the four chairs weren't bolted to the floor. That seemed to suggest I wasn't going to be placed under arrest. I pulled my phone out to check the time but a NO SERVICE! notification in red letters came up on the screen. Not surprising.

A moment later, the door opened, and my friend, Lieutenant Aaron LaZelle, stepped in and said, "Hi, Dev." He took a step toward me and stopped, turned and said something to a person standing just out in the hall. I couldn't make out what he was saying. He talked for maybe twenty seconds, then closed the door and headed over to me. I was sitting in the chair with my arms crossed, not looking very happy.

He casually tossed a file on the table as he sat down and said, "Why the face? You don't appear to be happy."

"Oh, I don't know. Maybe because you sent two squad cars to drag me out of my house when all you had to do was tell me on the phone you wanted me to come down. Maybe because they basically surrounded my house, and I'm sure my neighbors are wondering what I've done this time. Maybe because you know your close personal friend Detective Sergeant Norris Manning hates my guts and will do anything to see me locked up behind bars and then placed in the electric chair."

He smiled and shook his head, "Come on, Dev. You know we don't have the death penalty here in Minnesota."

"I'm sure Manning would gladly find a way to put me in a state that does have it, or try and bring me up on some Federal charge. Why didn't you just ask me nicely to come down?"

"For your own protection, Dev. And for your information, Manning is the one who suggested you may need protection."

"Manning? What the hell does he know? And, since when, has he ever been concerned with my well-being?"

Aaron ignored my questions and said. "Do you know a gentleman by the name of Hubert Holly?"

"Are you kidding me, Hubert Holly? Is this about that fiasco Friday night? God. I was helping S.R. Investigations. Scarlett Raunchnoble asked me to accompany her to the groom's dinner for Hubert's daughter and her husband to be. Only it turns out the wedding never happened."

"Yes, we're aware of that. We have several eyewitness statements attesting to the fact that the daughter was assaulted and ended up in the hospital overnight."

"Assaulted? Where did that come from?"

"Come on, Dev. You should know better than that. You think I'm going to ask you a question I don't know the answer to?"

"I'm just saying whatever information you have is wrong."

Aaron opened a file and pulled out a photograph obviously taken on a cellphone. I was lifting fat Crystal Holly into the front seat of Scarlett's car. The look on my red face suggested I might not be able to accomplish the task. "This ring any bells, Dev? She can't walk. Given the amount of blood, it looks like she's been stabbed in the rear, and we happen to know that you brought her to the ER at United Hospital."

Thirty-three

I sat quietly for a good fifteen seconds, relishing the moment. Aaron was a good friend, a dear pal. But I'd lost count of the times I'd been wrong about something, and he had pulled my feet out of the fire. Now here it was, laid out right in front of me like it was being presented on a silver platter.

"What's so funny, Dev?"

"I'm just enjoying the moment, Aaron. Whoever gave you that image had some awfully bad information. About the only thing you said that's correct is that I took her down to the ER at United. She wasn't stabbed, Aaron. She sat down on a picnic table bench in her parents' backyard and got a sliver in her butt about the size of a ten gauge nail. That's why all the blood, and believe me, she was bleeding profusely. I did tell a highway patrol officer that she had been stabbed, but that was only because he was going to ticket me for speeding. He followed us into the ER, then when I told him she was stabbed and he saw the blood, he helped me place her on a gurney and push it into the ER. He took off after that, so I never had the chance to set him straight."

"You're kidding. A sliver?" Aaron said.

"Yeah, 'fraid so, and let me tell you, it was big." I chuckled a little and said, "So, you gonna give me a lift home?"

"Not quite yet. Tell me what you know about Hubert Holly."

"Hubert Holly? What the hell is everyone so interested in him for? I don't know that much about him except that he's very rich, has a pain in the ass wife named Addison, a son named Justin who was going to be the best man, and a spoiled daughter named Crystal who is really heavy and I don't recommend carrying her."

"You happen to know where his wife is?"

"Addison? No. Last I heard she'd left strict instructions with the staff that she was not to be disturbed. That was yesterday after the wedding fiasco. I think she spent the better part of the day with her therapist, and I believe she's got a one-way ticket to Paris on a flight tonight."

"And you know this how?"

"I did the groom's dinner gig with Scarlett Raunchnoble, S.R. Investigations. That's the only reason I was there on Friday night at the groom's dinner in the first place. Then yesterday, I did a little investigatory work on a fellow named Brendan Bishmann. He was going to marry Crystal Holly, but he left in the middle of the dinner. I know that yesterday he moved out of the apartment he was renting, but I have no idea where he went. I also happen to know that the name Brendan Bishmann is an assumed alias he's been using for at least the better part of a year, maybe longer."

Arron was writing furiously and finally said, "Interesting. What's his real name?"

"No idea, honest."

He looked up at me and said, "Okay. Back to Hubert Holly for a moment. Do you know where he might be?"

"You can't find him? Last I heard he and Scarlett, umm, Scarlett Raunchnoble, were meeting guests who had arrived for yesterday's wedding ceremony. They told everyone there was a medical emergency, and the wedding had been postponed. I know Scarlett tried to call him at least four times yesterday evening, but he never answered."

"But a medical emergency wasn't the real story?"

"Right. Apparently Bishmann, the groom, broke things off literally at the Friday night dinner and left. We've heard a couple of stories, the bride told him she was pregnant, but he wasn't the father. I've only been involved with these privileged crackpots for about forty-eight hours, Aaron, so at best, this is pretty much secondhand information. You should probably talk to Scarlett Raunchnoble and her staff for more up to date and accurate info. Be a better idea than hauling me out of my house on a Sunday morning. Have you thought of calling Hubert Holly himself and talking to him?"

"Interesting you say that. Your phone number was one of the last calls to go through to him."

"Yeah, and I didn't make the call. Scarlett did last night while we were having dinner. She kept getting dumped into his voicemail, so I suggested she should maybe try to reach him on my phone. But how did you know that? Did he give you his phone?"

"Did he answer the call?" Aaron asked, ignoring my questions.

"No, she got the same result, dumped into voicemail. You should give him a call from here."

"At this stage, there's really no point in doing that," Aaron said, shaking his head.

"Why the hell not? Aaron, what the hell is going on here?"

"Hubert Holly's dead. His body was discovered around sunrise this morning."

Thirty-four

Aaron was just pulling into the Ramsey County Medical Examiner's office. It's on University Avenue next to Regions Hospital and the 35E Interstate. If it weren't for the sign out front, the one-story nondescript building would be a real drive-by.

"I really appreciate you coming over with me to identify the body, Dev."

"I didn't really volunteer. If you'll recall, you told me I could just walk home if I didn't want to do this."

"Hey, no problem, Dev. You don't want to help out our investigation and identify the body? Go ahead and hop out. I won't stop you."

"I'll do it. You know me, always willing to help."

Aaron pasted a fake smile on his face and said, "That's the spirit."

"Where did you tell me he was found?"

"Over in the Highland Park end of town. Nice little area where we used to go parking with girlfriends after dances. There are three or four of those parking areas along the River Boulevard. This was the one right off of Hartford and the Boulevard."

"Oh, I've got some good memories of that place. Do you happen to remember Jeannie? She—"

"So not interested," Aaron said as he pulled into a parking place with a sign that read 'RESERVED FOR POLICE VEHICLES VIOLATORS WILL BE

TOWED'. We climbed out and entered a small lobby with three faux leather couches, a couple of chairs, and a coffee table with stacks of cremation society brochures.

The receptionist sat behind a bulletproof glass window. She waved, flashed a sparkling smile, and as we stepped into the lobby, she called, "Hey, Aaron."

"How's it going, Carol? You still on that softball team?"

"Yeah, made it one more year, but my recovery time seems to get a little more extended every season. I had a knee problem that pretty much benched me for most of July. I thought you said you were going to make it to one of our games this season?"

"Yeah, believe me, I would have loved to. Been a busy summer, unfortunately."

"Tell me about it. You know we almost had to rent a refrigerator truck this summer to store folks."

"Yeah. That would have been interesting. Hey, we're here to identify the vic they brought in this morning."

"I heard he was some rich guy," Carol said, then looked me up and down and decided I apparently wasn't a rich guy.

"Supposedly. Can you buzz us in?"

"Yeah. I'll let them know. You'll be in the back viewing room," she said as the door buzzed, and Aaron opened it. I followed him in, and we walked down a long hallway to the viewing room.

The place looked the same as the last time I'd been here. Offices were on both sides of the hall. Framed landscape watercolors hung on the walls about ten feet apart. We passed three viewing rooms and entered the one furthest down the hall. It was always referred to as the Back Viewing Room, rather than number four, which corresponded to the number on the door. I never understood why.

The room was painted off-white and had one wall with a large window. A white Venetian blind on the other side of the glass was covering the window. The room had a beige carpet and a small cabinet with a box of Kleenex sitting on the top of the cabinet.

"You got something going with the receptionist?" I asked.

"Carol? You kidding? She's married and has three kids. Her husband works for the city. He's an architect or an engineer or something."

"Just the way she talked, it sounded like she was interested."

"Three kids? She doesn't have time to be interested. I dated a friend of hers a couple of times, and that's how I met her. Well, and this place is becoming like a second home, I'm down here so often. Relax, she was with her husband when I met her." The blinds suddenly went up, and a guy in a white lab coat waved at Aaron, then flicked a switch on the wall and said, "Hey, Aaron, how's it going?"

"Same shit, different day. This is a friend of mine, private investigator, Dev Haskell. Dev, Doctor Gary Skarla. Dev offered to identify the victim officially."

Gary Skarla was dressed in a white lab coat and wearing blue latex gloves. He wheeled a gurney into place alongside the window. I never quite got over the initial sight of the gurney with the body covered by a sheet. No matter who you were, in this case, a prominent, wealthy attorney, everyone got the same treatment, the same gurney, and the same industrial white sheet.

It suddenly seemed to grow exceptionally quiet. Gary stepped to the side, took hold of the white sheet covering Hubert Holly's head, and gracefully pulled it back, neatly folding it just under Holly's chin. Then he stepped back and politely waited. He must have done this at least a few thousand times, and he was still ever the gentleman. I focused on Hubert Holly, and Gary faded into the background.

Holly's eyes were closed, and he would have looked completely peaceful if it weren't for the two dime-sized bullet holes in the center of his forehead, maybe an inch apart and one slightly higher than the other. They seemed to effectively eliminate the idea of suicide.

I looked at Gary, nodded, and said, "Yeah, that's him, Hubert Holly."

Gary gave a quick nod, carefully pulled the sheet back over Holly's face, and lowered the blinds.

"All right, Dev, many thanks. Sorry you had to do that, but we couldn't reach any of the family, and you just happened along. You okay?"

"What? Oh, yeah. Unfortunately, I've seen a lot of dead people, and it still gets me thinking. It's funny in a sort of weird way. Hubert Holly, the guy's got all the money in the world, and he can't buy another sunrise." I shook my head. "It's too bad, and it reminds us we're both awfully damn lucky, Aaron."

"Yeah, come on. I'll give you that lift home."

Thirty-five

Aaron pulled to the curb in front of my place. "Thanks for your help, Dev. Much appreciated."

"Yeah, sure. Hey, you said Manning wanted me brought in for my own protection, but you never told me, protection from what or who?"

"To be honest, I was just trying to get on your good side. Then I remembered you don't have one. Go on, get out."

"You owe me a beer. Make it a couple of beers," I said. "Good luck trying to find who did that to Hubert Holly. If I can be of any help, just let me know."

"You'll be the first person I contact, Dev. Thanks again," he called as I climbed out of the passenger seat.

I waved goodbye and watched him drive off. As soon as he disappeared around the corner, I hurried into the house, let Morton out, then pulled my cellphone from my pocket and called Scarlett. She answered on the third ring. "Yeah, Dev, what's up? And before you ask, no, I can't join you tonight, so don't go out and buy the makings for more cosmopolitans because I won't be drinking them. In fact, I won't be drinking them ever again."

"Gee and I just got back from the grocery store. I was counting on cooking a special dinner for you."

"Really?"

"No, I was just kidding. Hey, you ever get hold of Hubert Holly?"

"No, he's still not answering. I just get automatically dumped into his voicemail, you know, before it even rings. I don't know what he's thinking. He's never—"

"He's not thinking, Scarlett. I just came from the medical examiner after identifying his body."

"What? Dev, if this is your idea of a joke, you are way the hell off—"

"Hey, Scarlett, believe me, I would never joke about something like this. Apparently, his body was found early this morning. Sunrise, as a matter of fact. Here in St. Paul."

"What was he doing?"

"You mean, why was he in a parking area along the River Boulevard overlooking the Mississippi? I've no idea. I'd guess that's one of the many questions the police have, not that they were in any frame of mind to give me information. Do me a favor. Give me the phone numbers you have for Hubert."

"Why, it's not like he's going to answer. Oh, my God. I just can't believe this."

"Can you give me his numbers, home, office? I've got his cell on my phone from your call last night, please, Scarlett. I'm going to try to track him."

"You? Dev, you're talking some sophisticated technology and—"

"Scarlett, will you give me the numbers, please?"

"Okay, crabby, calm down. You ready?"

"Yeah, go ahead." I wrote them down as she gave them to me then repeated them back to her.

"Correct. I just can't believe this. You're sure?"

"I found this out from Aaron LaZelle. He's a pal of mine. Heads up the homicide unit in St. Paul, and yes, it was definitely Hubert Holly at the medical examiner's. You should call Aaron. He'll fill you in on some of the details, and I know he'd like to hear from you. You got a clean space on the wall where you can write down his number?"

"Yeah, go ahead."

I gave her Aaron's number and then sent a text message to Preston with Hubert Holly's numbers, telling him to try to track the phone. I got an almost immediate reply, 'Visitors.'

I didn't know if that meant the police, a woman, or the pizza delivery guy. I decided to drive over and check things out. I pulled over to the curb about a half-block away from Preston's mother's house. A big black Cadillac Escalade was parked in front of the house. A guy was leaning against the passenger door, smoking a cigarette. I could see absolutely no advantage to going into Preston's just now, so I turned off my car and waited.

It took the better part of a half-hour before that big blonde guy from the night before strolled out with Fat Freddy Zimmerman and some other lowlife. They all climbed in the Escalade. I watched as it rocked from side to side as Fat Freddy oozed into the front passenger seat. A moment later they took off, made the first left, and disappeared. I waited another ten minutes just to be sure they weren't coming back before I pulled in front of the house and hurried to the steps leading down to the basement.

The door wasn't just unlocked. It was open. I stepped inside and hurried down the hallway calling Preston's name and moving a little faster with every step. "Preston? Preston, you okay? Hey, Preston?"

He was seated behind his computer screens, wearing a navy blue sweatsuit with a bloody nose and tears running down his face.

"Preston, you okay, buddy? What'd they do to you?"

"Just slapped me around a little, that's all. I'm okay, Dude," he said and wiped his upper lip with a bloody Kleenex, which only served to smear blood across the side of his face.

"Hold on. Here, put your head back. I'm gonna get you a towel. Go on now. Put your head back. Yeah, good. Now, keep it there for a minute. I'll be right back." I grabbed a grungy towel from the bathroom then looked in the freezer for some ice. There were two empty ice trays. I grabbed a bag of frozen chocolate chip cookie dough, wrapped the towel around it, and hurried back to Preston.

"Here, put this against the bridge of your nose. You're gonna be okay. It doesn't look like it's broken. Which one of those jerks did this to you?"

"You saw them?"

"Yeah, Fat Freddy and two other guys. The big blonde guy hit me last night."

"Dude, what is with that guy? I didn't even do anything, and that prick punched me."

"They're jerks. Look, keep that head back. Here," I said, rolling up a piece of Kleenex and handing it to him, then rolling another. "Plug your nose with these to stop the bleeding. Yeah, good. You're gonna be okay, Preston. Did they tell you they're going to come back?"

"No, nothing like that. I just don't like dealing with them. That jerk Freddy just laughed at me, told me I better find Brendan Bishmann and fast if I knew what was good for me. How come they're looking for him? Tubby wasn't at the dinner Friday night, was he? How do they even know him?"

"You got me. Did you tell them I was looking for him?"

"No. I wouldn't do that to you, Dev. They don't know I work on stuff for you, and I'm not about to tell them."

"Thanks, Preston, I appreciate that. I've never told them about you, and I won't mention anything to them. You know, since they don't know you've already been checking out Bishmann, you think you might feed them information, keep me twenty-four hours ahead of them?"

"I'd be happy to do that. Just promise me you'll keep a low profile. I don't want them knowing we're involved in any way."

Thirty-six

Preston's nose eventually stopped bleeding. I took the towel with the now thawed cookie dough from him and tossed the towel on the bathroom floor. I turned on the oven, arranged the dough on a cookie sheet, and placed it in the oven. As the basement filled with the scent of baking chocolate chip cookies, Preston seemed to get back on track.

As he ran his fingers across the keyboard, he said, "I still haven't found the real name of this Bishmann guy, but he's been moving a lot of funds into offshore accounts. At least I'm guessing it's him."

"Describe to me the term a lot of funds."

"I'm talking millions from a couple of personal bank accounts, what looks like some kind of trust fund, and a real estate account, it's all across the board. He's using servers in Ukraine, the Balkans, and Latvia. Those are just the ones I've been able to track so far. He's moving funds into numbered accounts in Panama, Brazil, Argentina, and the Seychelles."

"Is it a government or some sort of black ops thing?"

Preston shot me a quick look and shook his head. "No, nothing like that. But it seems pretty clear he's probably done this before. He seems to know what he's doing."

"And it's a million dollars?"

"No, it's millions, more like three and half-million so far. From what I can tell, this started last night around midnight."

"What the hell?"

"You ready for the next bit of news?"

"What?"

"One of the accounts belonged to Fat Freddy's boss."

"Tubby Gustafson?"

"Yeah, the guy drained five hundred grand from a real estate account before the password was changed. I'd say Mr. Gustafson somehow found out someone had access and was able to change security on his other accounts."

"But what about the rest of the money? You said three and a half million. Where's the other three million coming from?"

"Small world, Dev. It seems to all be coming from the guy whose phone number you gave me."

"Hubert Holly?"

"Yeah, well, I mean, a couple of the accounts were joint accounts. A person named Addison. Who's that?"

"Jesus, that's his wife."

"Well, I think they're close to being broke. Then there was a fund of some sort." Preston scrolled up on his screen for a long minute. "Yeah, here it is, an investment fund, emptied out about four-thirty this morning. All in all, a total of three-point five million in funds went to a numbered account in Panama. Fifteen minutes after that, the funds were divided between seven different accounts in Brazil. Thirty minutes after that they were sent to Argentina, I think. I'm still trying to track all of those. The ones I've found went to the Seychelles."

I was suddenly on the phone to Scarlett. "Come on, pick up. Pick up. Come on Scarlett. Will you pick—"

"Hi, Dev, I'm dealing with a situation. Let me call you back. Okay?"

"No. Scarlett. I just learned someone is draining the Holly accounts."

"What?"

"Someone is emptying the Holly accounts. It looks like they've drained the trust fund account, some joint accounts. Can you figure out how to put a hold on the rest of those accounts, maybe change the password? Whoever is doing this is very good and apparently knows what the hell they're doing. I suspect it's Bishmann."

"Confirmation," Scarlett shouted to someone.

"Better check the trust fund account, too. Where are you?" I asked.

"Hubert's office, here in his house. An automatic message from the bank on one of his accounts said a transfer had been made. All the passwords were filed on his computer in the cloud."

"I wonder if he had the password for a Tubby Gustafson account. It looks like that was drained to the tune of five hundred grand."

"The password has been changed on that account," Preston shouted then went back to tapping keys.

"Yeah, you hear that. The password on that account—"

"I heard, I heard," she said then whispered, "This is an outright disaster. Listen, I'll check with you later. I better go. Addison is about ready to jump from a bridge."

"You might want to have a couple of people there for security. Tubby Gustafson is not going to be very happy about this. Is she still flying to Paris this evening?"

"Under the circumstances, no. The police were here earlier and confiscated her passport, not that she was planning to leave now. You have someone working on this?" Scarlett asked, she was still whispering.

"Yeah, someone with a lot more technical expertise than me. He's trying to track this stuff, but it's moving from country to country. The servers are apparently scattered around Eastern Europe. Are your people on this?"

"Just getting started. We haven't even been here for an hour. They really just finished setting up the equipment. Right now, Addison is on the phone with her therapist, trying to get a stronger prescription."

"Good luck with that."

Thirty-seven

I phoned Scarlett twice more over the course of the day, but she didn't answer. I was just checking in anyway and didn't really have any new information. Preston had followed the transfers to accounts in Panama, Brazil, and then to Argentina. He was still trying to track things in the Seychelles, but that was as far as he'd gotten.

"How much time you think that's going to take?"

"To find out where they've moved it to? Not sure, Dev. Certainly a few more hours, maybe even a day or two, security on this is really tough."

"And Tubby's crew is bound to be back here. You want to pack up and come to my place?"

"Wouldn't that be the next place they look?"

"Not unless you told them you were doing work for me."

"Far as I can recall, I never mentioned it to them. No offense, Dude, but it still doesn't sound any safer than here. They pulled you out of there just the other night, didn't they?"

"Well yeah, but—"

"I'll take my chances here. Besides, other than tell them where the money's headed to, I don't know what else I could do."

"Bishmann is the key. We find him, and maybe we can restore these funds," I said. I wondered if Bishmann was the guy behind Hubert Holly's murder. I was thinking Scarlett mentioned Addison but never brought up the daughter, Crystal. Maybe she knew where Bishmann might be or, even better, maybe Bishmann had contacted her.

"Preston, I'm going to leave you to it. Keep tracking those transfers and see if you can figure out where this Bishmann character is. If he has any sense, he's out of town by now."

"Dude, if he has any sense, he's out of the country," Preston said. He didn't look at me but continued to focus on the screens and run his fingers across the keyboard.

I waited a long moment then said, "Stay in touch. I'm going to check some things out. I'll call you later this afternoon. You need any help, give me a call, Preston." He waved without looking at me as I headed out the door to sunshine and sanity. I hopped in my car and headed home. As I pulled into the driveway, my phone rang. I hoped it wasn't Preston.

"Mmm, Dev, honey. I wasn't sure you'd answer," a sexy voice said.

I was immediately breathing heavily and said, "Hi, Sharon. I wasn't sure I'd hear from you."

"Well, I first wanted to apologize for the other night. I was so excited to have you all to myself I guess I sort of overdid it with the pink Prosecco. And then, second, I should have phoned you a lot sooner, but I was so embarrassed about missing the opportunity I, umm, wasn't sure you'd even want to talk to me."

"Oh no, Sharon. Honest, nothing like that. I've just been really busy working on a case, and it all suddenly just blew up."

"Mmm, does that mean you might have time for me tonight?"

Wow. Talk about my luck changing.

"Dev, I promise you a night you'll never, ever forget. Just give me one more chance, please."

How could I refuse? "Sure, you want to grab dinner somewhere? You choose, and I'll pick you up."

"I choose to have dinner here at my place, and I'm not sure we'll even have time for dinner. Be here at seven, and you better rest up."

"Seven, I'll be there. What can I bring?"

"Not Prosecco. I don't want to miss a minute, and Dev, thank you so much. Mmm-mmm, I can't wait. I promise to be a very naughty lady. See you tonight. Bye, bye, bye," she said and hung up.

I debated about hurrying over and buying a lottery ticket since my luck was running so well, then decided maybe a shower and shave before the evening's festivities would be a better idea.

I hurried home and let Morton out. I shaved and hopped in the shower. After a long, hot shower, I pulled on a clean pair of jeans and found a shirt that looked halfway decent. I let Morton back in, gave him a dog biscuit, then instead of Prosecco, I picked up some flowers and headed to Sharon's.

When I called her on the phone in the security lobby, she answered before the first ring was even finished. It had barely started to ring when she picked up the phone and said, "Dev?"

"Yeah, hi, Sharon. Here I am."

"Oh, thank you, thank you, thank you. Get your hot body up here," she said as the security door began buzzing. I took the stairs two at a time up to her third-floor condo. As I climbed to the top of the last flight of stairs, the door to her condo opened, and she stood there waiting for me. She was wearing an extremely short black skirt and a white blouse. The blouse was completely unbuttoned, and there wasn't the slightest hint of a bra.

"Get that delicious body of yours in here. I want to eat you alive," she called when I was barely even halfway down the hall. She lifted her skirt up, exposing herself as an encouragement as if I needed any. I started walking faster and faster so that, by the time I reached her, I was almost running.

Thirty-eight

Sharon grabbed my arms and pulled me inside, then pushed me back against the front door and began kissing me all over my face. After a long minute or two, I pushed her back and stuck the bouquet of flowers between us just to let me catch my breath.

"Here, Sharon, they're for you. Thanks for inviting me over."

"Are you kidding? Thanks for coming on such short notice." She ignored the flowers, reached up, and began to unbutton my shirt.

After she'd undone the third or fourth button, I gently pushed her back and said, "Here, take these flowers and put them in some water. Then you can start up where you left off."

"Let's skip dinner and get right to my dessert. Namely you." She stepped back and took the bouquet of roses from me. She raised them up to her face and inhaled deeply. "Mmm-mmm, you are such a darling. I'll put these in water and then it's going to be your turn. No," she said, cutting me off before I could give some clever answer. "From now on, you are to follow my every command. Come on back to the kitchen."

She took hold of my hand and led me into her kitchen. It smelled of garlic and chicken and something sweet baking. "Oh, baby," she said and deeply inhaled the roses once more.

It sort of struck me as odd because when I bought them at the discount rack, I'd sniffed them and couldn't smell a thing. Not a complaint, they were turning out to be the best six dollars I'd ever spent.

She took a crystal vase from the cabinet beneath the kitchen counter, filled it with water, and placed the roses in the vase. The roses were still wrapped in cellophane and had a rubber band around them to hold them in position along with a small envelope of some sort of powder that was supposed to make them remain fresh longer.

She left the vase in the kitchen sink. As she strutted over to me, she opened her blouse, exposing herself. She placed her hands on my shoulders, backed me up against an antique oak chair with a pressed back and a cane seat, and gently pushed me until I sat down. The chair creaked as I settled onto it.

Sharon knelt down in front of me, pulled my shirt open, and began kissing my bare chest, working her way down to my belt. She unbuckled my belt and pulled it out of the belt loops on my jeans. She wrapped the belt around my stomach and buckled it behind me, attaching me to the chair.

She stood in front of me and pulled a roll of grey duct tape from a drawer beneath the kitchen counter. "I want to do all the work myself, wrist, please."

I held up my right wrist. She wrapped a length of tape around my wrist. "Tell me if it's too tight," she said.

She stepped behind me, gently kissed my ear, and whispered, "Pull your arm back here, baby. I want to get started and can't wait another minute."

I quickly pulled my arm behind my back, and she attached the tape to one of the spindles on the chair, then did the same with my left arm.

"Oh, so kinky," she said, now back down on her knees in front of me. She ran her tongue over her upper lip and said, "Ready, Baby? I've been dreaming of this all afternoon."

"Yeah, yeah, I can't wait either."

She suddenly stood, smiled, and walked out of the kitchen.

I waited for a long minute. The excitement began to disappear, and I called, "Sharon? Hey, Sharon? Sharon, where are you going? Sharon? Sharon, I'm all ready. Shar—"

"She's busy," a male voice said as a man stepped into the kitchen. I was ready to jump from the chair but couldn't thanks to my belt and the duct tape, besides, Brendan Bishmann was holding a gun.

Thirty-nine

Bishmann was wearing jeans, a blue golf shirt, and he had about a three-day growth on his beard. The beard was red, but it was definitely him, Brendan Bishmann."Please don't try to do anything clever. It's not going to work," he said. "What in the hell are you doing?"

"Getting ready to leave town. I don't want any trouble. I've accomplished all that I came here to do, and now it's time to leave quietly."

"But Hubert Holly? I mean, what did he ever do to you? You're acting all high and mighty and sounding sanctimonious, but he's dead. You stole all that money from his family, left them virtually penniless, and now you're fleeing the scene."

He smiled and said, "And just how in the hell do you think they got all that money? You think Hubert Holly scrimped and saved to gradually build a fortune? You buying into all that Man of the Year sort of bullshit? Maybe instead of checking to make sure some poor slob listed the right college major and didn't fudge thirty days working at a previous place on his job application, maybe you should investigate some of these wealthy bastards who apparently are above the law. You might find some surprising information once you begin turning over a rock or two. That includes your long-time pal Tubby Gustafson. So before you start preaching to me, as long as we're on the subject, just remember, you are known by the company you keep, Haskell."

"I don't know anything about Hubert Holly other than someone put two rounds between his eyes. But I do know—"

"You can stop right there because you're right. You don't know a damn thing about Holly. And, before you decide to get on your high horse, let me tell you something. I did not kill Hubert Holly. Got that? It wasn't me."

"Well, if it wasn't you, then who the hell was it? And before you get off your high horse, you might just want to consider returning the funds you stole from him. Stole from his family."

"His family? You mean the two spoiled brats who will never work a day in their life because they have a trust fund that allows them to look down on everyone else? Or, do you mean his wife, who's been a kept woman for so damn long she has no idea what the rest of the world goes through on a daily basis?"

"You can say whatever you want, Bishmann, but at the end of the day, what you've done is a crime. As far as Hubert Holly goes, if you didn't kill him, then who did?"

"I guess that's for you to figure out, Haskell. All I know is I'm leaving with a clear conscience and taking what is rightfully mine. Sharon," he called down the hall. "Sharon, you about ready?"

"Just a moment, Artie."

“So she’s your investment banker,” I said.

Bishmann shook his head. “You’ll never get it, Haskell.” He picked up the roll of duct tape and wrapped a length around my chest a number of times. Then he did the same thing with my legs, attaching each leg to one of the legs on the chair. When he’d finished, he stepped back to admire his handy work, then pulled off an eight-inch strip and taped it over my mouth.

“There, perfect. I should have started with that one. I’d say it’s been a pleasure, but actually, it hasn’t, Haskell.”

I suddenly heard a strange noise coming from the hallway. A moment later, Sharon appeared, wheeling a suitcase. She had a dark sweater pulled over her blouse. She looked at me taped to the chair and then glanced at Bishmann. She didn’t look happy. “I’m sorry, Dev, but we umm, we have a flight to catch.”

“Show him your ticket, Sharon,” Bishmann said.

“Oh yeah, see, we’re flying Delta, and we have to hurry.” She waved a small paper folder with the red triangular logo and the word ‘DELTA’ in blue letters. “Maybe some other time.”

“Be sure to give my best to that fat piece of shit, Tubby Gustafson. Let’s be off, darling. We’ve got a flight to catch,” Bishmann said. I watched as they headed toward the front door. Sharon turned and mouthed the word ‘Sorry’. Bishmann said something I couldn’t quite hear, and they hurried out the door. A moment later, the door closed, and all was quiet.

Forty

I waited for a long moment, half-expecting the door to open, and Sharon would rush in with tears in her eyes and apologize. It didn't happen. My arms strained against the duct tape, the chair creaked, but nothing happened. I could push my legs slightly and lift the chair, maybe a quarter of an inch off the floor. I slowly began to make my way over toward the kitchen counter, a fraction of an inch at a time. I finally got the chair positioned in front of the counter, and with my knees against the counter, I pushed against the back of the chair. The chair creaked, but nothing seemed to happen. After pushing maybe a dozen times, the back of the chair seemed to have loosened, and I could push further back.

I kept pushing for the next twenty minutes or so, gradually loosening the back of the antique chair until suddenly there was a loud 'SNAP,' and the back of the chair definitely loosened. A few more pushes and the back was suddenly disconnected. I moved my arms back and forth until I got my right arm free. In seconds, I was sliding the belt around so that the buckle was in front and I could unbuckle the belt. Once that was accomplished, I began pulling off the tape.

As soon as I freed my ankles, I stood, pulled my cellphone out of my pocket, and speed-dialed Aaron LaZelle. "Come on, Aaron. Answer, please. Pick up the phone, Aaron. Come— Aaron, thank God. I just—"

"Let me call you back, Dev. I'm in the middle of something and—"

"He just left, Bishmann. He and Sharon are catching a plane."

"What are you talking about?"

"Bishmann. The guy who shot Hubert Holly, he just left. He said they had to catch a plane. They're probably leaving the country."

"How do you know this?"

"Long story. Look, get someone out to the airport. Brendan Bishmann isn't his real name. It's Artie something."

"Artie? You mean like Arthur?"

"Yeah, or just Art or, hell, I don't know. Aaron, they left about a half-hour ago. He taped me to a chair. I guess Sharon is his girlfriend, or God, maybe even his wife. She's a blonde in a short black skirt and a white blouse. She had a Delta ticket. Sharon Sanders. Bishmann was wearing jeans and a blue golf shirt, and he had about a three-day growth on his beard."

"I'm on it. Call you back in a couple of minutes," Aaron said and hung up.

I punched in Preston's number. He answered on the fourth ring. "Still working on it, Dev. It's gonna be sometime tomorrow before I can have anything definitive. I think—"

"Preston, that Brendan Bishmann guy. His first name is Artie. Maybe Arthur, or Art or even Arturo."

"That's good news, Dev, and narrows it down a little, but that's still a hell of a big pool."

"Yeah, except that I think he's flying out on a Delta flight tonight. Probably international. If those funds end up in the Seychelles, maybe that's where he's headed, and he'd probably have a link in Atlanta or Miami."

"How'd you find this out?"

"Let's just say a date gone bad. Can you check it out?"

"I'm logging into Delta's system now. Let me call you back, Dude," Preston said and disconnected.

I headed toward the door when my phone rang. "Yeah, Aaron."

"Where are you now?"

"I'm in Sharon Sanders condo. She asked me over here, and then he suddenly appears. It was a setup, but it doesn't make any sense. They tied me to a chair. She waved the Delta ticket in front of me, thought it was funny, and they left."

"Where's this condo?"

"It's on Portland Ave, just off of Summit. There's a park next to it, uhh, Nathan Hale Park. Close to the University Club."

"I've got a team heading out to the airport. Stay there. I'm going to the airport. If we don't get this guy, I'll swing by."

"You should be able to get him. I told you, he's flying out on Delta."

"Yeah, that's what has me concerned. Look, I gotta go Just stay there, and I'll call you when I know something."

Forty-one

As long as I had to wait, I decided to look around. Sharon had some unopened mail in a recycling bag in a closet off the kitchen. Four of the envelopes were addressed to Resident, but the fifth envelope was addressed to Sharon Sanders. I tossed it on the kitchen counter and headed for her bedroom. The four-poster bed with the silk drapes was just as I remembered. The digital clock was still on the dresser. I opened one of the top drawers on her dresser. It was full of thongs and socks. I pulled open the drawer next to it, bras. The drawer below that had a number of blouses and shirts. The bottom drawer held sweaters and what looked like a running outfit

The closet doors were open, exposing more clothes, all neatly arranged on hangers. For someone who was theoretically leaving the country, conceivably for good, she sure hadn't packed very much. Shoes, boots, heels, clogs, three pairs of sandals, two pairs of flip-flops, one of which was all silver and sparkly, and three pairs of running shoes were all arranged on racks in the closet. None of it was making much sense to me.

I called Preston.

He answered on the third ring. "Yeah, Dev, I'm still checking."

"You finding anything?"

"Nothing on the name Arthur or Art. I had a few hits on the name, but one is nineteen, and three are over seventy. I checked direct flights to Pairs, Amsterdam, London, Dallas, Atlanta, Miami, JFK, and Los Angeles, nothing."

"And that's on Delta?"

"Yeah, although the Amsterdam flight was in conjunction with KLM, but still nothing."

"Strange. Okay, anything turns up let me know."

"Yeah, will do," he said and hung up. I went through the bedroom looking for something that might suggest Bishmann or Artie, as Sharon had called him, was here, but came up empty-handed. Same thing in the bathroom. Not so much as a toothbrush or a razor, although it did look like he was starting to grow a beard.

I walked back into the kitchen, smelled garlic and something sweet, and opened the oven. There was a casserole dish with chicken and rice on the top shelf, and below that, a pie on a cookie sheet. I grabbed a hot pad and pulled them both out of the oven. The pie had definitely been in there too long but still appeared to be edible. The chicken was overcooked but not burnt. I let it sit for a moment while I opened the refrigerator. There were three bottles of white wine lying on their side. One of the bottles was only half-full. I decided it might be a good idea if I just left them in case Aaron wanted to get fingerprints or something.

My stomach was rumbling, so I opened the silverware drawer, took out a knife and fork, and stood in front of the chicken casserole dish and started eating. It was a little overdone but still good. I finished a chicken breast, and a good portion of rice then moved over to the cookie sheet with the pie.

It was an apple pie. The upper crust didn't look all that burnt, but it tasted pretty bad. The filling was okay, so I focused on that, removing a forkful at a time from beneath the crust. The pie tin eventually cooled down with the help of some ice cream, and I wandered into the living room and clicked on the TV. I was halfway through the Netflix movie when my phone rang.

"Yeah, Aaron, you find anything?"

"Yeah, the condo building. I'm just coming up the steps to the front door. Buzz me in. What's the unit number?"

"309, I'll buzz you in just a second." I pulled the pie tin with the burnt crust and the melted ice cream off my stomach and set it on the coffee table. Then walked over to the front door and pressed the security buzzer for a good fifteen seconds. I was beginning to wonder if Aaron had made it in when I heard him cough as he was coming up the final flight of steps.

I stood with the door open and watched as he walked down the hall toward me. For just a brief second, I thought of Sharon standing in the doorway with her blouse undone and lifting her skirt. In the end, nothing more than a major league setup, and I fell for it, hook, line, and sinker.

"You touch anything?" Aaron asked and then stared at me.

"What are you staring at?"

"You've got lipstick all over your face."

I automatically rubbed a hand across my cheek and glanced at my fingertips. Sure enough, there was a hint of pink lipstick. "Oh, sorry about that, part of the setup they had for me."

"Setup?"

I went on to tell Aaron about my arrival. Sharon's suggestion of nonstop sex, which basically eliminated consideration of any alternatives, like Bishmann hiding around the corner, being taped to a chair, or the two of them running off.

"Nice work," Aaron said, shaking his head and stepping past me into the condo. He stood for a moment and looked around. "You touch anything?"

"Yeah, the TV remote, some drawers in the bedroom. Handle on the oven and the refrigerator. I had a little to eat, so a fork and a knife. What did you find at the airport?"

"In a word, nothing. Delta had a number of flights going out this evening. No one matched the description you gave or the names. We must have checked a half-dozen flights. I've still got six guys out there, plus we alerted the TSA folks, although I think, at this stage, it's pretty much a dead end."

"But she was waving her ticket," I said. "Delta, you know with the red logo and blue letters."

"And this Bishmann didn't react, didn't say anything."

"No, he just said something like, 'Let's get going, we gotta catch a flight.' She said thanks for the night to remember or some jerky comment, and they left."

Aaron nodded. "I'd say we were set up. Bishmann doesn't strike me as being this stupid. The only mistake he's made so far is having us find Hubert Holly's body. If it weren't for that, we wouldn't even be this far."

"Yeah, one of the things he said was he didn't have anything to do with killing Hubert Holly."

"Maybe, but he knew he was dead? I don't know."

"It's been on the news, hasn't it?"

Aaron seemed to think about that and said, "Yeah, six o'clock tonight. I think."

"Well, okay. Anyway, it sounds like he's in the process of disappearing into thin air again."

"It's starting to sound like he's maybe had a lot of practice at this sort of thing," Aaron said and shook his head.

Forty-two

Aaron told me not to touch anything else. He called the crime scene unit, and they arrived thirty minutes later. Between the time he called, and when they arrived, we walked through the place, and I pointed out a number of obvious things, like all the clothes left behind. I mentioned that Sharon didn't take much and had packed a small suitcase, although she had larger ones in the back of her closet. I indicated the envelope I'd pulled out of recycling lying on the kitchen counter with her name, Sharon Sanders. I told him about being taped to the antique chair, now in a number of pieces next to the kitchen counter. In the end, we stood outside in the hallway and waited for the crime scene team to arrive.

At one point, the woman in the unit next door popped her head out and asked what we were doing. Aaron showed her his badge and asked if she had heard anything. She said she'd been up at the lake for the past few days and had only been home for a half-hour or so.

While we waited, Aaron got a call from his team out at the airport. They had come up empty-handed, and two guys were going to check a ten o'clock flight scheduled to fly to Jamestown, North Dakota, but they didn't sound too positive.

I checked in with Preston while Aaron was talking to the crime scene unit. He had nothing. He sounded tired, and I had the feeling he was about to crash, so I told him to knock off. Then I reminded him to double lock the door just in case Fat Freddy or some of Tubby's thugs decided to show up.

Aaron finally sent me home and said if they found anything at Sharon's, he'd let me know, maybe. He didn't sound all that positive. Morton was standing on the couch looking out the window as I pulled into the driveway. When I stepped inside, he barked a greeting and hurried through the litter from the kitchen wastebasket to the back door. I couldn't really blame him. It had been hours since I'd been home, planning to spend a raucous night with Sharon but instead ending up with Aaron.

I grabbed a shower, just to get the remnants of duct tape off my wrists and loosen some of the kinks in my neck. I toweled off, put on a bathrobe, and let Morton back in. I poured myself a Jameson and turned on the TV. The news was the same, and I quickly changed the channel. I sipped my whiskey, watched thirty minutes of a movie I'd already seen, then turned off the TV, washed my whiskey glass, and went to bed.

As per usual, I was up before Morton, and I had just about finished breakfast when he came downstairs. He let me give him his morning scratch and then waited by the back door. I let him out, filled his food and water dish, and turned on the computer. The term no news is good news bounced around in my thick skull, and after checking my emails, I turned off the computer. I let Morton back in, and once he was finished with breakfast, we headed down to the office.

We were in before Louie arrived, but then again, it was barely eight in the morning. I poured yesterday's coffee down the drain and made a fresh pot. I was halfway through my second cup before Louie showed up.

"Hey, you two are in bright and early. What's going on?"

"Just wanted to get down here and back in the groove," I said.

"Busy weekend?"

"More like a worthless weekend." I brought him up to date on what had happened; the Groom's dinner and Bishmann leaving in the middle of it. Crystal's sliver, and running her to the emergency room. I told him about the canceled wedding, Hubert Holly's murder, and my trip with Aaron to the medical examiners. I finished up with Brendan Bishmann, aka Artie, apparently way past the third date with Sharon. I purposely left out any mention of Tubby Gustafson and Preston Leadbetter, which reminded me I needed to call Preston around ten. Any time before that and I'd just get dumped into voice mail.

Louie shook his head as he filled his coffee mug, then took a noisy sip. "God, it sounds like I lead a really dull life."

"Count your blessings. This was more like the weekend from hell."

"So no sign of this Bishmann, or Artie, or whatever his name is and your latest heartthrob, Shelia."

"Her name's Sharon, not that you need to remember. She's out of the picture as of last night."

"Yeah, Sharon. Amazing. You know, Dev, it almost sounds like she was setting you up, right from the get-go. The whole three-date deal and having too much to drink and falling asleep. You said she was up in the middle of the night cleaning up the kitchen and doing dishes? You ever think it might have been this Bishmann guy setting you up, and he had something going with this Sharon the whole time?"

That gave me pause.

"And then, remember when you got the call from Tubby Gustafson about something stolen out of the vault at Bare Facts? If this Bishmann guy got the passwords and is emptying accounts of his potential in-laws, maybe he got the combination to that vault of Tubby's from Hubert Holly's records?"

"I don't think Holly would have given that to him. He was a highly successful, sharp attorney who—"

"Yeah, I know that, but didn't you say your pal Scarlett told you Holly and his wife have a place in Hawaii? What if Bishmann had access to the Holly house while Hubert Holly and his wife were in Hawaii? He gets all the account numbers and passwords, and then maybe, you know, looking around, what if he finds the combination to Tubby's vault?"

I started thinking. "So take it a step further. What if Tubby found that out and he's the one who had Holly killed? Tubby's out a big chunk of cash. Bishmann has drained all the Holly accounts plus whatever he stole from Tubby, and now he's set for life."

"Could be he's already got a new alias and is traveling under that," Louie said and gave a loud slurp from his coffee mug.

Forty-three

I got off Facebook and phoned Preston Leadbetter at exactly one minute after ten. “Hi Dev,” was how he answered. “I was just about to call you.”

“You got anything on a Delta flight that Bishmann and Sharon Sanders might have taken?”

“No, sorry, but I came up empty-handed. I didn’t find anything. Sharon Sanders definitely didn’t fly Delta, United, or Sun Country yesterday, and she’s not listed as having a reservation for any future flight, at least that I could find. Same thing with Bishmann. I did a search on the names Arthur, Art, Artie, Aiden, Alex, Alexander, Oliver, and Ollie, set up a subset with an age parameter of thirty-two to forty-two, and the few that came up were easily dismissed as soon as I started looking at them. They’d been employed for years, most of them had photos, wives, families, in short, a history that immediately eliminated them.”

“Shit.”

“Not so fast, I may have found one thing. You mentioned Bishmann filed a character reference for a guy last spring.”

“Yeah, that’s right, Darrin Yardly,” I said. Louie glanced up from the file he was reading with a quizzical look on his face.

"Turns out this Yardly did some time, twelve months to be exact, up in Lino Lakes for possession with intent to distribute. This was back in two-thousand-ten."

"Yeah, he seems to have been in and out of trouble. Not surprising on the intent to distribute, he died from an overdose last spring, a couple of weeks after receiving a suspended sentence."

"Yeah, I saw that. Thing is, while he was in Lino Lakes, a guy named Arthur Walker Junior was also up there. Doing time for assault. You interested in who he assaulted?"

"Okay, who?"

"An attorney by the name of Hubert Holly. Seems Holly represented a real estate developer who was accused of not paying small contractors in two-thousand-nine, right during the great recession. Holly gets the real estate developer off. One of the contractors' businesses fails, and he gets assaulted by a former employee."

"I'm not following," I said.

"The real estate developer Holly represented was none other than Tubby Gustafson."

"What?" I half-shouted.

"Yeah, and the contractor that was assaulted after his business failed was Arthur Walker Senior. Artie Walker's father. The father never recovers from the assault, goes on disability. His wife develops cancer and dies in two-thousand-thirteen. Arthur Walker Senior dies a year later in two-thousand-fourteen. He died at his son's home. Get this, Dev, Arthur Junior, the son, is a locksmith by training."

"A locksmith?"

"Yeah, opening safes and fixing locks on doors, that sort of thing."

"And someone emptied out Tubby's vault at Bare Facts," I said.

"And I would guess there's about a ninety percent chance that someone was Artie Walker Junior. I'm thinking it looks like payback time."

"He told me he didn't shoot Hubert Holly."

"Maybe. But just based on the facts, at least as I explained them, sounds to me like he could be a pretty likely suspect."

"You going to give Tubby this information?

"Eventually. But I plan on feeding it to him piecemeal. It'll be a couple of days before he has all this. In the meantime, I'll be delving deeper into Artie Walker. Maybe there's a lake place or a condo in Florida. Somewhere he's keeping a low profile until things quiet down."

"A bankrupted father, I don't know. I wonder how come Crystal Holly's father didn't recognize him? I mean, if this Artie Walker character assaulted Hubert Holly and was sent to jail, you'd think Holly wouldn't forget what he looked like."

"I'm guessing plastic surgery. I've got his photo from police records. I'm sending it to you now." I could hear Preston's fingers clicking across the keyboard. A moment later, my computer dinged, alerting me to an incoming email.

"I think your email just came in. Hang on, let me take a look." I clicked on the Yahoo link and then clicked on the file. After a couple of seconds, four images appeared. I studied the closeups of the face. There were three, one looking straight ahead and then a left and right side view. Yeah, it was the guy I'd seen yesterday in Sharon Sanders' condo, Brendan Bishmann. Although his hair was still curly in these pictures, it was red. The nose, the chin, and the cheekbones were definitely different, and I could see how Hubert Holly may not have put it together. The fourth image of Arthur Walker Junior standing was taken with a height chart in the background indicating his height at an even six feet.

"Yeah, Preston, this is the same guy I saw yesterday. You're right. Plastic surgery and a lot of it. Just for starters, now he's got a chin like Kirk Douglas."

"Who's that?"

"Kirk Douglas? Umm, he's Michael Douglas's father. He was an actor, too."

"Huh. You don't say. Interesting."

"You find anything current on this Artie Walker Junior guy?"

"I'm just about to start that. I gotta tell you, Dev, just in case you haven't figured it out. This dude is good."

Forty-four

Louie looked at me and asked, "He sent you some current photos of the guy?"

"No, these are from maybe eight years ago. I had current ones from the wedding info Scarlett had, but check this out. Lots of plastic surgery." I turned my laptop toward Louie. He got up and walked over to my desk. He leaned down and stared at the pictures.

"He's a redhead?"

"Yeah, anyway he was, and my guess is very soon he will be again. He's probably shaved his head at this point. He has a new nose. This one in the police picture looks like it was probably broken at some point. He doesn't have that slight curve in his nose anymore or that bump. Now he's got a Kurt Douglas chin and more pronounced cheekbones. Add to that almost eight more years, and you can see how he would have fooled Hubert Holly. Plus, get this, he was trained as a locksmith, so I'm guessing opening that vault of Tubby's wasn't that big of a deal."

"Especially if he had the combination," Louie said.

"Yeah, there is that."

Louie gathered three or four files, placed them in his briefcase, and said, "I got a court appearance in just over an hour, and I want to set my client straight before we go in there." He gave me a wave and headed out the door.

I picked up my cellphone and phoned Scarlett Raunchnoble.

"S.R. Investigations," the sweet voice said.

"Catherine?"

"Yes. Is this Dev Haskell?"

"Lucky you, it is." She didn't react. After a long moment, I said, "Is Scarlett available."

"One moment and I'll connect you." She sounded like she couldn't wait to get off the line with me.

Scarlett picked up after two rings. "Good morning, this is Scarlett."

"Hi, Scarlett, Dev Haskell."

"Hi, Dev. I was just thinking about you."

"Hopefully, on a positive note. You learn anything further on the Holly accounts?"

"My accountant is at the bank now with three attorneys and the head of the IT department from Hubert's firm. It's going to be a long, arduous task. Obviously, the bank is not excited about taking a loss, let alone a major loss like this."

"How much are you talking?"

"It's up to almost four and a half million. I think all the passwords have been changed by now, but it appears that whoever did this had some method of bypassing the secondary security questions."

"Secondary security questions?"

"Yes. On these accounts, the primary security was the ten-digit password which the individual apparently had, but then there were a series of security questions asked in addition to the password. Somehow the individual either had those passwords as well or was able to bypass the bank system. The bank is investigating now, with the IT person from the Holly firm right there."

"Four and a half million, you'd think the bank would have more than enough insurance to cover that."

"I'm sure they do, but still, you can imagine the stress."

"Yeah. Anything yet as far as funeral arrangements?"

"Nothing at this point. Addison has her therapist at the house. She's basically medicated to the point of being out of the loop. The daughter, Crystal, is holed up in her condo and not answering the phone. Young Justin is willing to help, but he's in a holding pattern at least until his mother regains a semblance of her sanity. I've got people at all three locations just in case. We're not expecting any problems, but you never know."

I didn't want to tell her about Bishmann turning out to be Artie Walker Junior. At least not yet. "Can you tell me about Hubert's relationship with Tubby Gustafson?"

"Not much to tell. As far as I know, he represented Mr. Gustafson on some real estate transactions. I don't know much about them other than, given the level of clients Hubert worked with, I'm guessing the transactions would have been rather large and involved. A number of investors, that sort of thing."

"You aware of any difficulties with Tubby paying contractors?"

"Difficulties? You mean like late payments or questions about the quality of work?"

"Yeah, or maybe just stiffing some guy. You know, a small contractor. You have someone pull that on you while you're basically living paycheck to paycheck, and in short order, you could be out of business."

There was a long pause before she spoke. "I suppose something like that could have happened. I'm not aware of anything specifically."

"How long have you been working with Hubert Holly?"

"We've had his firm as a client for almost five years. This past weekend, providing security at the wedding was highly unusual. Usually, we'd provide security for one of their clients, invariably someone from out of town — a Hollywood type, perhaps the music business. Occasionally, an investor in one of their client's projects from outside the US would come to town. They usually brought their own security and would then interact with us as the local eyes and ears organization."

"You aware of anyone thinking they got a raw deal from Hubert?"

"A raw deal?"

"Yeah, you know I'm guessing from time to time he had to represent an individual or company on one side of a dispute, and at the conclusion, the person on the other side comes away with the feeling that they got a raw deal."

"I think that's part of the business. In a dispute, it's rare everyone comes away happy. In fact, my sense would be that oftentimes no one comes away happy, but the dispute is settled in the court system, hopefully, according to the law. I mean, the mere fact that you'd have attorneys involved suggests that things may not have gone well up to that point."

"Yeah, I suppose."

"What are you looking for, Dev?"

"I'm not sure. It just seems that, I don't know, this Bishmann character set to marry Crystal, the daughter, and then Hubert is murdered. If he is as clever as we think, absconding with all these funds, why murder Hubert Holly? It doesn't seem to add up," I said, hoping I planted a seed.

"Well, if not him, who?"

"I'm not sure."

Forty-five

I was staring out the window thinking about my phone call with Scarlett, not sure if she knew something and was hiding it, or was she really in the dark? I saw the black Cadillac Escalade pull up across the street, and a moment later, Fat Freddy climbed out of the driver's seat. The front passenger door opened, and the big blonde guy who cold-cocked me the other night stepped out. He moved his head from side to side and rolled his shoulders.

A woman pushing a stroller with two little kids in it walked past, and the blonde jerk apparently said something to her because she got a frightened look on her face and picked up the pace, hurrying around the corner. That seemed to bring a smile to the blonde guy's face. I suppose it was always a pleasure for him to ruin someone's day.

Fat Freddy opened the rear passenger door, and I saw Tubby sitting in the seat talking on the phone. Fat Freddy stood there with the door open, blankly staring down the street as cars whizzed past. The blonde guy continued rolling his shoulders and then turning from side to side at the waist. I wondered if Tubby had suggested he might make some sort of instructive point if I happened to present something Tubby didn't want to hear. I unlocked my desk drawer, pulled out my .45, and placed it on my lap. A moment later, Tubby oozed out of the rear seat and, still talking on the phone, led the three of them across the street. A bus coming down the street had to slow to a stop while they crossed. Wisely, the driver didn't honk.

I heard the staircase begin to creak, and a moment later, a red-faced Fat Freddy opened the office door. Tubby stumbled in behind him, breathing heavily, followed by the blonde guy. Speckles of perspiration dotted Tubby's flushed forehead. I wondered if the blonde guy had to push him up the stairs with both his hands on Tubby's fat ass.

"Honest to God, Haskell. No wonder you never have any business."

As the blonde guy stepped into the room, Morton gave a low growl. "Grrr-grrr."

"Morton, that's enough. Mr. Gustafson is a friend," I said.

"Oh please, really," Tubby gasped and sank into the client chair with the least amount of duct tape.

As Fat Freddy sat down and tried to catch his breath, I said, "Can I get you a cup of coffee, Mr. Gustafson? To what do I owe the pleasure?"

"Watch yourself, Haskell."

"Yes, sir," I said and tried to look like I'd just been put in my place.

"I want to hear what you know about this Brendan Bishmann person," Tubby said as he straightened his tie.

"Brendan Bishmann? The guy who ran out of the dinner the night before his wedding? Not much. I think I may have mentioned before that the first time I'd even heard of him was maybe an hour or so before that dinner. I don't know what he does or where he's from. I was just working that gig on an hourly rate. I drove Crystal, the bride to be, to the ER and she—"

"Silencio, you moron. I've heard all this before. I didn't ask you what you did that evening. I asked you what you knew about this bastard, Bishmann."

"Not much, sir. I know he lives at seventy-seven Oxford Street, just off of Lexington Avenue."

"And how do you know this?"

"One of the things we had to do was review a list of all the guests who were planning to attend the dinner Friday evening. Not only did they have photos of everyone, but they also listed where people lived. Quite a few were from out of town."

"Too much information. I don't care about people from out of town. For the last time, try and pay attention, Haskell. I'm asking you about Bishmann. Give me that address again."

"Seventy-seven Oxford Street. If you take Summit Avenue and turn, heading north on—"

"Enough. Frederic has the address," he said, looking over at Fat Freddy. "What does this Bishmann do?"

"I'm not sure, sir. I think he's involved with a hedge fund, but I haven't confirmed that. Weren't you going to look into him?"

Tubby shot a look at Fat Freddy. "We seem to have hit a bit of a wall in that process."

"I wish I could tell you more, sir. Quite honestly, I got the sense that the information about Mr. Bishmann was on a need to know basis, and apparently, I didn't need to know."

"Any sense is just about the last thing you have, Haskell."

"I'm afraid I can't argue with you there, sir. Maybe Mr. Holly's wife would be able to provide a better update."

"She's indisposed at the moment."

"Have you considered contacting S. R. Investigations? They hired me for that evening, and I'm sure they would have more up to date information. I can give you their phone number."

Tubby shook his head and said, "I knew this wouldn't be worth the effort. Once again, I wonder why I even bother. Let's go Frederick. We've wasted too much time here already."

Fat Freddy jumped out of his chair as Tubby stood. The blonde guy took a step back, and Morton suddenly barked. All three of our visitors jumped, and the blonde guy took a step toward Morton, looking like he might be getting ready to kick him.

"Do that and your dead," I said, pointing my .45 directly at him.

"Haskell. Oh, for God's sake, put that thing away before you hurt yourself. Fredrick the door, please," Tubby said.

Fat Freddy hurried to the door and opened it. He gave me a quick glance as Tubby headed down the staircase and hurried to catch up.

The blonde guy stared at me as he slowly backed up toward the door, and I kept my .45 pointed at him. "You and your damn mutt are on limited time, dip shit."

"If I were you, I'd get myself the hell out of here before I change mind and shoot your worthless ass."

His grey eyes seemed to grow even colder as he pointed his finger at me and looked like he was going to say something, then maybe thought better of it. He shook his head, slowly backed out of the door, and headed down the stairs, catching up with Tubby and Fat Freddy.

I watched them as they crossed the street and climbed into the Escalade. For the first time that I could remember, Fat Freddy didn't look up and give me the finger while he stood out on the street. The blonde creep looked up, shook his head, and stared for a long moment before he climbed in the passenger seat.

Forty-six

As soon as they were out of sight, I left Louie a note and then put Morton in the car, and we drove over to Scarlett's office. I didn't want to leave Morton alone in the office in case that blonde creep somehow showed up looking for trouble. I pulled into the parking ramp, put the leash on Morton, and we headed into Scarlett's building.

Catherine was sitting at the receptionist counter. She pasted on a fake smile as I walked in, but once she saw Morton, her smile spread across her face, and she stepped out from behind the counter. "Oh, now who is this?" she said, bending down and rubbing Morton behind his ears.

Morton's tale began wagging, and he shoved his nose under her skirt.

"This is Morton. He's a service dog," I lied.

"Oh, well, hello there, Morton. It's so nice to meet you," she said, clearly excited to see him. She looked up at me and said, "You here to see Scarlett?"

"Yeah, I don't have an appointment, but hopefully, she'll have a minute."

"Let me just check," she said, giving Morton a final rub before heading back around the counter. She picked up the phone, and a moment later, said, "Yes, I have Mr. Hassle out here in the lobby. He doesn't have an appointment but was hoping you might have a moment." Another one-second fake smile as she listened to whatever Scarlett said. "Okay, will do," she said and hung up. "If you'll have a seat, it should just be a couple of minutes."

I settled into the cream-colored leather wingback chair. Morton circled a couple of times and then curled up on the floor next to me. He seemed to give a long sigh suggesting this was bound to be another boring exercise and placed his head on top of his front paws.

Catherine picked up the phone about five minutes later, listened, and said, "I'll send them back now. No, a lovely service dog named Morton. Yes, he is." She hung up and said, "You can go back now, sir. Do you remember the way?"

"Yeah, I think I can find my way." We headed down the hallway to Scarlett's office.

I knocked on the door and opened it just as Scarlett called, "Come on in. Well, the two of you, and who knew you had a service dog?" she said in a tone that made it clear she wasn't buying my tale. "What can I do for you?"

"Just thought we'd stop by and bring you up to date. I had a visitor or, should I say, visitors this morning."

"Oh, that doesn't sound too promising. Police?"

"If only. No, Tubby Gustafson and two idiots."

"Eew. Not fun. What did they want?"

"Information on Brendan Bishmann, not that I really have any. I just wanted to let you know they were there and to be prepared if they decide to pay you a visit."

"I appreciate the heads-up. Hang on for just a moment." She picked up her phone and pressed a number. "Yeah, Tommy, sorry to bother you. I've got Dev Haskell in my office. Yes, that's him. He received a somewhat unpleasant visit earlier this morning from Mr. Gustafson and two of his staff. You might want to alert folks. Maybe position someone in the reception area. I don't want Catherine to be out there alone. No, nothing like that. It would just seem like a good idea to be prepared. Hopefully, at the end of the day, it will turn out to be an overreaction on my part. Yes, that would be perfect. Thank you," she said and hung up. "So, information on Bishmann?"

"Yeah. I'm coming to the conclusion that Bishmann drained the Holly accounts, but killing Hubert Holly doesn't seem to add up."

"Why not?"

"Why not? Because I think he's had this whole operation planned for months if not years. From the relationship with Crystal Holly at exactly the time her parents are in Hawaii for an extended period to walking out in the middle of that dinner on Friday night. It just seems too orchestrated, and then he simply vanishes, and by the way, there's no record of him for the preceding thirty plus years. It's all seems too carefully planned out. Except that suddenly and apparently on a whim, he murders Hubert Holly in a small parking area on the River Boulevard in the middle of the night. It just doesn't add up."

"But isn't that exactly the reason he could murder Hubert Holly? Because he knew or thought he knew, that he could get away with it?"

"Why take the chance? He's gotten away with enough money to live very comfortably for the rest of this life. Stealing those funds has the police looking for him, sort of, maybe, except he's not going to be hanging around town. But a murder, they'll be on it, as will everyone else in law enforcement all across the country. I just think he planned the financial aspect and had no intention of shooting Holly. Why even meet up with the man when he was busy draining his accounts and transferring funds all over the world?"

"Maybe to let Holly know that was exactly what he was doing and then shooting him so he would be unable to stop him."

"Maybe. But here's a question for you. Friday night, Bishmann leaves the dinner, and things quickly go down the drain. You knock on Holly's office door, and he tells you he's busy and on the phone. Who was he talking to?"

"Well, that's what he said, but I sort of took that as an excuse. He just didn't want to see anyone at that point, which I sort of understand. Imagine his embarrassment. Dev, all his friends, his business associates, his extended family, everyone who meant anything to him was at that dinner, and they all saw the rug essentially being pulled out from underneath him. No one would like that, let alone a highly successful, prominent attorney like Hubert Holly."

“Exactly, everyone that mattered was physically there. So who would he have called?”

“Like I said, I have no idea, and I’m not sure he was even calling anyone.”

“There’s one way to find out.”

Forty-seven

I pulled in behind Scarlett's dark blue, sporty Acura NSX. We had just pulled into the circular drive in front of Hubert Holly's home. We were parked behind a black SUV with an official-looking sign resting on the dashboard that read 'SR. INVESTIGATIONS' and, below that, the image of a gold badge. I left Morton in the back seat.

"I'm guessing that's one of your guys," I said, nodding at the SUV as we headed toward the front door.

"Yeah, that's Roger. I think I mentioned I have someone here as well as the children's homes. I don't expect any trouble, but just to play it safe."

"I can't say I blame you," I said.

The front door opened, and I recognized the guy as one of Scarlett's team from the night of the groom's dinner. "Hi Roger, everything all right here?" Scarlett said as we stepped into the entry.

"Everything is wonderfully boring," Roger said. He smiled and extended a hand. "Sorry, but we never really had the opportunity to chat the other evening, Roger Essen," he said.

"Dev Haskell," I said as we shook hands. "Yeah, bit of a crazy evening."

"Is Addison up and around?" Scarlett asked.

"I haven't seen or heard her. If you want, I can go upstairs and knock on her door. She's been cooped up in her room since late Saturday. With the exception of her therapist, I'm not sure anyone has seen her. The cook leaves breakfast, lunch, and dinner outside the bedroom door. Sometimes she eats, and sometimes she doesn't."

"The therapist is here every day?" Scarlett asked.

"Yeah, three times a day, morning, noon, and night. I'm guessing he's administering some sort of *medication*, but I don't know that for sure." He sort of drew out the word medication, suggesting a pretty heavy dose of something.

"Okay, we may as well get started. We want to check out Hubert's office phone and see if there's any record of phone calls Saturday night. Don't let us interrupt," Scarlett said.

"You kiddin'? This is the most activity I've had all day — not a complaint, by the way. I'm going to do my rounds. Just text me if you need anything. If you decide to leave, the door locks automatically, so you'll need to contact me in order to be let back in."

"Thanks, Roger. Come on, Dev, Hubert's office is this way," she said, heading toward a short hallway beneath the grand staircase. The door to the office was eight panels and looked to be mahogany. It had an elaborate brass doorknob. Interestingly, there was a peephole in the door, so if you were in the office, you could see who was out here in the hall before you opened the door.

Scarlett turned the doorknob and stepped inside. I don't know why I should have been surprised. The entire house was decorated to an extreme, and Hubert's office was no exception. There was a massive fireplace with antique tiles around it and a carved wooden mantel. Over the mantel hung a six-foot-high beveled glass mirror in an elaborate gold frame. Two of the walls had floor to ceiling bookcases with a ladder attached to a railing in the event you wanted one of the books from an upper shelf.

The books all appeared to be law books. Centered at the far end of the room was an elaborately carved desk with lions heads on either corner and a massive lion's head centered on the front of the desk. The top of the desk was covered with leather that had elaborate gold embossing all along the edge. Behind the desk was a credenza of carved mahogany, built to match the desk. Three cut crystal decanters rested in the center of the credenza. Each decanter had a silver label hanging around the neck. The labels read, 'WHISKEY.'

Above the credenza hung a painting of Hubert Holly, standing behind a chair and holding some sort of rolled up papers, looking like he was going to speak before congress or the Supreme Court.

"Apparently, Hubert thought very highly of himself. Nice digs. Just for point of conversation, what did Hubert charge an hour?"

Scarlett smiled and said, "If you have to ask, you can't afford."

The phone on the corner of the desk looked antique, although it had push buttons rather than a dial and above that a small screen. Scarlett picked up the receiver, punched in three numbers, and began to scroll through the display. "Okay, a couple of calls Friday afternoon, here's an incoming one from me at four-thirty-four that afternoon. An outgoing call to Crystal at five-twenty, another at five-forty, another at five-fifty-five."

"Probably calling, wondering where in the hell she and Bishmann were," I said.

"No doubt. A couple of calls from me, one from your phone, that was me, also."

The next call is outgoing at eight-seventeen. I don't recognize the number. That call lasted six minutes. An incoming call from the same number at eight-forty-two that lasted three and a half minutes. Another incoming call from that same number at eleven-fifty-seven, that call was barely a minute and a half. I wonder who that is?"

"Mind if I have a look at the number?"

"Go ahead. Help yourself," Scarlett said and stepped to the side.

I glanced at the number. Unfortunately, that's all I needed was a glance. I recognized the number immediately.

"What's wrong? You don't look too happy. You know who made those last three calls?"

"Yeah."

"Well, who, Dev? It looks like that could have been the last person Hubert Holly ever talked to. Who is it?"

"Tubby Gustafson. That's his office number."

Forty-eight

Scarlett did a double take and then said, "You're kidding me, Tubby Gustafson? I can't believe it, Tubby—"

"You already said that, Scarlett. A couple of times."

"But, oh my God. I mean, I know Hubert represented him once or twice but—"

"I'd say based on the phone calls, the first one coming from here to Tubby, the relationship might have been a little closer than representing Tubby once or twice. This is the whole reason Bishmann was involved in the first place."

"What are you talking about? What does Hubert's particular relationship with a client have anything to do with Brendan Bishmann?"

"I don't know. It just does," I said, kicking myself for opening my big mouth.

"What aren't you telling me, Dev?"

"I don't know what you mean."

"Yes, you do. Look at me. You're holding out on me. You look like a little boy caught peeping through the keyhole. Now, what aren't you telling me?"

"Okay, okay, just promise me you're not going to get all mad and—"

"Dev, for God's sake, we're in the house of the man Brendan Bishmann murdered."

"He didn't murder Hubert Holly."

"How can you be so sure?"

"Because he told me."

"He told you? When? What are you talking about?"

"Okay, so just calm down. Here's what happened." I went on to tell her about my going to Sharon's condo, Bishmann suddenly appearing, him telling me he didn't murder Hubert Holly as he and Sharon made their way out the door. I went on to give her Preston's information, the prison photos of Artie Walker from Lino Lakes, where he met Darrin Yardly, and how Artie Walker was a locksmith. I told her about the two bags Tubby said were taken from his vault. How Hubert Holly defended Tubby in the lawsuit brought on by Arthur Walker Senior and how Arthur lost his business, and it destroyed the remaining few years he had.

I described the plastic surgery and how Brendan Bishmann was the name of a child who died at the age of one month back in 1983. When I finally finished, Scarlett stood for a minute with her mouth half-open, and then she just dropped down into Hubert Holly's desk chair. She placed her head in both hands and just shook it back and forth.

"I just can't believe this. God. I was warned. They said, don't contact you. Begged me not to do it. But of course, I knew better. I thought it would be fun to work with you, and now I'm up to my neck in this shit storm that is all your doing!" She screamed the last five words and glared at me, ready to kill.

"Why is this all of a sudden my fault? All I did was find out this information. I'm not the lawyer. I'm not the cheating real estate developer that ruined a family and everything a guy had worked for his entire adult life."

"What did you say his name was?"

"Bishmann? His real name is Artie Walker. He did a year, maybe a year and a half, up in Lino Lakes. That's where he met—"

"Stop You already told me all of this. Did you happen, in one of your free moments, to pass this on to your Lieutenant friend in the police department?"

"Umm, that was sort of going to be my next stop."

"Your next stop? What? You're waiting to see who else is going to be killed? Who else will wake up in the morning and find their accounts drained? Honest to God, Dev, I have never in my life seen such a, a, oh for Lord's sake, just get out of my sight. Go down to the police department and get them brought up to date. Maybe there's a chance the murderer is still in town, and they can get him."

"I told you, Bishmann, err, Artie Walker, said he didn't kill Hubert Holly."

"Oh, well, there you go. Problem solved. After all, who wouldn't believe someone who just left a family penniless?"

"Oh, yeah, you mean like Hubert Holly and his late-night phone call pal Tubby Gustafson did to the Walker family." I glanced around the office with the bookshelves, the carved desk, and the crystal decanters, no doubt filled with the best whiskeys. I looked up at the painting of a smug-looking Hubert Holly holding what apparently were very important papers.

"The Walkers are just the one family we know of. How many people did Holly run over and leave in the ditch to get this place? Yeah, I'll go tell the cops what I know, and I'm genuinely sorry Hubert Holly was murdered. But you know what, Scarlett? I don't think he was an innocent victim." I stormed out of the library and met Roger coming down the hall.

"Everything all right, Dev?"

"Let's just say a matter of differing opinions."

"Oh, with Scarlett? Amazing. Relax, we've all been there."

"I think this one is pretty serious."

"They all are. Hey, nice to see you. You take care."

"You do the same, Roger. I'd be careful if you're going in there. She's looking to take someone's head off."

"Won't be the first time."

I climbed in my car and headed back into town to meet with Aaron. I took the West Seventh Street exit, which was the longer route, and called him while waiting for a light to change. I got dumped into voicemail. "Yeah, Aaron, this is Dev. I've got some new information on the Holly murder. I'm coming down to tell you about it. Hope you're around."

Once the light changed, I pulled into the right lane, letting everyone anxious to get where they were going pass me. Although I took my time, it still seemed like only a matter of few minutes before I pulled into the parking lot across the street from the police station. I dodged two large potholes and had just pulled into a space and parked when my phone rang.

I hoped it was Scarlett, calling to apologize and suggesting maybe dinner and a roll in the hay would put us back on track. No such luck. "Yeah, Dev, it's Aaron. Sorry I missed your call. What's up?"

Forty-nine

I was sitting in Aaron's office. Detective Norris Manning was seated next to me. He was not my biggest fan, to put it mildly, and he seemed to be squeezing the arms on the chair in an effort to stop from jumping up and attacking me. Behind him were two homicide detectives, Lewis and Andretta, leaning against the wall. I knew them barely well enough to say hello. "How damn long have you known this shit?"

"I just picked up some rumors yesterday and wanted to check things out instead of having you guys chasing all over town on something that wasn't true. Like I said, once we got back into Hubert Holly's office and I saw the phone call record from Friday night, suddenly what this Artie Walker guy told me sounded like it might be true. He was pretty adamant he didn't shoot Holly. The last phone call to Holly's office came through around midnight, and it was from Tubby Gustafson's phone. His office phone, to be exact."

"Would have helped to know that, Dev. And you can explain it any way you want, but you know you were withholding information on a murder."

I just sat there. Unfortunately, Aaron was right.

"Do you think the knowledge of a phone call from Gustafson's office coming through to Hubert Holly around midnight might be of interest to us? Especially when Holly was murdered not long after that phone call.

No other calls on his office phone or his cell phone after that, and he's murdered just two or three hours later. His body was spotted around sunrise by an early morning jogger. You think your information might have been pertinent to our ongoing investigation?"

"Yeah, I know it was."

"So, why in the hell didn't you tell us, Dev? What were you waiting for? You trying to protect some piece of shit? You trying to protect your pal, Tubby Gustafson?"

"Come on, Aaron. You know he's not my pal."

"I gotta tell you, Dev. Right now, I'm not so sure."

"I know. I was just being stupid."

"Stupid doesn't begin to cover it. I'd call you an absolute dumb son-of-a-bitch, but that doesn't even begin to cover it."

"I, I don't know what I was thinking. I—"

"I've half a mind to lock you up and charge you, Dev."

"I think that would be a good idea, sir," Manning said.

One of the detectives leaning against the wall smiled, then quickly wiped the smile off his face when Aaron gave him a quick look.

"What else did you happen to find out about this Artie Walker character?"

"What else?"

"Yeah, you know, like the name Brendan Bishmann might be an alias. That his real name just might be Arthur

Walker Junior. That he was trained as a locksmith and served time in Lino Lakes for an assault on Hubert Holly some years back, anything like that happen to cross your desk?"

Damn it, Aaron already knew. "Well, some of it might sound familiar."

"Oh, for God's sake. I'm going to give you one option and only one," he said, holding up his hand with his index finger extended. "You screw this up. You even think of lying to me, and I'm turning you over to Detective Manning, and he will escort you down to your cell. You'll be held pending a court date, which may be months away. And, if you think I'm kidding, you just try me."

I knew he wasn't kidding.

He ran his fingers across the computer keyboard, waited a moment, and then said, "Okay, we've got the forensic report back on Hubert Holly's murder. Holly was shot twice, at close range, with a nine-millimeter. We've got two shell casings and a couple of fingerprints. The fingerprints matched up with an individual who has a rather lengthy criminal record, although there doesn't seem to be any link we can find to Hubert Holly. Now here is your one and only chance. You know a guy named Harold Gunkel?" Aaron said.

I shook my head. "No, I don't. Honest, Aaron, I've never heard of him."

Aaron turned his computer screen, so it faced me and said, "See if this might ring a bell."

I stared back at a face with cold grey eyes, sharp cheekbones, and blonde hair. The jerk with Tubby Gustafson earlier this morning. The guy I pulled the gun on when he made a move to kick Morton. The blonde-haired bastard who knocked me out.

Fifty

I stared for a long moment. "Oh man. Yeah, I recognize him. Don't know him, and I never heard his name before. What did you say it was? Harold something?"

"Harold Gunkel. His fingerprints were on the shell casings and Hubert Holly's car door."

"Harold Gunkel. The guy is a real asshole."

"When was the last time you saw him."

"The last time? Just this morning, when Tubby Gustafson showed up to pay me a visit. This prick Gunkel was with him along with Fat Freddy Zimmerman."

"Why did they come to see you?"

"They wanted information on Brendan Bishmann."

"And?"

"And what? I didn't tell them anything. I just suggested they talk to Holly's wife, Addison, maybe she could help. She's been knocked out on some therapist hack's medication since she got the news her husband was murdered. Probably wouldn't be able to tell them her own name, let alone anything on Bishmann, and certainly not Artie Walker."

"And Harold Gunkel was with them?"

"Oh yeah. I pulled a pistol on him when he made a move to kick Morton. Warned him nicely, he better not do that or it would be the last mistake he ever made. Bastard blindsided me one night and brought me to Tubby Gustafson's house."

"What for?"

"At the time, Tubby wanted me to find Brendan Bishmann. Neither one of us knew the guy's real name was really Artie Walker. I'm guessing Tubby still doesn't know that. The thing that pops into my mind is if this Harold Gunkel's fingerprints are on the shell casings at the scene of Hubert Holly's murder, Tubby has no idea. He's still thinking that Artie Walker, aka Brendan Bishmann is the killer.

"Why would he care?"

"There's another part to the story."

Aaron frowned and said, "What the hell is that?"

"You got info on Artie Walker. He assumes the alias of Brendan Bishmann, right?"

"Yeah, I already said we know all that, no thanks to you."

"Yeah, okay. So, a week or two ago, Tubby has one of his thugs steal my car, and some other thugs bring me to Bare Facts, his strip club. Ruined the date I was on, by the way, this gal named Sharon that was apparently a setup because—"

Aaron shot a quick look at Detective Manning and rolled his eyes. "For God's sake, get back to telling me about Tubby."

"Yeah, okay, okay. So his thugs walk me into the office in Bare Facts. This is at night. The place is jammed, two or three women dancing on stage. Anyway, Tubby is in the office sitting behind the desk, running a bunch of numbers on an adding machine. You know, the old kind with paper tape. There's like five feet of tape off the back of the adding machine, and Tubby is not a happy camper. There's this antique looking vault set into the wall behind him. A big thing with a black steel door about five inches thick. The door is open, and he tells me someone broke into the club, opened the combination lock on the vault behind him, and stole two big cargo bags. This happened a little after three in the morning. He has no idea who did it, and he wants me to find out who it was and then tell him. I'm guessing he probably didn't report the robbery to you guys."

"Not that we're aware of," Arron said and gave a nod to one of the detectives leaning against the wall who immediately left the room. "So, what was in the cargo bags?"

"He never told me. In fact, all he wanted me to do was find out who took them, and he'd deal with whoever it was. My guess is it was cash. I'm basing that on him running the numbers on the adding machine. I don't see him doing that if it was drugs."

"And this vault is in the office of Bare Facts?"

"Yeah, the office is just down the hall from the restrooms. Kind of a funny looking lock on the door now that I think about it."

"Funny how?"

"Just a strange sort of keyhole is all, but nothing like I'd ever seen before."

"So how does this tie into Artie Walker and Hubert Holly?" Aaron asked.

"Okay, Artie Walker does time in Lino Lakes for an assault on Hubert Holly."

Aaron's eyes grew wide. "His assault was on Hubert Holly?"

"Yeah, I thought you guys knew that. Walker's father, Arthur Senior, was a small-time contractor. He did work for a real estate developer, who ended up stiffing him, and he lost his business. The real estate developer was Tubby Gustafson, and the attorney who defended him and got Tubby off was Hubert Holly. That's why Artie Walker Junior assaulted Hubert Holly. Go forward a number of years, Artie Walker Junior's parents have both passed away. Artie has a bunch of plastic surgery done, he assumes the alias Brendan Bishmann, and last spring has an affair with Holly's daughter, Crystal, while her parents are in their winter retreat over in Hawaii. I don't know this, but I'm guessing that gives Artie Walker Junior access to Holly's home office and computer, where he gets the information to a number of bank accounts, and maybe, he also gets the combination to the vault at Bare Facts. The same vault where Tubby has stashed two cargo bags full of cash."

"Jesus Christ."

"Yeah, well, I don't think Bishmann, I mean Artie Junior, was involved in the murder. The fingerprint you found on the shells and Holly's car, more or less, confirms my suspicion that Artie Walker didn't have anything to do with the shooting of Hubert Holly. This Gunkel creep did that, maybe at the behest of Tubby, but I don't know that, and it doesn't sound like something Tubby would do. I can't see how it would benefit him."

Aaron tapped his fingers on his desk, deep in thought. After a long moment, he looked over at Manning sitting next to me, and Lewis still leaning against the wall. "Okay, you two can take off. See what you can make of this mess. For God's sake."

"You want me to bring Haskell down to a cell?" Manning asked, sounding hopeful.

"No, I'll deal with him here."

Manning looked like he was about to say something, then maybe thought it would be better to keep his mouth shut. He gave a groan as he rose out of his chair, and the two of them headed out of the office. Aaron got up from behind his desk and closed the office door.

"We could have been a lot further down the road if you had cooperated from the start, Dev. Back up for a moment. You mentioned a woman named Sharon?"

"Yeah, the woman I dated a couple of times, Sharon Sanders. You met me in her condo."

"Yeah, well, that condo isn't really hers. It turns out she's just subleasing the place."

"Is her name really Sharon Sanders?"

"As far as we know. Dev, you should have told us all this stuff."

"I get it, Aaron, but I was still putting everything together. Do you really want me calling you a half-dozen times a day when you're in the midst of an investigation telling you I've got another possible lead, ninety percent of which are going to turn out to be dead ends?"

"It would have been nice to know this is all I'm saying."

"Aaron, I don't want to—"

He held his hand up, suggesting it might be a good idea to stop. "I'm going to need your help with something."

"What's that?"

"I want you to go to Tubby Gustafson and tell him we're in the process of identifying fingerprints on the shells."

"Why do you want me to do that? Just go in there and arrest this Gunkel creep that did the shooting."

"It would be best for all involved if we didn't arrest him on Tubby's property. Just trust me on this, Dev."

"But, Aaron. I— You sure this is what you want me to do?"

"Yeah, and we'll be right behind you, so don't worry."

Fifty-one

I took Morton home, and I did worry. In fact, I was very worried. If I was going to go to Tubby Gustafson and tell him the cops had prints on Hubert Holly's killer, I didn't want Morton anywhere near that creep, Harold Gunkel. He was likely to do something crazy. I took the nine-millimeter pistol from my bedside table and stuck it in the front of my belt then pulled a sweater on to cover it up. I took a small twenty-two caliber weapon from my closet and strapped on an ankle holster.

I let Morton back into the house, gave him a dog biscuit as a treat, and looked at him for a long moment. God, if this went wrong, I might never see him again.

"You've been a great friend, Morton. I'll be back in a little while. Love you, man," I said and reached down to give him a hug. He quickly picked up what was left of the dog biscuit and moved a half-step away so he wouldn't have to share. I sort of laughed and said, "Perfect. Be good." Then I hurried out the door and into my car.

I somehow made it through every traffic light along the way and didn't have to stop once. It was the fastest trip I'd ever driven to Tubby Gustafson's. The front gate was closed, and I had to step out of my car to use the speaker at the entrance. I pressed the button, looked up into the camera, and waited.

"Yeah," a voice said over the speaker. He didn't sound friendly.

"Hi, I'm Dev Haskell, and I'd like to see Tub, err, Mr. Gustafson. I don't have an appointment."

"Just a minute."

He came back on maybe a minute later. "What exactly is this about?"

"An ongoing police investigation. I have some information Mr. Gustafson will find interesting."

I waited another couple of minutes before he came back on. "You can just tell me, and I'll pass it on to the big man."

"Tell you what. You can just wait until the cops arrive, and then Mr. Gustafson can deal with it. Sorry I took up your time."

"Haskell, you're ruining the moment," Tubby suddenly shouted. "What the hell is so important?"

"Oh, hi, Mr. Gustafson. I've just come from the police department. The homicide guys hauled me in. I picked up some information, but I'm thinking it's for your ears only."

"All right, but this better be good. I'm very busy, and you're interrupting."

Suddenly, the iron gate began to roll to the side. I jumped back in my car and drove through as soon as there was enough room. The gate rolled closed behind me. I pulled up to the front door as two guys came out of the house. I parked a few feet from a big old, chrome-covered Harley as one of the guys stepped off to the side, and the other headed toward my car. As I got out, he looked in the windows to make sure no one else was in the car.

When I came around the front of the car, he said, "Put your arms out on either side. I'm just gonna do a quick search."

"Okay," I said as I put my arms out at shoulder height on either side. Just as he began patting my left arm, I said, "I got a nine-millimeter in a sticky holster tucked into the front of my belt."

He didn't even blink like it was just an everyday occurrence, which at Tubby's house, I guess it was. He patted the right arm, did a quick check at the back of my belt, then lifted my sweater and pulled out the sticky holster with my pistol. "You can get this on your way out," he said and nodded at the other guy off to the side. "Okay, Hassle, go on in."

So much for being thorough. The guy off to the side waited for me at the front door and then led me inside and down the hall to Tubby's office. Another thug was standing just outside the door. He knocked on the door and waited until Tubby growled, "Send him in."

The guy opened the door and flashed a funny sort of smile that maybe suggested 'Good luck.'

Four lights were positioned at the corners of the massage table set up in the middle of the room. A large container of massage oil sat on the edge of the desk. Tubby Gustafson was lying on his back, naked except for the white towel draped over his midsection and the two slices of cucumber, one over each eye. His large, red, pocked marked nose resembled a traffic cone standing in the middle of the street.

The two Asian women I'd seen the other week were attired in small, black thongs. Both of them were giggling as they hurried through the secret door in the paneling at the corner of the room.

Lying on his back and not removing the cucumber slices over his eyes, Tubby said, "You seem to have a penchant for choosing the worst possible time, Haskell. What exactly do you want?"

"Sorry to bother you, sir. But I thought you'd want to know just as soon as possible. I've just come from the police department. They were in the process of reviewing the forensic evidence related to the Hubert Holly murder."

"Humf. No doubt they'll be looking for this bastard that ran out on his daughter. What the hell was his name?"

"Umm, Bishmann, sir. Brendan Bishmann, and actually no, that's not who they'll be looking for. The name I overheard was Gunkel. Harold Gunkel."

Tubby suddenly bolted upright. The cucumbers fell to the floor, but fortunately, the towel was wedged in place by one of the folds in his massive stomach. "Gunkel? Harold Gunkel?"

"Yes, sir. I've never heard of him before, but the police were saying he has a pretty extensive criminal record. I just thought you should be made aware, you know in case . . . Well, I mean, you know a lot more people than I do."

Tubby shook his head as his face began to grow redder. "Always the bearer of bad news, Haskell." He swung his legs over the edge of the massage table then inched his fat ass toward the edge as the table creaked and rocked back and forth. Unfortunately, as he slid off the table, the white towel fell to the floor.

"Oh, Jesus," I said, not meaning to. I quickly turned away as Tubby waddled and jiggled over to his desk.

He picked up the phone and shouted, "Find Peaches and send him in here. Now!" He slammed the phone down and thankfully reached for the silk paisley robe draped over his desk chair.

Fifty-two

Fifteen minutes of listening to Tubby rant as he paced back and forth while occasionally sipping from the crystal whiskey glass in his hand was just about to send me over the edge. Fortunately, the office door finally opened.

"Here he is, boss," a voice said as the blonde guy was sort of pushed into the office, and the door closed behind him.

He looked first at red-faced Tubby and then at me and said, "You want me to deal with this problem, Mr. Gustafson?"

Tubby drained his whiskey and set the glass on his desk. "Some recent information has been brought to my attention," Tubby said.

"I'm not sure what you mean, sir."

"I'm afraid you probably do. Dimwit here overheard the cops saying they're coming here to make an arrest."

"An arrest, excuse me, sir. But you're listening to what in the hell Haskell says? He's obviously lying. That's all he ever does is lie."

"Seems they found your fingerprints on a shell casing in Hubert Holly's car. Found another one on the car door."

"That doesn't make any sense. I don't even have a nine-millimeter. I carry a Colt Super 38 Semi-Automatic."

Tubby eyed him and said, "I never mentioned it was a nine-millimeter."

"I think you just did, sir." The blonde guy's eyes were shifting left and right, and all of a sudden, his arms were slightly extended like he was ready for trouble.

"No, I didn't, Gunkel. You shot him. You shot my damn lawyer, Peaches. Why in the hell did you do that?"

"But I didn't, sir. I was here the whole time. That night, I was in this very room. You and Holly talked a couple of times on the phone, and you went upstairs for your massage just after eleven."

"But the last call to Holly's phone came from this office number at eleven-fifty-seven that night," I said.

"How do you know that shit?" Peaches growled.

"I checked Holly's office phone record earlier today," I said. "You can check with Scarlett Raunchnoble," I said to Tubby. "She was with me today in Holly's office. You set him up, Peaches. You told him to meet you at—"

Peaches suddenly pulled out his pistol. He took a step forward to fire at me, slipping on a cucumber slice as he did so and giving me just enough time to jump beneath the massage table. I heard glass breaking and looked up as Peaches held his hand up to his forehead. Tubby, now nowhere to be seen, had thrown his crystal glass hitting Peaches in the forehead. I pulled the twenty-two from my ankle holster and fired twice as Peaches ran for the door.

The guy who let him in five minutes ago stepped into the office and was pulling his gun out just as Peaches gave him a forearm beneath his chin, and the guy's eyes rolled back in his head. His skull bounced off the door frame, and he dropped face-first to the floor.

I kept my pistol pointed toward the door. A moment later, someone else stepped in and fired a round in my direction. The crystal whiskey decanter behind Tubby's desk shattered. Suddenly, from behind the desk, Tubby shouted, "Stop shooting, you Moron. You're wasting my whiskey." From outside, I heard what sounded like a motorcycle suddenly starting up and speeding off.

Fifty-three

Tubby was seated in his desk chair, sipping a whiskey. Aaron and Detective Manning were sitting on the opposite side of the desk. The guy Peaches had forearmed was in the back of an ambulance en route to the hospital. The guy who shot the whiskey decanter and I had pulled chairs alongside the desk. We sat there silently listening to the back and forth between Tubby and the detectives.

"Mr. Gustafson, you're telling me you have no knowledge of the call to Hubert Holly?" Manning said. He held a pen and a notebook in his hands.

"That's correct, Detective. I was, mmm, indisposed at that moment."

"Indisposed?"

"Yes, I was meeting with two individuals regarding a sleep therapy procedure. Peaches or, should I say, Mr. Gunkel, was performing his nightly duty of straightening up my office." Tubby raised his hand, essentially taking in the room. The shards of crystal from the whiskey decanter lay scattered across the credenza just below the whiskey splatter and the bullet hole in the wall. A puddle of blood just inside the door to the office was in the process of being scrubbed up by a maid.

"Once Mr. Gunkel completed his task of straightening things, he would leave for the evening. That work would normally take all of two or three minutes. I had already retired upstairs for some final therapy. I presumed he would have departed just a minute or two later. You're proposing that, apparently, was not the case."

"So," Manning said. "You're suggesting that he remained in this room and then placed the call to Hubert Holly at eleven-fifty-seven?"

"Yes, that's correct."

"And can anyone corroborate your statement?"

"It's a mere presumption on my part as to Gunkel's activities. However, my security system can provide a video recording of my whereabouts at that precise time and would be able to document the fact that I was not in this room and that I did not make a phone call to Hubert Holly at that time."

Manning shot Aaron a quick look and said, "Really, a video recording of your whereabouts?"

"Yes."

"Would it be possible to view this?" Manning asked.

"It would, but I would like this to remain private, and I must caution you that, once I turn it on, you would be required to watch the entire recording."

Manning cleared his throat and nodded as he said, "I think we can all deal with that, sir."

Tubby raised his eyebrows and said, "Very well. If you would turn your attention to the flat screen mounted on the wall." Aaron and Manning looked off to the side as I and the guy next to me turned almost completely around and stared at the blank screen.

We could hear Tubby clicking the keyboard on his computer. I glanced over, and he raised his eyebrows and actually flashed an evil smile at me. A moment later, what had to be at least an eighty-five-inch flatscreen mounted on the wall came alive with the image of a gigantic four-poster bed and three candles lit on two bedside tables, one on either side of the bed. The TV was quiet for a good thirty seconds, although you could tell time was passing because the candles were flickering. Besides that, in the lower right-hand corner of the screen, the date and the time were recorded. The time was in the mode of a twenty-four-hour clock, currently reading 23:45:17, meaning, 11:45 PM and 17 seconds. The seconds were piling on.

Manning looked like he was about to say something when suddenly the sound of distant female voices could be heard. A moment later came the unmistakable sound of a door opening, and the voices grew louder.

Tubby's physical therapists, the two Asian women, suddenly appeared on the screen. Both were dressed in short silk robes. One carried what looked like two stemmed wine glasses, while the other carried a number of scarves in her hand. The woman with the scarves tied two to the headboard and two to the footboard. She then removed her robe and dropped it onto the floor. She crawled naked onto the bed and took the two stemmed glasses from her partner, who proceeded to drop her robe onto the floor before she crawled onto the bed. The women exchanged a lingering kiss and took a sip from their wine glasses.

"We will, umm, need to see you at some point, Mr. Gustafson," Manning said, sounding more than a bit uncomfortable.

Tubby smiled and said, "I should be along shortly."

Tubby stepped into the room maybe a minute later. A full eleven minutes before the final phone call had been made to Hubert Holly. He held a crystal whiskey glass and was dressed in the same paisley silk robe he was now wearing. As he came into view, one of the naked women handed her glass to the other and slid off the bed, talking in a language none of the five of us watching could understand.

Tubby set his glass on the bedside table and turned to face the woman. She smiled and said something that sounded seductive as she untied the belt around his massive waist. She rubbed her body against Tubby as she stepped behind him and pulled the paisley robe off his shoulders. She hung the robe from a hook on the wall, hurried back into the bed, and then both women grinned and beckoned Tubby into bed.

"I think we've seen enough, Mr. Gustafson," Manning said as everyone turned away from the screen before they had to watch naked Tubby climb into bed.

"Are you sure? We're not even at the good part. It goes on for forty more minutes," Tubby said.

"No, no, I think we've seen more than enough," Manning said.

"I'll make a copy and send it to you, Detective. What's your email address?"

Manning glanced over at Aaron, who nodded, and Manning took out a business card and set it on Tubby's desk.

Fortunately, Tubby turned off the sound, although the video continued to play. He smiled at Aaron and Detective Manning. "Any other questions, gentleman?"

"No, no, I believe that just about covers everything."

"Don't let me keep you from apprehending Mr. Gunkel," Tubby said, as he flashed a smile and stood.

For a moment, it looked like he might undo his robe and expose himself. Manning gave a quick glance at the TV, Tubby now in the bed on all fours, and he quickly headed for the door.

"Feel free to contact me should you have any other questions, gentlemen," Tubby called as they disappeared out the door.

Once they were gone, the smile quickly faded from Tubby's face, and he looked at me. "What the hell have you got to say for yourself, Haskell?"

"I'm just glad my movement got Gunkel's attention, and he fired that shot at me, giving you the chance to duck behind your desk, sir."

He seemed to think about that for a moment and said, "You can get yourself out of my sight, too."

I didn't have to be told twice.

Fifty-four

I gladly left Tubby's office and headed down the hallway. I retrieved my nine-millimeter from the guy at the front door. As I stuck it back into my belt, he looked back down the hallway toward Tubby's office and asked, "Did he ask where you got the gun?"

"You mean that twenty-two in my ankle holster? No, he didn't say a thing, and I didn't volunteer any information. When someone is shooting at you, you're not going to even think about the guy shooting back. You're just glad he can do it. I think I fired twice, probably missed him by a mile, but it was enough to move him out of the room."

"Thank God he didn't hit the boss."

I stepped outside, looked at my car, and said, "The Harley that was parked out here, did that belong to Gunkel?"

"You mean, Peaches? Yeah, fancied himself a biker, but I don't think he would have cut it — too much of an asshole. You want to be tight with a bunch of bikers, you better be true to your pals, and that was the last thing Peaches was. By the time we knew what was going on, that slime ball made it out the gate and disappeared."

"Better keep an eye out for him all the same."

"Oh, yeah. You do the same, man. Thanks for giving the boss the word on the cops and Peaches and for chasing him out of the office."

"Ycah, it'd be too soon if I never saw that creep again."

I didn't feel like going down to the office and just sitting there looking out the window. I called a pizza place near my house and placed an order for a medium pizza with everything. I stopped at the liquor store and picked up a six-pack, picked up the pizza, and headed home. Morton was on the couch, looking out the window. He barked a couple of times as I pulled into the driveway and then disappeared. He was standing at the door when I opened it with his tail wagging.

"Hey, Morton. Man, am I glad to see you. We are going to have a relaxing night eating and watching a movie of no redeeming social value. Come on. Let's get you outside, and then we can both chill out."

Morton hurried toward the back door. I let him out and placed three slices of pizza on a plate. I pulled the beers from the six-pack and put five of them in the refrigerator. I called Morton back in, gave him a treat, then headed into the den with my beer and pizza.

I was not in the mood to do any thinking. I just wanted to be entertained, so I clicked on Netflix and brought up The Big Lebowski. No thought required. I'd seen it over a dozen times and still loved it. Once Morton got the message that I wasn't going to share any pizza with him, he settled down next to my feet and drifted off to sleep. After the better part of a six-pack and all but the last piece of pizza, I apparently did the same.

We stumbled upstairs together around eleven. Just to play it safe, I climbed into bed, still wearing my ankle holster, and placed my nine-millimeter within easy reach on the bedside table. Thankfully, there was no need for either, and due to the effects of the six-pack, I slept soundly through the night.

I was up before seven the following morning, shaved, grabbed a hot shower, and headed down to the kitchen. I had the ankle holster strapped on, and my nine-millimeter in the sticky holster tucked into my belt. I was eating toast with about a half-inch of raspberry jam slathered across the top while on my computer. When Morton finally came downstairs, I gave him the perfunctory rub behind the ears and let him out. Once he was back in the house and had finished eating, we got ready to head down to the office.

I called Aaron, hoping he'd tell me they had arrested Peaches, but I ended up leaving a message. I checked the street out front through the sitting room window then looked out the kitchen windows for any hint of Peaches. Thankfully, I didn't see him. I put Morton in the back seat, and we headed down to the office.

Fifty-five

Morton and I arrived in the office before Louie, so I made a fresh pot of coffee. I assumed my position seated at my desk, scanning the apartment building across the street through my binoculars. I'd been at it for maybe twenty minutes, coming up with a big fat nothing when I saw the dark blue Acura NSX pull to the curb behind my car. Scarlett.

I quickly put the binoculars back in the desk drawer, pulled a handful of files out of a file drawer, and set them in two piles on my desk. I took out my legal pad, folded a number of blank sheets over the top then quickly scribbled some notes on the facing page. I heard the stairs begin to creak lightly as Scarlett made her way up to my office. I pulled out my cell phone and placed it next to my ear then began speaking nonsense until she opened the office door.

"Leo, let me call you back," I said into the dead phone as I waved Scarlett into the office. She was dressed in tight black leather leggings. There was a brass zipper about six inches long down at the ankle of both legs. She had on black velvet boots with block heels, a loose-fitting white top, and looked like a million bucks. A wonderful, subtle scent of perfume floated through the air as she pulled back one of my client chairs and sat down.

"Yeah, got it, Leo," I said, writing down a made-up phone number on the legal pad. "I'll get back to you." I pretended to turn the phone off before I set it down on the desk. "Hi, Scarlett. Can I get you a cup of coffee? I just made a fresh pot."

"You going to have one?"

"I got one going."

"Yeah sure, why not," she said.

"You take it black, right?"

"Yeah," she said. Fortunately, the coffee was actually behind her, so she didn't see me dump Louie's half-empty mug from yesterday into the sink. I refilled his mug and brought it over to her

"Here you go," I said, setting the steaming mug in front of her as I walked around my desk and settled into the chair.

She took a sip and said, "Umm, Dev, I hope I'm not interrupting your day. I wanted to maybe say, I guess I might have seemed a little upset yesterday. It's just that this whole Hubert Holly thing has been extremely difficult. At the end of the day, he was my client, and he was murdered." She took a sip of coffee, set the mug on the edge of my desk, and stared at the mug.

"No need to say anything, Scarlett. There was nothing you could have done to prevent it. The fact is that Hubert was in his office at midnight and then got in his car and drove off to some out of the way place. With all due respect, it was beyond stupid. He didn't even talk to Tubby Gustafson. It looks like one of Tubby's thugs called him, and God knows why, but Hubert drove off to meet him."

"It wasn't Gustafson?"

"Nope. The cops are looking for the guy. They've got a BOLO out on him. His name is Harold Gunkel, nickname Peaches, and I dare say, Tubby's group is no doubt out and about checking under every possible rock. If the guy has any sense, he's a thousand miles away from here by now."

"You think they'll find him?"

"I don't know. The thing is, if Tubby's gang finds him first, they aren't about to turn him over to the police. And if the cops find him, I can't see the guy being taken alive. Killing a high-priced lawyer and an upstanding citizen for no apparent reason, he's got to be certifiable at this point."

"Are you going to look for him?"

"Absolutely not. I want nothing to do with him, and as far as I'm concerned, the sooner he's eliminated, the better. The guy is a danger to anyone who has the misfortune to come into contact with him. Any word on funeral arrangements? Is Addison anywhere back to whatever normal is for her?"

"Nothing on arrangements, and slowly but surely, Addison seems to be coming around. We're working on recovering the funds, but that's going to be a very long process. In the interim, I'm going to have a conversation with her about putting the Sunfish Lake property on the market."

"You think she'll do that?"

"I don't think she has a choice. I've had some initial conversations with Hubert's partners. Thankfully, they're all on board." Scarlett took a sip from the coffee mug then set it back on the desk. She slid the mug a decent distance away from her, signaling she was finished. "Anyway, I just wanted to thank you for all your help. I'll get a check cut for you. You should see it by the end of the week." She held her hand out to shake.

I had been hoping for something more, but I get it. I shook her hand and said, "Maybe we can have dinner some night. Be nice to catch up once things quiet down."

"Sure thing." She smiled, held onto my hand for a long moment and looked like she wanted to say something but, in the end, didn't.

I watched her out the window as she crossed the street and climbed into her car. A moment later, she headed up the street. I watched out the window long after she disappeared from sight. Eventually, Morton got my attention. He was standing at the door and looking at me. No doubt wondering why I wasn't picking up on the fact I was supposed to take him for a walk outside.

Fifty-six

We met Louie at The Spot that night. He was just finishing his whiskey as we walked in, which meant it was my turn to buy the next round. I signaled Mike by raising Louie's empty glass. He nodded and continued filling the glasses of the women he was talking to. Louie grabbed a couple of pork rinds from his bag on the bar and handed them down to Morton lying at my feet.

"So, what's the latest on Hubert Holly's murder?" Louie asked.

I started to bring him up to date. He didn't ask any questions. Instead, he just shook his head occasionally, suggesting he couldn't believe what I was telling him. When I was finished, he handed more pork rinds down to Morton and said, "You know, about the only good thing in this whole fiasco is it makes average idiots like you and me look half-way decent."

I signaled Mike again for our drinks. "Yeah, and that's saying something. God, I can't believe it, but I'm actually looking forward to being on the phone confirming past employment and academic qualifications on job applications."

"Boring is good," Louie said, then yelled, "Hey Mike," and raised his empty glass.

Mike gave a nod and reached for a clean glass and the Jameson bottle. A moment later, he filled a beer glass and headed our way. "Thanks for your patience, gentlemen. I was in the process of getting a phone number."

I glanced down the bar at the group of women, all nice looking. "Which one?"

He shook his head. "That's all the information you two are getting." He headed back down the bar and took up his conversation with a redhead. I couldn't really blame him. She looked fun. I stayed for one more beer, and then Morton and I headed home. I was beat and looking forward to a quiet night stretched out on the couch, watching something of no redeeming value.

The knocking on the door woke me. Morton moved a little, then gave a sigh and settled back to sleep. I got off the couch and walked out to the front door. There was a deliveryman standing on my front porch. He had a box in his hand, and his back was to the door, watching the traffic pass on the street. I figured he probably needed a signature.

I opened the door and said, "Can I help you?"

"You're the one who's gonna be needing help, dip shit," Peaches said as he tossed the box aside, revealing what looked like an incredibly large gun pointed at me. He stepped inside, closed the door behind him, and turned off the porch light. "This place should work out just fine," he said, looking around.

"Every cop in a five-state area is on the lookout for you. Your best bet is to get your ass out of town."

"Yeah, I bet you'd like that, wouldn't you? Give you a chance to get hold of all that money Hubert Holly left behind."

"Money Holly left behind? Are you kidding? In case you don't know, there isn't any money. All his accounts were drained. His wife is gonna have to sell that fancy house they live in."

"What are you talking about? The guy's a millionaire a bunch of times over. Said he'd give me a hundred grand if I killed that Bishmann. Once he said that I figured he'd pay way more if I didn't shoot him. Stupid bastard didn't have a checkbook on him. He only had sixty bucks cash, and I knew he'd call the cops. Shit."

"Yeah, well, see, the guy posing as his future son-in-law drained his accounts, or at least he's suspected of doing that. I'm not kidding you. There's no money there. By the way, the cops got your fingerprints, and they're looking for you. Just in case you haven't figured it out, Tubby Gustafson is after you, too. So probably the smartest thing you could do is go right back out that door and head south."

"Oh my God, maybe you're right. There's just one little thing I have to take care of before I go."

He suddenly swung the pistol, hitting me across the chin. I stumbled back and automatically had both hands up to my face. I couldn't see, and he punched me hard in the stomach, literally lifting me up off the floor.

"Not so tough now, are you, dip shit? Bringing the cops down on me. I had a sweet deal going with Gustafson, and you screwed that up. So guess what, dip shit? You're going down." He hit me with a solid right and then a left.

I tried to move back and get out of his reach, but he seemed to be all over me. I was down on my knees with my hands covering my head. Peaches stepped back and kicked me on the side of the head. I saw stars as I went down on the floor. He jumped on top of me, punching me in the face. Suddenly, there was a deep throaty growl, and Peaches was on the floor, screaming. His gun slid across the floor.

Morton had him by the arm and wasn't about to let go. Peaches was swinging at him, hitting him. Morton growled deeper and louder as I staggered onto my knees. Peaches suddenly hit Morton hard in the head, and he yelped and released his hold.

I was still dizzy and started to crawl for the gun on the floor, but Peaches got there first. He was on his knees, in the process of grabbing the gun and pointing it at me as he shouted, "You just don't get it, Haskell. You are—"

I jumped at the sound of the gunshot as a red dot appeared on Peaches' forehead, just above his right eye. I was aware of someone stepping in from the hall and blinked in an attempt to focus.

“Are you okay? You going to be all right?” the voice said softly, but it wasn’t directed at me. The figure leaning over Morton held a pistol in his left hand and was softly rubbing his right hand over Morton’s head.

Peaches was lying his back with his legs curled beneath him, and a glassy stare to nowhere in his grey eyes.

“Bishmann? Err, Artie Walker?” I said, still trying to clear my head.

“That bastard was going to kill you.”

“Yeah, thanks. He was going to kill both of us,” I said and crawled over on all fours to Morton.

Walker stood and took a step back. I rubbed a hand over Morton’s head, and he licked my arm.

“I think he’s going to be okay. How’s your head?”

“It’s going to hurt for a couple of days but better than that bastard,” I said, looking over at Peaches. “What the hell are you doing here?”

“I made him bring me,” a woman’s voice said from behind. I turned, and there stood Sharon Sanders, looking radiant.

Fifty-seven

Artie Walker said, "She's not kidding. She's got something to say." He picked up Gunkel's gun and stuck it in his belt, then released the clip from his pistol, ejected the chambered round, and handed the empty pistol to me. "Grab onto this. When the cops come, I'll expect you to tell them it was you that shot him. Sharon, three minutes. I'll be out in the car. I'll leave this clip on your front porch, Haskell."

I took hold of the empty pistol and watched as Artie Walker opened the front door and limped outside. "Thanks, umm, I don't know what to say. But thank you, glad you were here," I called after him.

He raised his arm and gave a little wave without looking back.

My nose was bleeding, and I wiped my hand across my upper lip, which only succeeded in smearing blood across the side of my face.

"Oh Dev, I'm so sorry. I don't know where to begin. Well, actually, I do. Here," she said, opening her purse. She handed me a small packet of Kleenex. "Stuff a couple of these up your nose to stop the bleeding. You going to be okay?"

"I think that bastard broke my nose. I was just about to take him out when Artie—"

"Dev, don't kid yourself. He was going to kill you. We've been out on the street for the last two nights waiting for him to show up."

"Waiting? But why didn't you—"

"Now, don't say anything. Look, I just want you to know I really enjoyed our dates. Well, except for having to Uber home that night from Antonio's. I was really looking forward to getting to know you better." That last line covered a lot of ground. "But Artie and I have been together for a couple of years, and after what Hubert Holly and that Gustafson person did to him and his family, I felt I would do anything I could to help him pay them back. I just didn't think part of that was going to be meeting someone as nice as you. You can be a wonderful gentleman on occasion."

I looked over at Peaches with the hole in his forehead and the glassy stare. "I'm just glad you two were here. How did you get in?"

"Artie knows everything about locks. He wanted me to just what I had to say, and we'd leave. He wanted me to send you a postcard, but I just couldn't. He's actually a very nice guy, despite what everyone in town is probably thinking right now. Besides, I knew that animal would show up here sooner or later." She shot a disgusted look at Peaches and shook her head.

"Well, you've got a lot of folks looking for you, so if I were you guys, I'd get the hell out of town. I promise I won't say anything. But really, you better go."

She nodded, leaned over, gave me a kiss, and then walked out the door. Morton was suddenly on his feet and stretching. I got him a biscuit and waited another ten minutes before I called 911.

Fifty-eight

I was seated on the staircase in my entryway while the EMT applied a green splint to my nose.

"I don't know about you, but I'm ready to call it a day," Aaron said.

The first ambulance had taken Peaches down to the medical examiner's once he was pronounced dead maybe a half-hour ago. They left without turning on the siren, no point in hurrying. Crime scene guys were photographing the spot where Peaches had been shot. I had wiped down Artie's gun and the shell casing and made sure my own fingerprints were all over both items.

"Anything you want to add to your statement?" Aaron asked.

I shook my head.

"Please hold still, Mr. Haskell," The EMT guy said as he stuck a length of tape across my forehead. Aaron smiled with every length of white First Aid tape that was draped across my face. I have to give the guy this much, he sure knew what he was doing.

Finally, he leaned back, gave me a long look, and said, "That should do it for right now. Call your doctor, make an appointment within the next forty-eight hours. Keep that head out of the water until after your appointment, that includes showers. If you don't have a doctor, you can go to the ER over at Regions. They'll set you up. Any questions?" He asked as he closed his case and stood.

"No, thanks for your help."

"Okay, now don't forget, get that nose checked out in the next forty-eight hours. I'll see you around, LT."

"See you, Jerry, and thanks. I know he was a difficult patient," Aaron said.

"See what you can do to straighten him out," he laughed.

"I asked you earlier, Dev, anything you want to add to your statement?"

"No, it pretty much covers everything. He shows up, starts beating the hell out of me, and I got his gun and shot him."

"Strange just the one round," Aaron said and looked at the bloodstain on my oak floor. Considering he'd been shot in the head, the stain was just a small one, maybe three inches in diameter.

"I just don't get why he even showed up here. Except to tell me he was going to get all sorts of money from Hubert Holly's accounts. I can't believe he would have been smart enough to do anything online. Who knows? Maybe he figured they would have stacks of cash piled up in the house, and he'd just barge in and take them. It's crazy. You guys were looking for him. Tubby Gustafson, no doubt, has his crew out trying to find him. He should have been a thousand miles from here. I just don't get it."

“Sometimes it just doesn’t make any sense,” Aaron said. He seemed to think for a long moment and then said, “Maybe most of the time it doesn’t make any sense.”

“I’ll be fine, although I’m not looking forward to wearing this splint for the next few weeks.”

“I don’t know, Dev. I think it’s an improvement.”

Fifty-nine

I was on the couch the following afternoon when someone knocked on the door. I debated answering and then remembered there was no way it would be Peaches. My face was black and blue, and my nose throbbed as I rose off the couch, but at least the bleeding had stopped. Morton stood, stretched, and followed me out of the den to the front door.

Scarlett stood on the front porch and waved when she saw me, but even with the smile, she couldn't hide the shocked look on her face. "What the— Oh my God! Are you okay?" she said as I opened the door.

"Hi, come on in. Good to see you."

"I had no idea. I heard the report on the news. They mentioned that Gunkel character was an intruder who was shot while breaking in, and I just knew it had to be your place."

"Did they mention me?"

"Lucky you, no, not a word. They just said it was in the city, no address." She lifted two bags, bottles clinked together in one, and a delicious scent of spicy food came from the other. "I brought dinner. Hope you don't mind. I invited myself. I can just leave this here if you're not feeling up to it. Just give me a call when you're feeling—"

"No, Scarlett. This is great. I could certainly use the company, and I'm really glad it's you."

That brought a smile to her face, and she said, "You just relax, and that's an order. You're under my tender loving care for the next twenty-four hours."

The End

Thank you for taking the time to read Mystery Man. If you enjoyed the read please consider leaving a review, it really, really helps. Thanks in advance . . .

Check out the sample of **Bow-Wow Rescue**. The next book in the Dev Haskell series.

Bow-Wow Rescue
Mike Faricy

Prologue

Seymour Smeelie filled the crystal glass with a half-inch of rum and handed it to the small man seated across from him. He was seated in the wingback chair, his feet almost but not quite touching the oriental rug on which the chair sat. “Thank you, Seymour,” the small man said without smiling.

“Thank you, sir. So very kind of you. Havana Club Anejo Especial, one of my favorite rums, and next to impossible to get here in the states. I was fortunate to obtain a bottle in Florida, but it cost a pretty penny, and though I’ve sipped it sparingly, it’s almost gone. However did you know? Oh, and umm, your driver?” Seymour said, indicating the large man quietly standing in front of the office door with his hands clasped in front of him.

The man had a large, shaved head with a number of scars and almost no neck, just that large head resting on massive shoulders. His nose had a peculiar bump, suggesting that on more than one occasion, he had been rather difficult to deal with. He wore a black suit and a starched, open-collar white shirt. “Would he care for a glass?”

“No, Bumpy’s driving, Seymour. Besides, one is too many, and that entire bottle would never be enough for him.” He set his glass on the edge of the end table as Seymour poured rum into his own glass and settled into the wingback chair opposite the small man. He waited a moment before he said, “It would appear there’s a problem, Seymour.”

Seymour took a hearty gulp of rum, liquid courage, although it didn’t seem to be working at the moment. “I can promise you, sir. This is simply a temporary setback. A modest, temporary setback.”

"Modest? This will be the third month I've not received payment. That's no longer modest, nor temporary, Seymour. It's an absolute disaster!" The small man shouted those last four words, causing Seymour to flinch. Rum spilled from his glass onto his suit coat and across his silk tie.

"I can assure you, sir, it's only a matter of time before—"

"I can assure you that your time is up." He nodded at the large man stationed at the door. "The contract," he said.

The giant stepped forward, reaching into the inside pocket of his suit coat. Seymour actually recoiled, expecting to see a gun emerge in the giant's massive hand. He exhaled once he realized it was merely a multi-page document.

"I'll need your signature, Seymour. Initial the three areas marked in yellow and then sign on the bottom of the second page. No need to date it."

Seymour blinked, attempting to focus on the document. At the moment, the stress of the situation seemed to be making it hard for him to breathe.

"Relax," the small man said, handing Seymour a pen. "Initial and sign. This is simply a backup. Should things not work out, I gain control, and everything reverts to me until we get them back in the profitable column, whereupon you regain control. I want both of us to be successful. The contract is valid until one of us passes away, and then everything reverts to the other. I'm a good twenty years your senior, so things definitely lean in your favor."

"But I'd like to have my attorney take a look and—" Seymour swallowed, or tried to, without much success. He felt his nose running, coughed, and shuddered from a quick spasm.

"Initial, Seymour. Yes, right, good, good. Now the next page, sign at the bottom. Excellent. Here, a toast to success," the small man said, raising his glass.

Seymour reached for his glass, almost knocking it off the table before he grabbed hold.

"Drink up, my friend, my partner," the small man said as Seymour attempted to do just that. He poured the liquid into his mouth and was vaguely aware of it running down his chin. As the first seizure struck him, he convulsed, falling from the chair and dropping to the floor.

"Get the contract," the small man said, pouring his glass over Seymour's face while he convulsed on the rug.

Bumpy pulled on a latex glove, picked up the contract, quickly stepped back, and handed the contract to the small man.

"Excellent. Now, if all goes well, this shouldn't be more than ten minutes." Five minutes later, he said, "Check for a pulse." Blood was running from Seymour's nose and mixing with the yellowish discharge oozing from his mouth.

The large man placed his gloved hand on Seymour's neck for the better part of a minute, searching for a pulse, then looked up and shook his head.

"Wonderful, check his pocket for keys."

Bumpy rifled through Seymore's pockets. He pulled out a set of keys and a wallet. He handed the keys to the little man, opened the wallet, and pulled out three twenty-dollar bills.

"Well done. Put one of those twenties back in the wallet, leave the bottle, Bumpy, and get my glass and the pen. Oh, and grab that other bottle out of his cabinet. We'll point the finger at the woman," the small man said. A minute later, they cautiously peeked out into an empty hallway and hurried to the elevator.

One

Taffy asked and stuck her chest and bottom lip out at the same time, just to make her point. "Oh, come on, Dev! Why do you always have to be such a party pooper?"

It was Thursday night, and we were sitting out on her friend's deck. They'd just hurried into the house after inviting us up to their lake place tomorrow. Based on the reaction Taffy gave me, I knew I was in a losing battle before it even began, but I had to try. "I would love a weekend away with you, Taffy. Honestly, nothing would be better. It's just that going up to Kevin and Stacy's lake place is not my idea of a relaxing weekend."

"Oh, right, I forgot it would be more fun for me to sit on the couch and watch you play video games."

"First of all, I don't play video games. And second—"

"Mmm-mmm, sorry, I forgot. I meant throw a football back and forth for six or seven hours while Stacy and I run around getting dinner ready and making sure that, at all times, you have a cold beer within easy reach."

"Where is this coming from? Why am I getting accused of stuff I don't do?"

"Well, if you don't like my friends, you can just say so. You don't have to beat around the bush."

"Taffy, I'm not knocking your friends. It's just that, whenever someone invites me up to their lake place, it never really works out. I know you aren't going to like it up there. Were you listening? They described the place as rustic. Now we can—"

"That's not fair. I like the lake. I like laying in the sun. I like listening to birds chirp, the sound of the waves, the whole back to nature thing, and I'd like to go for a ride on their pontoon boat. You could go fishing off the dock. Sleep in. I bet they've got a private guest room. Very private," she said, raising her eyebrows and thrusting her chest out again.

It was obvious I didn't have a snowballs chance. "Okay, if it means that much to you, yeah sure, we'll go. You like back to nature, okay, your call."

"Mmm-mmm, you're gonna love it," she said then kissed me on the cheek and whispered, "We can be really naughty, and no one will hear."

"Okay, you guys, dinner is served," Stacy called as she stepped onto the deck. She carried a platter with a half-dozen hotdogs in buns. Her husband Kevin was right behind her with a bowl of potato salad and thankfully, a pitcher of beer. Stacy set the hot dog platter on the picnic table, swatted the flies away, and sat down. "So, what'd you guys decide."

"We'll be up tomorrow," Taffy said, which caused both women to scream as they reached across the table and grabbed one another's hands.

"Oh, this is going to be so much fun," Stacy said.

"We're heading up bright and early tomorrow morning," Kevin said as he slathered mustard up and down a hotdog bun. "You guys come on up whenever you can."

Stacy got a concerned look on her face and said, "Taffy and I were thinking they could just ride up with us."

Kevin crammed almost half a hot dog into his mouth, chewed two or three times, and said, "Oh, yeah. I suppose we could do that. Mmm-mmm, we were planning on leaving around ten."

"Well, actually," I said just as Taffy slid her hand beneath the picnic table, reached over between my legs, and pinched my inner thigh. "Awe, umm, that would be great. Yeah, we can be here a little after nine."

Taffy smiled.

I reached for a hot dog.

"Thanks for saying you'd go up to their lake," Taffy said and stroked my arm. We were on the way home, and I'd just turned onto her street.

"Well, you made it pretty clear you really wanted to go, and then when you mentioned the very private guest room, you know," I said and gave her a look.

"Well, I'm maybe presuming that a little, but they probably do."

"What? I was hoping to have some, you know, *special* private time together. Just you and me."

"God, is that all you ever think about?"

"Yeah, probably. But that's because you're so good," I said, pulling to the curb in front of her condo. I turned off the car and started to climb out from behind the wheel.

"Don't, Dev. I'll just let myself in."

"Huh?"

"Besides, I have to pack tonight and get about a thousand things ready. Just relax. You'll get taken care of tomorrow night. Thanks," she said and leaned over to give me a peck on the cheek before she hurried out of the car.

I watched as she input her security code at the door, stepped inside, and disappeared behind the door. If this was the way the weekend was going to go, it was shaping up to be a long two days at the lake, and we hadn't even left town.

Two

I was up before my alarm went off the next morning. I tossed a pair of shorts, two t-shirts, my swimsuit, socks, and a baseball cap in a brown paper grocery bag and hurried downstairs. I put the coffee on, fired up the computer, filled Morton's food and water dish, and went online. I heard Morton hop off the bed and do his morning stretch about a half-hour later. He came downstairs, walked into the kitchen, stretched once more, and walked over to me for his morning heavy-duty scratch behind the ears.

I let him out and went back on the computer. I emailed Louie, my office partner, asking him to watch Morton for the weekend while Taffy and I headed up to the lake. No sooner did I send that email than I received an email from an old flame, Brianna Di Salvo, asking for an appointment today. Actually, the email read, *'Hi Baby, Need to see you today. The earlier, the better. Strictly business, unless…'*

It had been at least four years since I'd seen her. She'd dumped me two or three times before I finally got the message. Over the course of the next year, I'd learned I hadn't been the only guy in her life.

I replied, saying, *Long time no hear, Brianna. I can meet you at 8:15 this morning or anytime Monday.*

She called about ninety seconds later.

"Haskell Investigations."

"God, no other business sounds as sexy when they answer the phone."

"Brianna?"

"I knew you couldn't forget, Dev. Wonderful to hear your voice. Just confirming I'll be at your office at eight-fifteen. Are you still in the same place?"

"Yeah, Randolph Avenue, just kitty-corner from The Spot Bar."

"Oh," she said, not hiding her disappointment. "Well, anyway, I'll see you then," she said and hung up.

That was just an hour away. I let Morton in. Once he emptied his food dish, I tossed the dish in a bag with his dog food, and we headed down to the office.

Louie wasn't in yet, and I knew he had something at the courthouse scheduled for ten. He was one of the go-to guys in town if you were charged with a DUI, Driving Under the Influence. In the past four years, his client list had grown exponentially. He'd left the coffee pot on overnight, and there was about a quarter of an inch in the pot that had been going for the last twenty-four hours. I dumped it in the sink then checked to see if the coffee had damaged the porcelain. Fortunately, it hadn't.

I brewed a fresh pot, rinsed out Louie's mug, and sat at my desk sipping coffee and looking out the window for Brianna Di Salvo to show up. I was scanning the apartment building across the street with my binoculars, but unfortunately, the only shades that weren't pulled was a unit with a fat guy in boxer shorts. Not what I really needed to see first thing in the morning, let alone any time.

After about twenty minutes, a dark blue Mercedes pulled to the curb behind my 2014 ugly, pea soup green Dodge Dart. The door opened, and gorgeous Brianna stepped out of the car. She gave my Dart a quick look and shook her head as she crossed the street. A moment later, I heard the stairs begin to creak as she made her way up to the second floor.

I had my cellphone up to my ear and started a fake conversation as the door opened. “No, you’ll be much better off if you wait until this evening.” Brianna struck a pose in the doorway for a moment. She was wearing black hose, an extremely short designer skirt, and what looked like a five-hundred-dollar low-cut top. A diamond about the size of my eyeball rested on top of her massive cleavage. I waved her in and pointed to a client chair. As she approached, I continued my conversation, and a wonderful perfume drifted across my desk. “Knock on the door about seven tonight. He’ll answer. Make sure you have the backdoor covered, and you can make your arrest. He doesn’t own a gun but be careful. Yeah, okay, glad to help, detective,” I said and set the phone on my desk. Brianna and I studied one another for a long moment.

“Brianna, it’s been a long time, what three, maybe four years? It’s nice to see you,” I said as I rose out of my desk chair.

She extended her hand across the desk, nodded, and smiled, suggesting everyone always said it was nice to see her. When I took hold of her hand, she grabbed on with both hands and stroked the back of my hand.

"It's all my fault, and it's been way too long. Do you know I actually dream about you, Dev Haskell? I dream about you all the time. What was I ever thinking? You, well, you umm, look the same," she said, taking in my camouflage shorts and the navy-blue t-shirt that said, 'The Spot Bar.' "You haven't changed a bit. You're just the same as I remember," she said and shook her head. I wasn't sure she meant that as a compliment.

There were a number of ways I could have replied. Instead, I said, "Your email sounded somewhat urgent. What's up?"

"Well, would it be fair to say that, based on our history, we can be honest with one another?"

I wanted to say, based on our history, it would be the first time for you. Instead, I replied, "Absolutely, Brianna."

"And you're a private investigator. So, I'm guessing that covers a variety of, shall we say, circumstances you have been involved in over the past few years."

"Well, I investigate a number of different situations, everything from work history to extramarital affairs. On occasion, I've provided security for people. Usually, some individual arriving from out of town for a meeting or, in one or two instances, a court case."

"I have an individual I would like you to investigate."

"An individual? Just who would this be?" I asked.

"An individual who was, umm, an acquaintance. He's scammed me out of at least ten thousand dollars. His name is Seymour Smeelie. Now, I call him Seymour Smelly."

"Scammed you? How did that happen? A bad investment? Were you not paid for work or services?"

"Well, yes and no. We vacationed down in Florida this past winter. Seymour told me he was involved in purchasing stock options, and his accounts were tied up. Of course, I was only too happy to help. He told me I'd receive fifteen percent of the multi-million dollar deal he was involved in. But once the snow was gone and we returned up here to the world's biggest small town," she wrinkled her nose, "I haven't been able to contact him."

"Does this guy travel? Is he busy? I mean, surely you can—"

"Were you listening, darling? I said I haven't been able to contact him. He's blocked my email, Instagram, Facebook, Snapchat, Twitter, and he's blocked my phone number. Now, as of yesterday, he's filed a restraining order on me," she said as she reached into her designer purse and tossed the restraining order across my desk.

"Someone served you yesterday?"

"Yes, some fat, smelly creature with dirty fingernails. Oh," she said and shuddered.

"Wow, sounds serious," I said, hoping she couldn't tell how much I was enjoying her little problem.

"I'll say. Fifteen percent of a ten million dollar deal is one point five million I'm owed."

"I don't suppose this Seymour gave you a contract, a signed agreement, or anything along those lines?"

"That's beside the point. I do have a file full of receipts for everything from three months' rent in Florida to food, liquor, fishing rentals, massages, waxings—"

"He got a waxing?"

"Well, no. Actually, I did but at Seymour's request."

"So, what did you want me to investigate? It sounds like you might be better served by a lawyer, rather than me, but I gotta be honest, Brianna. Without a contract or a written agreement of some sort, I'm not sure you have much of a leg to stand on."

"Interesting you put it that way because that's exactly where you come in."

"What?"

"If you could provide some little incentive, you know, maybe break his leg. Or, better yet, break both his legs. That would work as an encouragement for him to make good on his promise."

I slowly shook my head and said, "Brianna, I'm sorry, but I don't really do that kind of work."

"Dev, honey, did I happen to mention you would get a very nice percentage as well? Say, ten percent. Let me do the math for you and just think of it. A hundred and fifty thousand dollars and all you have to do is get him to pay me. I don't care how you do it. I don't even have to know. By the way, there would most definitely be a very personal bonus thrown in. The type of bonus I happen to know you would really, really, enjoy." She took her time crossing her legs, revealing the top of her hosiery and the black garter belt.

"So, tell me more about this guy." I said, leaning forward and staring at her upper thigh.

She grinned, pulled a sheet of paper from her designer purse, and handed it to me. "I knew that personal bonus would get you. His name is Seymour, Seymour Smeelie, but like I said, now I'm calling him Smelly. I know what you're thinking, how inappropriate. Now, here is his address, both office and condo. His phone number, email account, usernames for Instagram, Snapchat, and Twitter, as well as his Facebook page and the security code to his condo."

I unfolded the paper and read through the information. I recognized the condo address as some pretty pricey real estate. "Brianna, I wish I could help you out here, but I just don't do that. Check with an attorney and see what they tell you, but my sense is you might be screwed unless you have a signed document or evidence of some kind that proves you were promised fifteen percent."

She took a deep breath and exhaled, then shook her head and gave me a look that brought back a lot of memories, all unpleasant. "I should have known better. When will I learn? I bare my soul to you, and all you can do is throw up your hands. I offer to provide every perversion and pay you more money than you'll ever see in your entire life, and this is the thanks I get."

She glanced around the office at Louie's picnic table desk and Morton lying in his bed, chewing on a toy. "This is what I get for trying to help you," she said as she stood. "Oh, by the way, the dreams I had of you, not to worry, they were really nightmares. I'll just deal with this myself." With that, she picked up her list, turned and strutted toward the door, putting an extra effort into her backside. When she opened the door, she glanced over her shoulder, cocked a hip, and said, "Enjoy the view, that's all you're going to get." She closed the door behind her and headed down the stairs.

I watched out the window as she crossed the street and climbed into her Mercedes. She lowered the driver's window, stuck her hand out, and gave me the finger before she headed up the street. I was in the process of writing Louie a note when he hurried into the office.

"Hi, Dev. Sorry, can't stop to talk. I have to grab a file and head over to the courthouse." He stopped and sniffed. "You wearing some kind of perfume?"

I shook my head no and said, "Long story. Louie, I have to go with Taffy up to the lake. You okay to watch Morton? I got his food and water dishes along with his dog food. I can pick him up at your place on Sunday. I'll buy you dinner."

Louie was rifling through a stack of files, found the one he was looking for, and tossed it in his briefcase.

"Yeah sure, whatever. I gotta run. See you," he said and hurried out the door.

I wasn't sure what I said had even registered with him, so I finished the note and left it on the picnic table. I gave Morton a rub and headed out the door.

Three

I made it over to Taffy's in record time. I pulled in front of her building then pressed her number on the security phone.

"Dev?" was how she answered a moment later.

"Yeah, Taffy. You all set?"

"Come on up. I've got one or two more things to pack." The security door suddenly buzzed. I pulled it open and took the elevator up to her third-floor unit. I stepped out of the elevator and headed down the hall. She opened the door to her unit when I was just halfway down the hall, gave a look at my camouflage shorts and t-shirt, and said, "That's what you're wearing?"

"Yeah, Taffy, good morning to you, too. Believe me. No one cares what I'm wearing. I could wear this every day, and no one would even notice."

"Well, I notice. Of course, too late now, I guess I'm stuck with it. Here, you can take these out to the car," she said and wheeled two suitcases out from behind the door. "I'll grab the rest of this and be right behind you."

"Honey, we're only going to be there for two nights, and most of the time, you'll be in a bikini. What's all this stuff?"

"Oh yeah, perfect. That'll work, fashion advice from you," she said, pointing and indicating my outfit.

I knew better than to respond. I dragged her suitcases down the hallway, stepped onto the elevator, and turned to hold the door. She was nowhere in sight. I held the door open for a minute or two until it began buzzing, then let it close and dragged her suitcases out to my car. I tossed the suitcases in the back and then leaned against the side of the car, waiting for ten minutes until she appeared. She was carrying a small pink case that I happen to know held about a thousand dollars' worth of makeup, and she had a yellow and blue computer bag slung across her shoulder.

She handed me the makeup case, and I set it next to her suitcases. As she pulled the computer bag off her shoulder, she said, "Careful, my laptop is in there."

"You think they'll even have internet access?"

"Dev. Really? Come on. Let's get going."

I closed the door once she climbed in and hurried around to the driver's side. The car started on the second try.

"Thanks for not driving us up there in this thing, Dev. It's liable to die in the middle of the woods, and no one would find us until next spring."

"We could have taken your car," I said as we turned onto Dale Street and headed toward Stacy and Kevin's.

"No. I think they're in some remote location on the lake, and you have to get there on a gravel road."

"Yeah, so?"

"Hello, I'm not driving my car on a gravel road." That was the last of our conversation until we pulled in front of Stacey and Kevin's house.

They lived in a story and a half cottage style home built in the 1930s in a nice corner of town. All the homes in the neighborhood were similar and built before the Second World War. Stacey and Kevin's was painted light green with white trim. It had a front porch with four large supports and an oak front door centered exactly in the middle of the house. Their car, a white Jeep Compass, was parked in front with the rear and both back-doors open. Kevin was loading the back of the car with grocery bags, two toolboxes, shovels, and a suitcase. I noted the single suitcase for the two of them but thought it might be wise to keep my mouth shut.

"Hi Kevin," we both called as we climbed out of my car. Taffy gave Kevin a hug and headed into the house. I began to haul out Taffy's luggage and then my grocery bag, lining it all up on the boulevard as Kevin pushed and crammed things into the back of the Jeep.

Once he filled the back area, he looked at Taffy's suitcases, the makeup case, and her computer bag and said, "I'm afraid that stuff is going to have to go in the backseat, between you two."

I shook my head and said, "Not a problem. Let's get it in there before the girls come out and make us rearrange everything."

Twenty minutes later, we were on our way, Kevin and Stacey in the front seats. Taffy and I in the back with her two suitcases and the computer bag stacked up between us. Her makeup case was on the floor with her feet resting on it. My grocery bag with the clean t-shirts, swimsuit, baseball cap, and socks, was on the floor next to my feet.

"Oh, we're going to have a great time. I can't wait until you see our place," Stacy said as we took off down the street.

Four

We drove two and a half hours up to Duluth and stopped for lunch. I offered to pay for lunch, and unfortunately, they took me up on it. We climbed back in the car and drove along the Lake Superior shore for another hour, and through the town of Two Harbors.

"Oh, you guys are so lucky," Taffy said. "I've just loved Lake Superior ever since I was a little girl and my folks would bring us up here. This brings back all sorts of wonderful memories."

Five miles later, Kevin made a left turn onto County Road 3, and we headed west, leaving Lake Superior and Taffy's memories behind us. We drove through the wilderness for another hour before Kevin turned off on a gravel road. According to the sign, we were headed toward Butt Lake.

"Oh. My. God. I don't believe it. Who would want to live there? Butt Lake, can you believe it?" Taffy laughed.

"Actually," Stacy said, turning around to look at Taffy, "that's our lake."

"No, come on," Taffy said, not quite catching on. With the suitcases stacked between us, it was impossible to elbow her.

"Yeah, that's where our place is," Kevin said. "Thankfully, because of the lake name, we could afford the property. Forty feet of lakeshore and once you get past the reeds and cattails, it's a great view."

"Oh, umm, good thing you found it," Taffy said in a failed attempt to recover.

Kevin turned on another gravel road and slowed. This road was in a lot rougher condition than the previous, and as slow as we were going, the gravel was still bouncing off the undercarriage and sides of the car. The lake occasionally came into view through the birch trees on the left-hand side. We passed three mailboxes and dilapidated structures that appeared to be lived in. At the fourth mailbox, Kevin slowed and turned onto a rutted trail that wound through the woods and over a slight rise. As we drove over the rise, I could hear the bottom of the car scrape the ground.

"You and I are going to level that out later today, Dev. It's the reason I brought the shovels," Kevin said. We cleared the rise and rolled down to little more than a shack with patches of different colored shingles on the roof.

"Here we are, our second home," Stacy said as Kevin pulled to a stop.

The "cabin" was a one-story structure that looked more like a work shed than something fit for human habitation. Along with the random patching on the roof, what I assumed had been a window at one time was covered by a sheet of warped pressboard. The two wooden steps leading to the backdoor were warped. The gray cedar siding hadn't seen a coat of paint since the Nixon administration, and most of the paint on the white trim had peeled off, exposing weathered and rotted wood.

"Okay, everyone out and grab something," Kevin said as he and Stacey opened their respective doors and hurried out.

Taffy looked at me with wide eyes, and her lower lip started to tremble.

"Come on. Let's get this stuff out of the car," I said, opening my door. I climbed out and reached back in, pulling out both of Taffy's suitcases. Two steps later, the mosquitos found us. I stopped twice and slapped a number of them on my arms and neck. Stacy and Kevin had run ahead to the door and unlocked it.

Taffy shot past me, slapping the air and mumbling, "Awe, icky, God, get away. Oh Jesus."

Kevin opened the door. Stacy hurried inside and stomped her feet a number of times. Kevin followed her in and did the same thing. Taffy was right behind them. She hurried inside and said, "What's that sound?"

Stacey ignored the question. As I stepped in, she pointed to the flowered sofa with the worn arms and the stuffing hanging out on the corners. "Dev, that's the Hide-a-bed. Go ahead and pull that out for you and Taffy. Kevin, I'll do the counters if you'll bring the suitcase into the bedroom."

I wheeled Taffy's suitcases over to the Hide-a-bed. She was still standing just inside the door with wide eyes and her mouth hanging open. I pulled the cushions off the Hide-a-bed, revealing mouse droppings, lots of mouse droppings. I quickly unfolded the metal frame with the mattress— more mouse deposits, lots more. I thought I saw something scurry out from beneath the couch and under a chair. Taffy was still standing at the door, awestruck. Her mouth hung open, and she was slowly shaking her head from side to side.

"Taffy, maybe you could give Stacey a hand while I get the rest of your luggage out of the car. Taffy? Hey, Taffy?"

"What?" she said, shaking her head and coming back to reality.

"Give Stacey a hand while I get the rest of your luggage," I said and headed out the door.

I half-ran to the car, slapped a couple more mosquitos on the way, and grabbed Taffy's makeup case and the grocery bag with my clothes. On the way back to the 'Cabin,' I noticed an outhouse about thirty feet away with a path leading to it. Taffy was going to go crazy.

Five

Christine Abner gave hugs to her three girlfriends, and they all promised to meet for lunch again next month. Now all retired, Christine and Mary Jane widowed, and all four fleeing the midwestern winter in different directions from January until April or May, there never seemed to be enough time to catch up. Updates on grandchildren, high school classmates, God forbid someone passing, who is doing what to whom, and suddenly the two-hour lunch was over.

They split the bill four ways, each leaving a two-dollar tip, pushed back their chairs, and stood. Christine made a show of draping her shoulder bag across her chest then raised her eyebrows as her three friends focused on the classic Saint Laurent monogram.

"Well just look at you. Tell me that isn't some knock-off you got at the state fair," Sandie said.

"What can I say? The perfect birthday gift from the perfect son-in-law."

"Your son-in-law gave you that? I don't believe it," Kate said.

"Yes, he did, and my daughter Debbie is very jealous. I think he might just be buying another for her birthday."

"God, you are something. That's a long way from teaching kindergarten for forty years."

"Forty-three years. Our monthly mortgage payment was less than this cost. I'm only carrying it in nice weather, not far from home, and never, ever out of my sight.

All four of them stepped out of the restaurant and onto the street. Sunglasses immediately came out of purses, and one more round of hugs before they were off in different directions. The other three were driving, but Christine only lived two blocks away, so she walked. She gave a final wave and headed up the street. She stopped at the corner and waved the car on. The young man behind the wheel smiled and waved a thank you. She crossed the street and strolled past Fitz's and then the Red Cow, two popular restaurants. She passed the parking lot for the senior residence and smiled a 'hello' to the two women sitting on the bench in front. She crossed the next side street and walked halfway up the block then climbed the half-dozen stairs up to her building, input the security code, and opened the door.

"Oh, please, allow me," the young man said from behind and pushed the heavy glass door open so she could step in.

"Thank you," she said and smiled, thinking, isn't it nice some people are still raised to have manners. She pulled her keys out from her purse to open the inner door.

"I'll take that," he said.

"What?"

"Your purse, give it to me."

"Who are—"

"I'm not kidding, lady," he said and jammed a pistol into her ribs. "Now, give me the damn purse before things get a whole lot worse." He looked around anxiously, although no one else was in the small entry.

"But, this is—"

He jammed the pistol into her ribs again, this time a lot harder, and she groaned and winced. "Uff, please don't. It means so much—"

He tore the handbag from her shoulder, shoved her against the wall, and ran out the door. She was too frightened to move.

Six

It was after nine. A half-moon was rising over the lake. Taffy was seated in the upholstered chair the mouse had run under when we'd arrived. "I don't want to stay here," Taffy whispered as a tear ran down her cheek.

"We're gonna have to for two nights. Remember?" I said.

Kevin and Stacey were busy cooking dinner on the two-burner stove. Hotdogs again. Kevin had been hoping to do steaks out on the fire-pit, but the mosquitos were so bad he could barely get the fire started, let alone stand out there and cook for fifteen or twenty minutes.

"I want to go home, Dev."

"We can't, Taffy. Remember, you wanted to ride up with Kevin and Stacey. So we could lie in the sun." I held my hands out, palms up, revealing the blisters from the four hours of shoveling Kevin and I did to even out the rise on the trail into this hellhole, and we were only halfway finished.

"But I thought it would be nice up here. I wanted to go out on their pontoon boat, and—"

"They don't have a pontoon boat, Taffy. As a matter of fact, they don't have a boat. But that's okay because they don't have a dock. As a matter of fact, that forty feet of shoreline is all swamp with cattails and reeds going twenty feet out before you actually get to the lake. Did you happen to see that rusted out Volkswagen Bug out in the water about twenty feet offshore? The thing looks like it's been out there for at least thirty years. If this is Butt lake, guess which part we're on."

"Please, I can't sleep here. Maybe we could get a hotel," she said, suddenly looking hopeful.

"Taffy, there aren't any hotels around here. We're in the middle of nowhere. Now, it's only for two nights. You can do that. We'll make the best of this situation, and let's just enjoy the fact that we have two people cooking us dinner."

"Cooking? Dev, I thought it was chocolate sprinkles from cookies all over the counter. You know what it was? It was mouse shit. Mouse shit, Dev. And there was so much it couldn't have come from just one mouse. It had to be from hundreds of mice. I'm telling you, there's a mouse herd in this dreadful place, Dev. Stacey just brushed it off the counter and into the wastebasket like it was no big deal. Then every once in a while, she would stomp her feet, and you could hear the little bastards running around inside the wall and behind the kitchen cabinet. It's not safe here, Dev. We're going to get eaten alive. I'm not kidding."

"Okay, you guys, dinner's ready. A repeat of last night, hope you don't mind," Stacey said.

"Are you kidding? No complaints, we didn't have to cook, so like my mom used to say, eat it or wear it," I said.

"Oh, that's so cute. Come on, you guys, and sit down," Stacey said and placed a platter of hotdogs onto a Formica topped table from the Eisenhower administration.

Kevin set three beer glasses stolen from bars and one greenish colored glass on the table. They all looked like they could hold sixteen ounces. The greenish glass was emblazoned with the Coca-Cola logo. He poured some red wine maybe a third of the way up, into all four glasses. I led Taffy over to the table, and she stomped her feet before settling into the rickety wooden chair. Once she was seated, she grabbed her glass and gulped down half of her red wine. Stacey and Kevin shot a quick glance at one another.

We finished the hot dogs in about fifteen minutes. I ate three and a half, the half coming from Taffy's plate. I ate her BBQ potato chips as well. Taffy was apparently on the liquid diet, and at this point, she was about two glasses of wine ahead of us.

Stacey told us to stay seated as she hauled the plates and hotdog platter over to the sink. Kevin hopped out of his folding lawn-chair, grabbed a bag of bite-sized Snickers bars from the cabinet, and tossed them on the table. I noticed something had nibbled through the side of the bag and eaten the better part of a Snickers bar.

"Aww, Jesus. Snickers, my favorites," Taffy said. She was a little too loud, and her words were somewhat slurred as she grabbed the bag and tore it open. She either ignored the nibbling or hadn't noticed. She turned the bag upside down, dumped the candy bars out onto the table, and dug in.

Kevin smiled, raised his eyebrows, and deftly swept what was left of the nibbled bar into his hand. Once the candy bars were gone, mostly consumed by the now very intoxicated Taffy, Kevin and Stacey begged off to bed.

"See you guys in the morning," Stacey said. "First one up turns on the coffee. Taffy, honey, I left the aspirin bottle out on the counter in case you might want two before you go to bed. Might make for a better morning."

"Oh, yeah. Well, you better close your door unless you want to watch. I'm gonna put Dev to work," Taffy slurred and drained her glass.

Stacey flashed a momentary smile and said, "Thanks for the warning."

Once they closed their bedroom door, Taffy got up, staggered to the kitchen counter, and grabbed the last remaining bottle of wine.

"Hey, we should probably just hit the sack. Things will be better tomorrow. Want me to get you a glass of water for the aspirin?"

She shot me a look that suggested I wasn't making any sense. She twisted the cap off the bottle, then poured half of the bottle into her glass and dropped the cap on the floor. I figured the best policy would be to say nothing.

We sat quietly for the next twenty minutes, Taffy working her way through the glass of wine, me thinking about Brianna's threat to have someone break Seymour Smeelie's legs. I finally broke the silence. "You about ready for bed, Taffy?"

She raised her head, brushed her auburn hair back with both hands, and attempted to look in my general direction. With her glassy blue eyes, I wasn't sure she could see me only four feet away.

"You know what I wanna do now?" she said as her head swayed back and forth like a plate spinning on a stick.

"I think maybe bed might just be the best thing. We can—"

"We'll be in bed," she gulped and let out a loud burp. "But don't you plan on going to sleep anytime soon, Mister. I'm in need of some special attention. Very special." With that, she took her glass, drained it, and attempted to get to her feet.

After a couple of tries, I took hold of her arm and half-lifted her out of the chair. She smiled and said, "Mmm, this is going to be a night to remember. I'm thinking maybe we should come up to the lake more."

"Good idea, Taffy. I'll remember that."

"Just you wait," she said then reached down and squeezed my thigh. "Oh, wow, you're ready."

I got undressed and pulled back the covers on the Hide-a-bed. Thankfully, there were no new deposits since I'd cleaned it off. Taffy attempted to perform a striptease in front of the window looking out on the cattails and swamp reeds but ended up falling into a chair. Fortunately, she landed on the cushion and giggled for a long moment. She was down to just her bra and thong and halfway fell onto the bed. I pulled her in, and as I lifted the covers over her, she started to snore. It couldn't have been more than ten minutes later when she bolted up in bed and headed for what she thought was the bathroom. Unfortunately, the only door led into Stacey and Kevin's bedroom.

I was up just as Stacey yelled, "What the hell!" I grabbed Taffy by the arm and directed her out the backdoor. We almost made it to the outhouse before she threw up. Yeah, definitely a night to remember.

To be continued…

What in the world is going on? Seymour Smeelie is poisoned in his office. Gorgeous Brianna Di Salvo offers herself as payment if Dev would just break a leg or even two on Smeelie. Taffy completely misjudges what turns out to be the weekend from hell. And now, Morton is about to run with a rougher crowd. You better grab your copy of **Bow-Wow Rescue** to see where this all ends up. Anyway you cut it, things don't look good Dev Haskell…

Books by Mike Faricy

Crime Fiction Firsts

A boxset of the first four books in four crime fiction series;

Russian Roulette; Dev Haskell series
Welcome; Jack Dillon Dublin Tales series
Corridor Man; Corridor Man series
Reduced Ransom!; Hot Shot series

Available on Amazon.

The following titles comprise the Dev Haskell series:

Russian Roulette: Case 1
Mr. Swirlee: Case 2
Bite Me: Case 3
Bombshell: Case 4
Tutti Frutti: Case 5
Last Shot: Case 6
Ting-A-Ling: Case 7
Crickett: Case 8
Bulldog: Case 9
Double Trouble: Case 10
Yellow Ribbon: Case 11

Dog Gone: Case 12
Scam Man: Case 13
Foiled: Case 14
What Happens in Vegas… : Case 15
Art Hound: Case 16
The Office: Case 17
Star Struck: Case 18
International Incident: Case 19
Guest From Hell: Case 20
Art Attack: Case 21
Mystery Man: Case 22
Bow-Wow Rescue: Case 23
Cold Case: Case 24
Cash Up Front: Case 25
Dream House: Case 26
Alley Katz: Case 27
The Big Gamble: Case 28
Bad to the Bone: Case 29
Silencio!: Case 30
Surprise, Surprise: Case 31
Hit & Run: Case 32
Suspect Santa: Case 33
P.I. Apprentice: Case 34
Rebel Without A Clue: Case 35

The following titles are Dev Haskell novellas:
Dollhouse
The Dance
Pixie

Fore!

Twinkle Toes
(*a Dev Haskell short story*)

The following are Dev Haskell Boxsets:
Dev Haskell Boxset 1-3
Dev Haskell Boxset 4-6
Dev Haskell Boxset 7-9
Dev Haskell Boxset 10-12
Dev Haskell Boxset 13-15
Dev Haskell Boxset 16-18
Dev Haskell Boxset 19-21
Dev Haskell Boxset 22-24
Dev Haskell Boxset 25-27
Dev Haskell Boxset 28-30
Dev Haskell Boxset 31-33
Dev Haskell Boxset 1-7
Dev Haskell Boxset 8-14
Dev Haskell Boxset 15-19
Dev Haskell Boxset 20-24
Dev Haskell Boxset 25-29

All available on Amazon.

The following titles comprise the Jack Dillon Dublin Tales series:

Welcome
Jack Dillon Dublin Tale 1
Sweet Dreams
Jack Dillon Dublin Tale 2
Mirror Mirror
Jack Dillon Dublin Tale 3
Silver Bullet
Jack Dillon Dublin Tale 4
Fair City Blues
Jack Dillon Dublin Tale 5
Spade Work
Jack Dillon Dublin Tale 6
Madeline Missing
Jack Dillon Dublin Tale 7
Mistaken Identity
Jack Dillon Dublin Tale 8
Picture Perfect
Jack Dillon Dublin Tale 9
Dublin Moon
Jack Dillon Dublin Tale 10
Mystery Woman
Jack Dillon Dublin Tale 11
Second Chance
Jack Dillon Dublin Tale 12
Payback Brother
Jack Dillon Dublin Tale 13

The Heist
Jack Dillon Dublin Tale 14
Jewels To Kill For
Jack Dillon Dublin Tale 15
Retirement Scheme
Jack Dillon Dublin Tale 16
The Collector
Jack Dillon Dublin Tale 17

Jack Dillon Dublin Tales Boxsets:
Jack Dillon Dublin Tales 1-3
Jack Dillon Dublin Tales 4-6
Jack Dillon Dublin Tales 7-9
Jack Dillon Dublin Tales 10-12
Jack Dillon Dublin Tales 1-5
Jack Dillon Dublin Tales 1-7
Jack Dillon Dublin Tales 6-10

All available on Amazon.

The following titles comprise the Hotshot series;

Reduced Ransom!
Finders Keepers!
Bankers Hours
Chow Down

Moonlight Dance Academy

Irish Dukes (Fight Card Series)
written under the pseudonym Jack Tunney

All available on Amazon.

The following titles comprise the Corridor Man series:

Corridor Man
Corridor Man 2: Opportunity knocks
Corridor Man 3: The Dungeon
Corridor Man 4: Dead End
Corridor Man 5: Finger
Corridor Man 6: Exit Strategy
Corridor Man 7: Trunk Music
Corridor Man 8: Birthday Boy
Corridor Man 9: Boss Man
Corridor Man 10: Bye Bye Bobby

Corridor Man novellas:
Corridor Man: Valentine
Corridor Man: Auditor
Corridor Man: Howling
Corridor Man: Spa Day

The following are Corridor Man Boxsets:

Corridor Man Boxset 1-3
Corridor Man Boxset 1-5
Corridor Man Boxset 6-9

All available on Amazon.

Contact Mike:
Email: mikefaricyauthor@gmail.com
Twitter: @Mikefaricybooks
Facebook: Mike Faricy Author
Website: http://www.mikefaricybooks.com

Thank you!

www.ingramcontent.com/pod-product-compliance
Lightning Source LLC
Chambersburg PA
CBHW071410200726
48294CB00002B/340

* 9 7 8 1 9 6 2 0 8 0 3 3 0 *